BOUND BY
DANGER

BOUND BY
DANGER

DANIELLE M. HAAS

Entangled Publishing, LLC
2614 South Timberline Road
Suite 105, PMB 159
Fort Collins, CO 80525
rights@entangledpublishing.com

Amara is an imprint of Entangled Publishing, LLC.

Edited by Alethea Spiridon
Cover design by Mayhem Cover Creations
Cover photography by neostock-geoff-apocalypse-hero
dorriss85.gmail.com, ssuaphoto, and maxym/Depositphotos

Manufactured in the United States of America

First Edition January 2019

AMARA
an imprint of Entangled Publishing LLC

To Scott, Abigail, and Vaughn. Thanks for letting me dream big.

Chapter One

The tight smile on Mickey's face made her cheeks hurt.

They'd only been in the air an hour and already her feet screamed in agony from being in heels and she'd wanted to smack at least one passenger. Why passengers thought it was all right to be rude to flight attendants was beyond her.

She glanced toward the front of the plane as the pilot slipped out of the flight deck. He stepped into the bathroom and the occupancy light turned red.

Dammit, he didn't shut the door to the flight deck. Does this guy ever follow protocol?

Mickey shook her head and pressed her teeth together. Leaving the door to the flight deck open while in the air was a major security breach, even if only for a minute while the pilot used the bathroom.

She glanced over her shoulder and spotted the other two flight attendants twelve rows behind her. She stretched onto her tiptoes and craned her neck toward them, but their focus remained on attending to passengers in the back of the plane.

Shit, she'd have to deal with this herself. She needed

to close the door to the flight deck, but the stupid drink cart blocked her path to the front of the plane. A flutter of movement caught her eye. A middle-aged man in the fifth row stood. A light brown baseball hat sat low on his head, casting a dark shadow over his face. His head swiveled from side to side and his eyes darted around the plane before he stepped into the narrow aisle. With squared shoulders, he strode toward the cockpit.

Panic tightened her throat and fear caused pressure to build in her chest, making it hard to breathe. She'd never trusted the security check flying out of Cancun, and something about the determined set of the man's shoulders had alarm bells blasting in her brain.

"Sir?" Her voice shook and she pushed her cart up the aisle at a quick trot. Perspiration clung to her palms and her hands slipped on the handle. Shrieks of protest sounded as the cart ran over passengers' toes in aisle eight and bumped against a hulking shoulder in aisle seven. She didn't care. The sinking feeling in her gut told her she had to stop the tall, lanky man in the tan jacket.

A soft *ding* sounded and the red occupancy light switched to green. Captain Fuller stepped out of the bathroom, blocking the path of the man in beige. Mickey drew in a deep breath, filling her lungs with air, and relief seeped into every fiber of her muscles. The man pulled something from his pocket with his left hand, and the light caught the smooth metallic sheath. "No!"

Captain Fuller frowned as the man drew his hand back and slashed the weapon through the air. The pilot's eyes grew wide and he doubled over. A knife stuck out of his side. Crimson seeped around the protruding knife, spreading out onto his crisp, white uniform like an intricate spider's web. Terror stole the air from her lungs. Gasps of horror sounded all around her.

The man shoved Captain Fuller back into the bathroom, pushed the door closed, and disappeared into the flight deck. The door slammed shut. Bile backed up Mickey's throat. The sour, acidic taste filled her mouth and burned her esophagus. She fisted her hand in her hair and scanned the plane. Wide-eyed passengers sat frozen to their seats, but a few hurried to their feet. None of the heroes-to-be were close enough to the front of the plane to make a difference. The door to the flight deck was already closed and locked from inside. Her breaths came out in sharp gasps. Screams echoed around the confines of the plane. She'd been trained for this, but her feet wouldn't move from their rooted spot.

Oh God, I don't want to die.

Someone pulled on her arm, and she stared down into the terrified eyes of a young woman. "What's happening? Is he okay? Do something!"

Hurried footsteps fell behind her, and she whirled around to see the other two flight attendants barreling toward her.

"What happened? Is Captain Fuller dead? What about the co-pilot? He's locked in there with that maniac. What do we do?" Panic drew deep lines on her co-worker's tense face and she spoke in a quiet, shaky voice.

Mickey focused on evening her breaths and her mind raced. None of them had ever dealt with this before. They had to stay calm. Or at least pretend to stay calm while they did something. She was in charge and she needed to act. Now. Mickey straightened herself and forced down the panic clawing at her throat. They had to get into the flight deck. She locked the cart in place, hitched her tight blue pencil skirt high on her thighs, and climbed over it. Her knees knocked a stack of plastic cups to the floor and something wet seeped into her skirt.

"Get this damn thing out of the way, and one of you contact Air Traffic Control," she yelled over her shoulder to the two other flight attendants and raced toward the front of the plane. She needed to get to the keypad on the cockpit door.

The nose of the plane dipped low and Mickey stumbled forward. Her palms slammed against the door to the flight deck and gravity pressed her weight against cold steel. Pain shot through her body like sparks from a fire. She sank to her knees and turned, pressing her back to the wall.

She closed her eyes, blocking out the screams, and tried to regain her equilibrium. The plane shook as it plummeted down at a sharp angle toward the ground. Chaos unfolded around her. She opened her eyes and air masks dangled above the passengers and they struggled to get them on. Luggage fell from overhead bins.

A strong hand gripped hers and hauled her to her feet. She tipped her head back to bring in the full length of the man in front of her. The intense gray eyes of the passenger she'd wanted to smack stared down at her. His mouth was set in a firm line, and his broad shoulders blocked out her view of the hysteria taking place in the cabin behind him. The plane shook even more, testing her balance, and she squeezed his hand. His unwavering stare brought a sense of calm over her.

"You need to get me in there." He nodded past her toward the cockpit.

She let go of his hand and her stomach pitched like the waves of a tsunami. She didn't have time to deal with a demanding passenger who wanted to play hero; she needed to get into the flight deck and figure out how to get everyone off this plane alive. But how could she do that if a psychopath was in control of the aircraft?

Captain Fuller.

She needed to make sure he was alive, and maybe he could still land the plane.

"Get me the hell in there."

They staggered as the plane dipped to the side. He fell forward, pinning her back to the wall. Her chest heaved in and out while her pulse spiked as the hard muscles of his body pressed against her. He reached behind his back and pulled a gun out from underneath his jacket. "I'm FBI."

A sharp gasp escaped her lips and her eyes searched his. The intensity never left them, but this time the gray steel gazing down on her gave her strength, courage to do whatever the hell she needed to get out of the plane alive. She choked down a sob, turned toward the keypad, and typed in the code. An FBI agent with a gun could do a hell of a lot more than she could.

The FBI agent pushed past her and swung open the door. He stormed into the flight deck while Mickey stared in horror at the man in beige sitting in the captain's seat, the co-pilot slumped over the controls in front of him.

The hijacker whipped around to face them, but before he could react, the FBI agent smashed his fist into the terrorist's jaw. The man's head lolled to the side. The agent grabbed a set of handcuffs from his back pocket and slapped them on the criminal.

"Do you know how to fly this thing?" the agent asked with a steady voice.

Mickey turned toward the cabin while the man sat down in the captain's chair. A few passengers stood in the tiny spaces in front of their seats while others sat still as statues. Chaos reigned, but she didn't have time to deal with them. Passengers were zeroing in on her; she held her hand up to stop approaching do-gooders.

She ran into the bathroom and found Captain Fuller hunched over on the floor. The bloodstained knife lay on the ground and the captain had both hands pressed against his wound. Thick blood oozed between his fingers. Mickey pressed her hand to her mouth to block out the overpowering metallic scent of blood.

Captain Fuller lifted his head to look at her. A grimace contorted the already deep lines of his face into small ravines. Sweat trickled down his brow. "Help."

"Do we have a doctor on board?" she yelled behind her and grabbed paper towels from overhead. She fell to her knees to press the paper towels against his side. She lifted his hands and placed them on the towels. A tendril of hair fell across her face and she used the back of her hand to sweep it behind her ear. "I'll be right back."

Scrambling to her feet, she stepped out of the bathroom and back into the narrow aisle of the cabin. The plane evened out. At least the mystery FBI agent could keep the aircraft steady. They still needed someone to land the damn thing. She scanned the terrified passengers and her gaze landed on the other two flight attendants rushing around trying to reassure everyone.

Mickey picked up the mouthpiece for the intercom and cleared her throat. "If there is a doctor on board, please come to the front of the plane."

A hundred worried voices assaulted her with a hundred different questions. Mickey took a deep breath and held up a hand, trying to quiet them. "I know everyone is scared, and I don't have any answers for you right now. But I have a badly injured man in need of assistance. Please, is there anyone who can help him?"

A young blond woman with a top knot and leggings stood up and walked toward her. She kept her gaze fixed on the floor and grabbed onto each seat as she passed by to keep her balance. She stopped in front of Mickey. The steel behind her green eyes stood in stark contrast to her timid body language.

"I'm in my second year of med school. I don't know how much I'll be able to help, but I'll try."

"You'll be great."

Mickey turned toward the bathroom with the girl at her heels. With no hesitation, the girl dropped to her knees and unbuttoned Captain Fuller's shirt to get a better look at the wound.

"Do you need anything?" Mickey asked.

"A medical kit if you have it."

Mickey closed her fingers around the hard metal of the keys in her skirt. Yanking them out, she strode to the locked cabinets that lined the wall.

"What can I do?" Allison, her fellow flight attendant, asked as she stepped beside Mickey. The slight tremor in her voice gave away the fear she hid behind her locked jaw and hard eyes.

Mickey handed her the keys. "Help with the captain while I check the flight deck. We need to land fast. I don't think we can do that without him."

"What about Bill?"

The image of the co-pilot slumped over the control panel flittered in her mind and she winced. "I don't know, but it didn't look good. Now get the med kit to the bathroom."

Turning the small corner, Mickey stepped into the flight deck. The man who'd hijacked the plane sat huddled on the floor behind the captain's chair with his hands handcuffed behind his back and his ankles tied together with a zip tie. His chin rested on his chest. The man who held everyone's fate in his hands turned and acknowledged her before facing the wide window that looked out to the sky.

"Have you checked the co-pilot? Is he dead?" She should see for herself, but lead weighed down her feet and she couldn't move.

"He's breathing. We need to land. How's the captain?"

"A med student is looking at him now." She twisted her hands in front of her. "He's lost a lot of blood."

"Is he conscious?"

"Yes."

"Then he can help me get this damn thing on the ground. I've radioed for help, and we can touch down in Atlanta. I need him in here fast."

Mickey's mouth fell open and she stared at the clean-shaven neck and the tousled dark blond hair in front of her. A shiver raced up her spine. They weren't out of the woods yet.

Hard gray eyes turned to her. "Go get him. Now."

His deep voice shook some sense into her. She stepped out of the flight deck and turned to look in the bathroom. She glanced past Allison, who stood in the doorway, and heaved a sigh of relief. The captain sat a little straighter on the cramped floor. White, wiry hairs curled in a matted mess on his bare chest and a flush brought some color to his cheeks. His shirt lay in a heap by his side.

The young woman sat on the floor, pressing white gauze to his wound. She glanced up. "He's lost a lot of blood."

Fuller shifted on the floor, using his hands to brace himself. "Did Bill call Air Traffic Control about making an emergency landing?"

Mickey's tongue swiped across her dry lips. "Bill's unconscious, but Air Traffic Control has been notified. An FBI agent is flying the plane right now, and he needs you to tell him how to land it."

The color on Fuller's cheeks instantly faded. He pushed up on his hands and collapsed on the floor as air wheezed from his clenched mouth.

"He really should stay down," the med student said.

"Then we'll all die in a damn plane crash. Not on my watch." His eyes met Mickey's. "Help me up."

Mickey pushed past the two women and bent down low. She grabbed the captain's arm, hooked it around her neck, and a howl of pain split the air. "Allison, keep your hand on his side while we walk him in."

They stepped out of the bathroom and into the flight deck. "Get the hell out of my seat, son."

The agent looked back, humor and appreciation softening the hard lines around his eyes. "Are you up for this?"

"I've been through worse."

The man nodded and stood from the chair. Mickey helped Fuller hobble to the seat, and then lowered him down. She grabbed Allison's hand and placed it over Fuller's wound. "I'm going to let everyone know we're preparing to land. Keep pressure on the wound and don't move your hand."

The heat of those gray eyes followed her out of the cockpit. She shook it off and stepped up to the intercom once more. "Ladies and gentlemen, we will be making an emergency landing in Atlanta. Please buckle your seatbelts and prepare for landing."

Walking up the aisle, she tried to right the cabin as much as possible while the plane descended. Her muscles throbbed with tension, but she pressed on. Outside the window, white, fluffy clouds appeared, and then disappeared. Terrified passengers hurled questions at her with every step, but she fixed a tight smile on her face and continued replacing luggage in overhead bins. The last thing she needed was for a piece of luggage to fall from the storage compartment and knock someone unconscious. The nightmare was almost over and then she could fall apart. But not until dirt sat beneath her feet.

When the outline of the city replaced the clouds in the windows, she walked to the back of the plane and took a seat next to Vanessa, the newest member of the flight crew. Vanessa reached over, took her hand, and squeezed it when the wheels touched down on the pavement and they taxied to a complete stop. Flashing red lights and screaming sirens announced the arrival of emergency vehicles. Applause filled the cabin as the door opened, and the FBI agent stepped out of the cockpit with the man in beige cuffed in front of him.

This man had saved them all, and she didn't even know his name. He led the hijacker to the door, but stopped suddenly and stared down the long aisle of the plane until their eyes locked. Mickey sucked in a breath and her heart jumped into her throat. He gave her a curt nod and then stepped out of the plane. Pride battled against the terror that had taken up residence in her bones. She'd been scared out of her mind, but she'd helped save the lives of everyone on board. The FBI agent, whoever he was, had acknowledged that with that one tiny gesture.

Her muscles went lax and she melted against the seat. She might have helped save the day, but she was going to need a very large drink soon.

Chapter Two

Sucking in a mouthful of humid air, Graham forced himself to swallow and pushed down the anxiety churning up his throat. Telling a mother a suspected sex-trafficker took her child never got easier. He loved his job at the bureau, but not this part...never this part. He'd much rather be back in Mexico chasing down suspects. But that wasn't an option right now. Especially since Sanchez had figured out who he was and hightailed it onto that stupid plane back to Chicago. Graham might have gotten the information he needed from Sanchez once he'd thrown him in a cell, but it hadn't been in time to stop Pete Bogart from taking one more girl. And a plane full of innocent people almost died because of his screw-up.

He turned toward his partner and nodded. Eric pressed the button for the intercom on the side of the apartment building and Graham waited for the moment he would bring a nightmare to a stranger's doorstep. Becca Stanley's family had no idea of the hell they were in for.

"Hello?"

"Ms. Stanley?" Eric's voice boomed from his large form, but a hint of compassion softened his delivery.

"Yes?"

"My partner and I are here to speak with you about your daughter's disappearance. We're with the FBI. Can we come up?"

No more words crackled through the speaker, but a soft *buzz* vibrated against the metal lock on the door. Graham opened the door and they hustled up three flights of stairs to the apartment Becca lived in with her mother. Images of young Becca Stanley flashed through his mind. Her curly blond hair and crystal blue eyes made her appear more like an angel than a child. Her cherub cheeks and heart-shaped mouth were the picture of innocence. He fisted his hands as a desire to beat the man who took her to a fucking pulp surged through him.

He'd failed Becca, and all of the other girls Pete Bogart had taken. He hadn't gotten the information he'd needed from Sanchez until it was much too late. Too late to keep Pete from taking more girls, but not too late to save their lives. He'd only gotten the name of the man responsible for planting a sex ring in Chicago from Sanchez the day before and hadn't had much time to get more information on the bastard. But now he had a name, and with the help of Suzi Stanley, he'd bust the sonofabitch if it was the last thing he did.

"You want to ask the questions?" Eric asked outside the closed apartment door.

Graham nodded and readjusted the file clenched in his fist.

Eric gave one curt nod and knocked on the door. A woman with eyes the same color as Becca's opened the door. Dark circles hung low under those blue eyes and tears streaked down her cheeks. She leaned against the side of the door and gazed at them with a far-off stare that suggested she'd taken something to dim her pain.

"Hi, Ms. Stanley. I'm Special Agent Graham Grassi and this is my partner, Special Agent Eric Short. We need to ask you some questions about Becca."

"Of course. Come in." She stumbled backward and Graham reached out to steady her. Ms. Stanley placed a hand over her heart and closed her eyes for a beat. For a second, Graham feared she wouldn't open them back up. Taking a deep breath, she opened her eyes and said, "I'm sorry. I can't… It's just…" Sobs interrupted her words and Graham led her to the sofa in the living room.

"This is a difficult situation and we're very sorry about what's happening. But if we're going to find Becca, we need you to answer some questions about the man Becca was with this morning." Graham sat down beside her and took a pen from the pocket of his jacket. He scribbled notes down on the notepad he had sandwiched in his file.

Ms. Stanley clasped her hands together on her lap and tried to regain her composure. "I've told the police everything I know."

"And they're doing everything they can to find Pete Bogart right now. An Amber Alert has been issued for Becca, and Pete's picture is being flashed across the state in hopes of gaining more information. But we've been investigating Mr. Bogart for a while and we need you to tell us how you and Becca met him."

"I don't understand," she said with a shake of her head. "You've been investigating him? You knew he was a bad man and let him hang around with young girls?"

"Why was he spending time with Becca this morning, Ms. Stanley?" Eric cut in.

Graham shot him a what-the-hell-are-you-doing look, but kept his mouth shut. He wondered the same thing but would have asked in a subtler way.

"Pete dated my best friend, Mickey O'Shay. Becca spends a lot of time with Mickey. Mickey's her godmother." Her gaze flitted between him and Eric and she wrung her hands. She sniffled back a sob and pressed on. "Mickey canceled their weekly get-together last minute and Becca was upset. It seemed perfect when Pete texted this morning wanting to see her. I figured an hour out of the house would take her mind off missing Mickey."

"Pete dated Mickey, as in they aren't dating anymore?"

"She broke things off a couple of weeks ago. Something about their schedules being too busy."

Eric took a step forward and angled his chin in her direction. "You didn't think it was odd that Pete would want to spend time with Becca after your friend broke up with him?"

A gasp escaped Ms. Stanley's parted lips and she clamped a shaky hand over her mouth.

Graham cleared his throat and shot Eric another warning look. The dude needed a little more tact today. Ignoring Eric's question, Graham cut into the tense silence with one of his own. "Did you or Becca ever visit Pete's house?"

She shook her head. "No. He and Mickey would pick her up."

"So you don't know where he lives?"

Again, she shook her head and the messy waves stuck to her moist cheeks.

Graham pulled pictures from his file of Pete with other missing girls in the city. "Do you know any of these girls?"

Ms. Stanley took the pictures and flipped through them. She lifted her head and fear invaded the blue of her eyes, turning them dark as night. "They look familiar, but I don't know them. Maybe I've seen them at the market or the park? Why did he take these girls?"

Graham glanced at Eric before he faced her. Time to tell

the truth about the monster who'd taken Becca. "Pete Bogart is suspected of being involved in running a sex-trafficking ring."

The pictures in her hand fell to the ground and Ms. Stanley covered her mouth with shaking fingers. "Oh my God. Not my Becca." The sobs she beat back before they returned with a vengeance. She cradled her stomach and fell against the side of the sofa.

Graham glanced up at his partner. One of them needed to stay and get more information from Becca's mom. One of them needed to go find Mickey O'Shay. Since he had already looked up Ms. O'Shay's information, he'd be the one paying a visit to the bombshell who he'd been shocked to discover was the flight attendant who'd zipped around a plunging airplane last night and helped him take down the hijacker.

Could she have been working with Pete all along?

• • •

Graham rubbed fatigue from his eyes as he sat on Mickey O'Shay's front stoop. He hadn't slept last night.

He couldn't believe his bad luck. It couldn't be a coincidence Mickey was working on the plane the night Sanchez had boarded and was connected to Pete Bogart. Especially since the man he'd followed onto the plane, and later taken into custody, was involved in the same sex-trafficking ring he suspected had taken Becca Stanley. He still couldn't believe the jackass had attempted to hijack a plane instead of going into custody.

But now he couldn't help but wonder if Mickey's actions were too planned out, as if she expected something to go wrong on the plane. Sanchez had sung like a canary and told them a lot about their operation. His vile excuse of a job was to take the new girls to Mexico to train them, and then transport them back to Chicago. The only person he worked with directly was Pete, but there were others. Sanchez had spoken to a woman in Chicago who was in charge of keeping an eye on the girls and breaking them down emotionally. Could that woman be Mickey?

Graham needed to get a grip. She should be home any minute now and he had to get a better handle of who she was and what she knew. The lives of three young girls depended on it.

The hot August sun beat down on him, causing rivers of sweat to pour down his back. Summers in Chicago were brutal and the linen jacket he wore to cover his firearm didn't help. Not even a slight breeze stirred the stilted air to cool him. He rested his forearms on his knees, his hands clasped together, as he watched people hustle along the busy street. Cars honked their horns as they crawled past and radios blared from open windows.

Dumbasses should have their air blasting.

Graham glanced at his watch. Ten minutes had passed since he buzzed the doorbell and no one had answered. He didn't have time to wait all day. He had shit to do. Rising to his feet, he grabbed the file folder sitting beside him and walked down the three steps to the cracked sidewalk. He rounded the corner, his grip lingering on the metal rail at the bottom of the stoop, and stopped in his tracks.

Mickey walked toward him with a pink yoga mat slung over her shoulder. Tight black pants showed off her sculpted legs and defined shoulders peeked out from her purple tank top. The mess of curly red hair piled high on top of her head bounced with every motion and long wisps of unruly strands curled around her face. Her gaze met his and her wide mouth curved into a smile.

Knots twisted in his stomach like a pretzel. Under different circumstances, he'd be smiling about seeing her again, too. But not like this. Not when he had to tell her that her goddaughter was missing and then figure out if she had anything to do with it.

Mickey stopped to stand in front of him and pushed back a coil of stray hair. She furrowed her brow and studied him, but the smile never left her face. "Hi."

Graham shoved his hand in the pocket of his khakis, rocked back on his heels, and let the file dangle at his side. The sun hung high in the sky behind her, causing him to squint despite his aviator sunglasses. He noted the dark circles under her eyes. She hadn't been sleeping, either. "Can we talk?"

Her amber eyes darted around him and she shifted her stance. "About the plane? I already gave my statement. I don't want to talk about it anymore."

"No, something else. Can we go somewhere private?"

A light blush colored her cheeks and her eyebrows rose. Dammit, he was giving her the wrong idea. He cleared his throat. "There's been an incident this morning and I need to ask you some questions."

"What kind of incident?" Her voice held a hint of weariness and she hoisted her yoga mat higher on her sunburned shoulder.

He ground his teeth together. She wasn't making this easy. He wanted to get her somewhere private so he could gauge her reaction when he told her about the girl. "I'd really like to sit somewhere to talk about this."

She folded her arms across her chest and pressed her lips together. The pleasure etched on her face moments before disappeared. "And I'd really like to know what's going on."

A young man in a suit and tie bumped into his shoulder as he hurried by. Graham grunted and staggered back before gaining his footing. Enough. He was hot and tired and he didn't have time to play games. If she wanted to do this the hard way, he'd play along. "I'll try one more time to be nice. We can go to your apartment and have a conversation, or I can take you to my office. The choice is yours."

Mickey's eyes hardened, sketching lines in their corners. "Fine." She stepped around him and climbed the stairs of the stoop. The faint scent of sweat and strawberries lingered behind her.

Following her, he climbed the two flights to her apartment and his dress shoes slapped against the wooden stairs. He pushed his sunglasses to the top of his head and tried to keep his eyes off the rounded shape of her ass. He was in enough hot water with his boss right now. He didn't need to add fuel to the fire by allowing himself to become attracted to a woman involved in one of his cases. He could already hear Harper berating him over conflict of interest bullshit.

She took a key out of a discreet pocket in the top of her pants and opened the door. Pushing the door wide, Mickey stepped over the threshold and threw her yoga mat on the gray sectional in the small living room. The door squeaked as he closed it behind him and he followed her to the kitchen. Mickey grabbed a clean glass from the cabinet and then banged the door shut. Water splashed out of the faucet and she filled the glass before bringing it to her full lips for a sip.

"Can I get a glass?"

Mickey shut off the water and sat down at the round distressed table nestled in the corner. "Sure. Once you tell me why you're here." The tight smile on her face told him her patience wore thin. She'd worn the same smile when he'd pissed her off on the plane.

He walked over to the table, sat down across from her, and placed the file in front of him. She placed her glass on the table and kept her gaze trained on his face. He studied her. How would her porcelain coloring change? Would lines ripple on her smooth-as-silk skin? Would tears burst from the corners of her eyes? He blew out a breath and dove in. "I'm here to tell you Becca Stanley went missing this morning around ten a.m."

Water sloshed over the side of the glass and dripped down onto the table. Her hand trembled and she set the glass down. "You can't be serious."

He watched her intently. Her forehead puckered as she took in his words, but no other signs of distress burst forward. "Trust me, this is no joke. I'd like to know where you were all day."

She jumped out of her seat and pulled her shirt from her body and said, "What does it look like? I was working out. What happened to Becca? I need to call Suzi. She doesn't have a lot of family. She'll need me." She started pacing across the kitchen and pressed the back of her hand to her mouth. "This has to be a mistake."

His gaze followed her. No tears sprang to her eyes, no asking who took the girl. Mentally tucking away his observations, he waited a beat before he said, "You need to answer some questions before you call Suzi."

She stopped moving and scanned the kitchen. "Where the hell did I leave my phone? Dammit!"

Mickey raced into the living room and threw decorative pillows and blankets off the sofa. Graham stood from the table and walked to the cabinet Mickey had taken a glass from. He grabbed a clear glass, filled it with water, and waited for her to find her phone.

Her head popped up from the front of the couch and she raised her phone in the air. She shot fire at him with her eyes. "She didn't call. I don't know what game you're playing, but Suzi would have called me if something happened to Becca. I love that girl with my whole heart." Mickey's voice cracked, but the heat never left her gaze.

Graham pressed the small of his back against the

countertop and set the glass down beside him. "Suzi didn't contact you because she was told not to. If you want to help us find Becca, it's important you tell me where you were today."

Mickey pressed the tips of her fingers into her eyes and drew a long breath in through her nose. She lowered her hands and tears hovered above her long lashes. "I went to yoga class this morning."

"What time did it start?"

Her cheeks sunk in as if she were biting them. "Nine."

That was hours ago. No way she'd been doing yoga until after three in the afternoon. He scanned the lean lines of her body. Well, maybe she had with a body like that. He forced his eyes back to her face. "What time did class end?"

"The class lasts an hour and a half. After class, I went for coffee with a friend." She lifted a hand to her forehead and her fingers rubbed her hairline. "By the time we finished, it was lunch. We intended to get a quick bite to eat but ended up talking for a while."

"About?" He picked up his water and took a sip.

Anger flashed in her eyes. "About how I almost died last night in a plane crash and the asshole who saved my life."

"Did you tell your boyfriend about how I saved your life?" He kept his gaze steady and gauged her reaction to his words.

She snorted and sat down at the table. "I don't have a boyfriend. Can I call Suzi now?"

"No." He picked up his glass and sat across from her. "What about Pete Bogart?"

She squinted and tilted her head to the side. The hair piled on top of her head bounced along with the movement. "How do you know about Pete?"

"I know a lot of things."

"Then you should know we aren't seeing each other anymore. I ended things a couple of weeks ago."

Suzi had told him the same thing earlier, but that didn't mean Mickey didn't know the truth about her recent ex. "When you were together, did the two of you spend a lot of time with Becca?"

Mickey straightened and her body tensed. "Sometimes. I try to see Becca once a week, and Pete would come along when he was in town. Becca's father isn't in the picture, and she liked having him around."

"Why didn't you see Becca this morning? Aren't Sundays the day you usually see her?"

"I needed some time to myself today." She dropped her gaze and wiped some crumbs off the table. "I wanted to get my head on straight before I spent time with her. She's a sensitive girl, and I didn't want her to pick up on my anxiety."

Graham slid the file toward her. "Did you know Becca planned on seeing Pete this morning?" He flipped open the file and a grainy picture of Pete and Becca eating yogurt on the street stared up at Mickey.

Mickey's head whipped up and met his gaze. "No. I haven't talked to Pete in two weeks, and Suzi didn't mention it when I called and canceled yesterday."

"He was the last person seen with Becca." He reached forward and fanned out the pictures in the file so all three were visible. Three photos of three different missing girls taken from various traffic cameras in the city. All with the same man. All with the man's face conveniently covered. He hadn't been able to obtain the bastard's identity until the call came in from Becca's mom this morning. "I've been investigating Pete for the past month. He has a connection with a sex-trafficking ring that recently moved here from Mexico."

A high-pitched laugh bubbled from Mickey and morphed into a hysteric groan. She shook her head, but her gaze never left the photo of her goddaughter. "This is all wrong. Pete's a good guy. He'd never do anything to hurt anyone, especially Becca. He adored her."

Graham waited a beat, studying her reaction. He wanted to believe she was telling him the truth, but he'd never been in this situation before. Instead of wanting to badger her with questions about her possible involvement, he wanted to take her in his arms and tell her everything would be all right.

"This has to be a mistake. I'm sure Pete lost track of time and will bring Becca back any minute."

Graham raised his brows and glanced behind Mickey at the clock on the wall. "Becca was supposed to be home five hours ago."

She grabbed her phone and her fingers flew over the screen. "Did you call Pete? Maybe they went to a movie or something."

He reached out and placed a hand on her arm. Jolts of electricity shocked his hand and he yanked it back. Mickey dropped her phone and stared at him. Clearing his throat, he asked, "Are you going to ask about the other girls in the pictures?"

"It can't be true. There has to be another explanation." Her voice was barely above a whisper. She dropped her gaze to the pictures and swiped the tips of her fingers over Becca's face.

Ring, ring, ring.

He grabbed his phone from his pocket and glanced at the screen. "I have to take this." He stood, turning away from Mickey, and talked to his partner. "What have you got?"

"Harper called and wants to see us as soon as possible."

Shit. He didn't have time to waste dealing with his boss, but if Harper wanted them in his office he didn't have a choice. He pressed his lips together and sighed. "I'm on my way."

He hung up the phone and faced Mickey. Digging in his

pocket, he grabbed a card and threw it on the table. "I have to go. Here's my card. Call if you think of anything I should know. I'll be in touch soon."

"Can I call Suzi now?"

The slight tremor in her voice tightened the knots in his stomach. He nodded. "Yes. If you think of anything that will help us find Becca, call me. The longer we go without finding her…"

She waved away his words and tears streamed down her face. "She's going to be fine. I know it."

"I hope you're right."

He turned and walked out of the apartment and back into the steaming heat of summer. The sun shone bright in his eyes, and he lowered his shades to hide the glare. His gut told him Mickey was telling him the truth, but his head knew he needed to keep an eye on her. Too much shit had happened around her in the last week. He couldn't ignore that. Either way, he'd just dropped a bomb on her.

Now it was time to watch and see how she picked up the pieces.

Chapter Three

The door clicked shut behind her and a shaky breath rattled from her throat. Finally, he was gone. She could breathe a little easier without him staring at her across the table with his accusing gray eyes. He'd be back, though, she was sure of it. But if seeing Agent Graham Grassi again meant he'd found Becca, then she'd welcome the opportunity.

She retrieved her phone, unlocked the screen, and pulled up Pete's number. Maybe she could clear this mess all up. She didn't blame Suzi for panicking and calling the police if Pete was so late in getting Becca home, but there's no way he took Becca for some sex-trafficking ring. Pete could be an ass sometimes, but he was a good guy. He'd always been so kind to Becca.

And she'd never be able to live with herself if she'd been blind to who he really was. The pizza she'd eaten for lunch churned in her stomach.

No way he could have carried on such a charade for four months.

No way she could have let a pedophile into her life...into

her bed. Unshed tears gathered at the corners of her eyes and she sniffed them back.

No, Agent Grassi had to have mixed up his facts. That was the only explanation.

Pressing Pete's contact information, she held the phone to her ear. Her heart pounded as it rang. One…two…three times.

Come on Pete, just answer the damn phone.

"The number you've dialed is no longer in service. Please hang up and try your call again."

Apprehension sent chills up her spine. She pulled the phone away from her ear and looked at the screen. She'd dialed the number programmed under Pete's name. The same number she'd called for months. Maybe he'd forgotten to pay his bill or something. She'd send him a text instead. If he was connected to Wi-Fi, it should still go through.

Hey Pete. Call me when you get this. It's important.

A small *ding* sounded from her phone and she glanced at the screen. Red letters appeared under the green box.

Message failed to deliver.

Her heart slammed against her chest. Her mouth got dry and tears burned her eyes. Doubt spiraled through her mind. She had to call Suzi. Clicking out of her messages, she pulled up Suzi's name and waited for her to answer.

Ring, ring, ring.

With every second that passed, Mickey's heart raced faster and faster. Why wasn't Suzi answering? She set the phone down beside the pictures. Her hand trembled as she picked up the one of Pete and Becca. They stood outside Becca's favorite frozen yogurt shop. The side of her mouth hitched up in a small smile. Becca's loose curls hung around her cherub face and her upturned nose wrinkled as she squinted toward the sky. Leave it to Becca to talk him into frozen yogurt so early in the day. She laid it back down and then picked up another picture. Her blood turned to ice.

A young girl around Becca's age stared up at Pete with a bright smile on her small face. The coloring of the girl was hard to identify in the grainy picture, but there was no denying Pete was the man who held her hand on the busy street. Even with the baseball hat pulled low over his face and his body turned at an angle. She'd bought him that hat when they'd went to their first Cubs game together. Disgust swirled in her gut and bile slid up the back of her throat. What was Pete doing with this girl?

She glanced at the time stamp in the upper right-hand corner. August 12, 3:25 p.m. Her sharp gasp rang loud in the empty kitchen. The day after her birthday. Pete had told her he'd be out of town that day. He'd booked a lavish suite at the Hyatt where they'd spent a romantic evening together, and he'd left before she'd even woken up the next morning.

Nausea rolled in her stomach, but she pushed past it and picked up the next picture. Another girl no older than eight held Pete's hand. This time he wore a different baseball hat and his back was to the camera. But it was him. She was sure of it. She forced her gaze to the time stamp. August 20, 5:45 p.m. The day before she flew back from Mexico and almost died. The day before she'd met Agent Grassi.

She dropped the picture on the table and picked up the card he'd left. *Graham Grassi. Special Agent, FBI.* What were the odds they'd been on the same plane that almost ended their lives, and now he was investigating the disappearance of Becca? She should have asked him why he'd even been on the plane in the first place. Usually, the crew was aware when law enforcement agents were on board. No one had known about Agent Grassi. And now her goddaughter's life was in his hands.

Becca.

Mickey hung her head in her hands and memories of her

goddaughter assaulted her. Suzi had been her best friend since the third grade, and the day Becca had been born was still one of the happiest of Mickey's life. She loved her like she was her own and had been a part of all of Becca's milestones. Her chest tightened and pressure built inside her. Each shallow breath she drew in became more painful than the last. Gasping for air, she leaned forward and pressed her forehead to her knees.

She needed to get it together. Falling apart wouldn't help anything. Straightening in her seat, she filled her lungs with a deep breath and then slowly released it through parted lips. Each breath slowed her rapidly beating heart and brought clarity to her frazzled mind. She had to talk to Suzi.

Mickey picked her phone up again and called Suzi. Still no answer. Tears slid down her face, splattering on the pictures and soaking through the glossy paper. Sniffing back her tears and wiping the wetness from her cheeks, she beat back her emotions and straightened her spine. She couldn't just sit here; she had to do something. Grabbing her purse off the counter, she slung it over her shoulder and ran out the door.

The humid air smacked her in the face as she stepped out into the sun. The curls around her neck tightened and sweat gathered at her temples. She pushed her hair back and rounded the corner to sprint the two blocks to Suzi's apartment. Her pace quickened as the building came into view, and she pushed past the fast-paced pedestrians to get to the door.

The setup of Suzi's building was similar to her own. She jogged up the three steps to the top of the stoop and pressed the buzzer connected to Suzi's apartment to get let into the building.

Crackling sounded through the speaker before a voice spoke. "Who's there?"

Mickey tilted her head, trying to pinpoint the high-pitched voice. She reached out and pressed her finger against the off-white button for the intercom. "It's Mickey."

A beat passed before more crackling split the air. "How dare you show your face here! This is all your fault. Get out of here before I call the police."

Suzi's mom.

She took a deep breath but couldn't keep the quiver from her voice as she pressed down on the button. "Mrs. Stanley, there's been a misunderstanding. I really need to talk to Suzi."

Seconds ticked by, but no other sounds came through the dirty speaker that sat flush with the weathered door. Mickey took a step back and shielded her eyes as she stared up at Suzi's third story window. The curtains were closed tight, the window shut. She pulled out her phone, but the door groaned open and Suzi's gaunt face and haunted blue eyes stared out at her before she needed to use it. The same blond curls Becca had inherited stuck out in all directions, as if Suzi had just rolled out of bed.

"Have you talked to him? Where did he take her? What has he done to my Becca?" As soon as she uttered Becca's name, Suzi's voice broke and a muffled sob escaped her twisted mouth. She took a step forward and pounded her closed fists on Mickey's chest.

Pain and shock rooted Mickey to the spot. She tried to grab Suzi's arm, but Suzi jerked away. Mickey wrung her hand around the strap of her purse and bit back a sob of her own. "I tried to call Pete, but his number's been disconnected. But I'll find him. I promise."

A strangled snort huffed out of Suzi's nose and the ice in her blue eyes sent a shiver down Mickey's spine. "You've done enough. You brought that sick bastard into our lives. And now he has my baby."

Suzi's words slammed into her much harder than her weak fists had and she staggered backward, nearly tripping down the top step. "I didn't know," she said, shaking her head.

"You dated him for four months. You didn't see any red flags? No gut feeling telling you that you'd let a monster into your bed?" Suzi's breath hitched and she pressed the back of her hand to her mouth. The dam burst and the flood gates opened. "How could you do this to us? Becca loves you."

Mickey's pulse raced in her ears and her stomach turned. "Suzi, you can't honestly think I had anything to do with this."

Suzi's shoulders slumped forward and defeat clouded her irises. "I can't think about anything right now except getting my baby back. Please, just leave."

She opened her mouth to speak, but the door slammed shut before anything came out. Her knees buckled and hot metal scorched her palm as she steadied herself with the rail. She'd lost her best friend and her goddaughter in one day. How had she not seen who Pete really was?

Guilt gnawed at her gut like a dog on a bone. Suzi was right. She'd brought Pete into Becca's life. She'd encouraged the girl to open up to Pete. Male role models were nonexistent in Becca's life, and Mickey had stupidly thought Pete could be the one. If it hadn't been for her, Becca would be home right now driving Suzi crazy with her constant chatter.

Reality crushed down on her. Suzi wasn't the only one who thought she knew the truth about Pete—so did Agent Grassi. Why else would an FBI agent have been waiting for her to get home earlier? The FBI didn't notify godparents about missing children. He had wanted to find out what she knew. Or in her case, didn't know.

Digging around in her purse, she searched for the card he'd left her. She needed to call him and straighten this out. Hell, maybe she had some information that could be helpful in finding Becca. A snippet of information Pete had mentioned that hadn't meant anything to her at the time.

Dammit, she hadn't grabbed the card. She stepped down the stairs and rushed toward home. Mickey rounded the corner toward her apartment, and goosebumps tickled her flesh. Stones scattered across the sidewalk behind her. She stopped and glanced around. The back of her neck tingled as though someone were watching her.

Get a grip. No one's watching you.

Quickening her pace, she closed the short gap to her building and hurried up the steps. She reached into her purse and rummaged around the bottom of her bag for her keys. Her heartbeat pounded and her fingers brushed against everything but her damn keys. The jagged outline of a small piece of metal skimmed the pad of her thumb and she clung to them like a lifeline.

The hairs on the back of her neck stood on end and she struggled to unlock the door. She closed her eyes, took a deep breath, and relief flooded through her as the key slid into the hole and she opened the door. The muscles in her thighs screamed from her earlier workout, but she pushed past the pain and ran up the two flights of stairs to her apartment.

She tried the handle, hoping her roommate had made it home, but no such luck. She jammed the key in the lock, yanked open the door, and hurried inside. Once the door was closed, she flipped the lock and leaned her back against the solid wood. The clawing sensation of fear subsided. She shouldn't be spooked. Becca was the one in trouble. But all of this had hit too close to home.

Pushing off the door, she walked into the kitchen and picked the business card off the table. She turned the white cardstock between her fingers as an image of the FBI agent with the cocky smile and intense gray eyes flashed in her mind. She'd actually been stupid enough to think he'd found her because he'd wanted to get to know her. Hope had bloomed in her for an instant, and then he had smashed that hope until it was nothing more than a swirling mist of nonsense. He didn't know a damn thing about her.

But that was about to change. No matter how big of an ass he'd been, he was looking for Becca. If she wanted Becca home safely, she needed to tell him everything she'd learned about Pete in the last four months. She grabbed her phone from her purse and then set her bag in front of her on the table. Her thumb swiped across the blank screen and she put in her password to unlock it before bringing up the call button. Her eyes darted between the card and her phone as she pounded in Graham's phone number.

Hard metal pressed against the back of her head and every muscle in her body stiffened. Warm breath skimmed over her bare shoulders.

"Don't move, or I'll blow that pretty little face of yours off."

Chapter Four

A dull ache pulsed behind his eyes and he rolled his head back and forth to ease the tension in his neck. Graham had chosen six years ago to join the human trafficking task force, but it didn't mean the cases didn't weigh on him.

Especially this one.

Something was different about how Pete Bogart handled himself. Graham and Eric had found next to nothing about the guy until Graham had interviewed Sanchez. He might be a slimy bastard, but he was smart. They couldn't find a name, a location, a fucking whisper in the wind about who he was. Not until Sanchez had given him a name...and not until Becca Stanley went missing.

Graham had looked at the other case files and spoken to the families of the other missing girls. None of the families had known Pete's name. None of the girls had spent time with Pete. So what was different about Becca? For a man who didn't mistakes, this had been a big one. Becca's mother could give them information about Pete and she could give them the name of the woman Pete had dated. A woman, once again, Pete had revealed his identity to.

The biggest question now was whether that woman was aware of everything Pete Bogart was or whether she was just another victim in his sick little game. It made his skin crawl.

He picked up a copy of the picture he had left with Mickey, the last picture taken of Becca with Pete from this morning. She'd been missing for five hours, and the more time that went by, the less likely they were to find her. He couldn't let that happen.

A sharp rap on the doorframe had him glancing up and staring into the deceptively calm brown eyes of his partner. Eric had been with the bureau for over twenty years and had been with the human trafficking task force since its inception. Graham considered himself lucky to be partnered with him and learned long ago not to underestimate his easygoing demeanor and receding hairline. His wrinkled shirts and slightly overweight build made him seem unassuming, but his mind was sharp and his instincts were usually spot on.

"Harper's ready to see us."

Graham groaned and fell back against his desk chair. The tension in his neck doubled. He hadn't been on the best terms with his boss the past month. "Can't you brief him while I keep working? We don't want to waste any time."

Eric narrowed his gaze and folded his arms over his broad chest. "You and Harper both need to get past what happened in Austin."

"I don't want to talk about it." He shoved the picture he'd been studying into a file and stood. "Let's get this over with."

They walked shoulder to shoulder down the wide corridor in silence. A sense of foreboding loomed inside him the closer they got to Harper's office. Eric was right, he needed to get past the part he had played in Austin, but knowing that didn't make it any easier. Guilt was his constant companion these days, and nothing he did made it go away. Hell, he wasn't sure he wanted it to.

A large hand came down on his shoulder and Eric pulled him to a stop outside of Harper's office. "Harper wants a briefing, and then we get back out there."

Graham nodded and followed Eric into the large corner office. His fingers curled around the edge of the file folder as it hung loosely in front of him. He stopped in front of Harper's massive walnut desk. Harper's gaze didn't lift from his computer screen, and Graham shifted his weight as the awkward silence dragged on. The muscles in his mouth tensed and he fought every instinct to roll his eyes. Leave it to Harper to call them in here and then make them wait until he was ready to speak.

Eric cleared his throat, and Harper held up one crooked finger, signaling for them to wait.

Graham glanced at Eric out of the corner of his eye, and Eric pressed his lips together to hide an amused smile. How could he find this funny?

Harper finally looked up and shifted his body so he leaned back in his black leather chair. The wheels squeaked until he stopped moving and his muscles relaxed. His brown eyes hardened as he asked, "What have you found out about the Stanley girl?"

"She was last seen with Pete Bogart at a frozen yogurt shop down the street from her apartment." Graham set the file folder on the desk. Harper flipped it open, but his gaze stayed locked on Graham. "I pulled the footage from a traffic camera on the corner and was able to get a picture of the two of them together. The mother hasn't heard from either Becca or Pete since nine a.m. this morning. She was supposed to be home by ten."

"Why did the mother let her daughter go with him?"

"Pete had been dating the mother's best friend for the past few months," Eric said. "The friend is Becca's godmother and she has a standing date with the girl every week. Pete often tags along for these outings, and the girl wanted to see him after the friend canceled today. The mother thought there was no harm in them spending an hour together."

"Have you talked to the friend?" Harper asked.

Graham's blood warmed as his mind went back to his meeting with Mickey. If he hadn't been able to stop thinking about her after seeing her on the plane, there was no way in hell he'd get the image of her in those tight black pants out of his mind.

A sharp elbow to the ribs brought his focus back to the present. "I talked to her earlier. As I wrote in my report, she's the same flight attendant that worked on the plane I followed the hijacker on. Her connection with both the plane hijacking and Pete Bogart was a red flag for me, and I wanted to gauge her reaction to the news about her goddaughter."

"That's one hell of a coincidence," Harper said. He drummed his bony fingers against the hard wood of his desk. "Did Sanchez mention anything about a woman helping Bogart when you questioned him?"

Graham shook his head and curled his hands into fists at his sides. It had taken all the self-control he had not to pummel Sanchez's face to a pulp when he'd questioned him. The bastard had almost succeeded in crashing a plane and killing hundreds of innocent people just to escape capture. And that would have been on his head, too. If Sanchez hadn't spotted him, he wouldn't have gotten spooked and resorted to such drastic measures.

"Yes, but he didn't have any information on her. The only name he gave was Pete's. He said he didn't know much more about what was happening in Chicago. He didn't even know the location of the girls. His role in this is limited to training the girls in Mexico, the sick fuck."

Harper raised his eyebrows. "Did you believe him?"

Graham shrugged. "Yeah. He shook like a leaf the entire time he was in the box. He would have given me anything to lessen his sentence."

"But we still have our eyes on the friend," Eric interrupted.

"Any other reason to suspect her besides the connection to Pete, the girl, and the plane?"

"Isn't that enough?" Graham asked with a snort.

Harper turned his sharp gaze in his direction. "Not after what happened in Austin last month. I trust you won't make the same mistake again. I need concrete evidence about this woman, not a hunch and a gut feeling."

Graham's nostrils flared. "There's also the issue of Pete only giving his real identity to her. I reviewed the case files for the other missing girls, and although Pete made connections with them and their mothers in weeks prior to their abduction, he gave each mother a different name. Why did he break pattern? Was he in a real relationship with Mickey and she was in the dark as she claims, or has she been in on it since the beginning?"

"These operations usually have a woman involved in keeping the girls in check," Eric said. "It's a woman who stays at the house to keep an eye on things. It's easier for the girls to become emotionally attached, and for the selfish bitch to use those emotions to mentally break down the victims." Eric slammed the toe of his shoe against the carpet as if to ground out his frustration.

Harper closed the file and slid it back toward Graham. "I'd say you need to find out what this woman knows as soon as possible. I've issued a BOLO for Pete Bogart, but chances are the guy's smart enough not to show his face around here. Something like this takes a lot of planning. He'd have a place set up to hide."

"If he's still in the city at all," Graham said. "And if he is, the chances of someone recognizing him are slim. How many blond-haired, green-eyed men with no distinguishing marks and of average build and height are walking around this city?"

"Too damn many. You two better get out there and start looking." Harper gave a curt nod and then returned his focus to his computer screen. Meeting over.

Graham grabbed the thin file and walked back to his small office down the hall. Reaching for his phone, he glanced back at Eric. "Where do you want to start?"

"Harper suggested seeing the godmother ASAP." Eric followed him in and took a seat on the hard plastic chair in front of his desk.

Fiery eyes that burned like dying embers popped into his head and his throat went dry. As much as he'd like to see what Mickey looked like out of her workout clothes, it wasn't a good idea. At least not tonight. He needed a little distance until he saw her again, and she needed time to let things simmer in her brain. Even if she were completely innocent, it'd be better to let little things Pete had said or done come to her over time instead of hounding her for information.

"No, I think it'd be better to see her tomorrow."

"Do you think she's in on this?"

He sighed and rubbed the palm of his hand over the two-day growth of whiskers on his chin. His hip rested against the side of the desk. "My first read is she's innocent. But dammit, she's tied up so tight into every aspect of this investigation, it doesn't sit well with me. We can't look past that. In most cases, the simplest answer is usually the right one."

"You said she didn't fall apart." Eric picked up a pen and tapped it against the side of the desk. "You don't think that's weird? If I found out someone I loved was missing, especially a child, I'd be pretty torn up."

"She went straight for denial. It won't be long before the truth smacks her in the face."

If she didn't already know the truth.

His mind went back to the small smile she'd worn when she first spotted him outside of her apartment. "It didn't help she and I have a history, even if a brief one. It threw her off seeing me again. I thought that might work to my advantage, but now I'm not so sure."

"You've got to stop second-guessing yourself, man. I agreed with you about speaking to her alone, that's why I stayed out of the way and talked more with Becca's mom." Eric dropped the pen and stood. "What's the plan?"

"Finding Becca is our priority, but to do that we need to go back to the beginning. We need to talk to the families of the other missing girls."

Eric nodded. "I agree. We also need to push on getting more information on Pete Bogart. We'll be more productive if we split up on this. Do you want the desk work or the families?"

His lips hitched up at the corner. "Seriously?"

Eric laughed and stepped toward the door. "I don't know why I even asked. Go ask the questions and meet me back here when you're done. If you get any leads, tag me. I'll do the same."

"You might not be able to ride the desk on this one, old man," Graham said with a laugh.

Eric scowled, making the lines in his face more pronounced. "Watch yourself, son. I'll put you behind your desk. I know how much you love paperwork."

"I didn't mean it." Graham winced and held up his hands in surrender. Being stuck behind his desk would be pure torture. Eric's preference for following a paper trail to track down a lead made him an ideal partner. "But in all likelihood one of us will have to go to Mexico and run down everything Sanchez gave us. And the last time I was on a plane from Mexico, it didn't go well."

"You brought in your man. I'd say it went well enough," Eric said with a chuckle.

Graham raised his eyes to the ceiling. "I guess it depends on how you look at it."

Eric smiled and gave a salute before walking out the door. Graham shuddered. No way in hell he was getting on a plane anytime soon. Not unless Mickey served him a cocktail with her long, lean legs peeking out of her hip-hugging blue skirt. He shook his head, forcing the image from his mind. He still didn't know the role she played in everything. For all he knew, the next time he saw Mickey, she'd be in handcuffs.

Chapter Five

The solid metal of the barrel pressed harder against the back of Mickey's head. All the blood drained from her face and she squeezed her elbows to her sides, trying to make herself smaller. Not that it helped. She had nowhere to run, nowhere to hide.

"Put your phone down," said the woman behind her. Her voice was full of grit, as if she'd gurgled a handful of rocks after smoking a pack of cigarettes.

Her hot breath brushed against Mickey's ear and her stomach heaved. Saliva filled her mouth and she swallowed hard to keep from getting sick. Something told her the woman holding her hostage wouldn't appreciate getting puke on her shoes. Slowly reaching forward, she placed her phone face up on the table.

"Take whatever you want," Mickey said in a small voice. "I don't have much, but take it all."

A harsh laugh raised all the hairs on her arms. "I don't want your shit. I'm here to make sure you keep your mouth shut."

"About what? I don't know anything." Tears clogged her throat. She pushed down the panic coursing through her and tried to focus. How the hell could she get out of this? Her eyes darted to her purse sitting on the table in front of her. If she could reach it, she stood a chance. But if she moved at all, she'd probably get a bullet in the brain.

"I saw the FBI agent leave here earlier. I know he was asking about Pete." The barrel of the gun sunk into her scalp and she winced. "What did you tell him?"

"I told him he was wrong. Pete couldn't have taken Becca. He's a good guy."

Holy shit. This crazy bitch knew Pete. What had she gotten herself involved in?

The woman snorted. "He's far from a good guy. You have no idea what he's capable of."

Mickey's ears tuned in to the hint of anger in the woman's voice. Maybe she could get her to talk, calm her down and talk her into leaving her alone. "How do you know Pete? Did he lie to you, too?"

"It's none of your damn business." The woman lifted the gun from her head and Mickey released a pent-up breath. "Sit down and put your hands on the table where I can see them. Don't even think about trying anything stupid. My partner's waiting downstairs. If you're lucky enough to get away from me and my gun, he'll snag your ass as soon as your feet hit the sidewalk."

She did as she was told. Sweat gathered on her palms, making her hands slippery on the wooden table. She pressed her teeth together to keep them from chattering and kept her gaze glued on her purse mere inches away from her hand. Running obviously wasn't an option. She had to get in there.

Footsteps fell behind her and traveled from one end of the kitchen to the other. The gun wasn't pressed against her anymore, but she had no doubt it was still trained on her. "I didn't sign up to kill people, but I have no choice. Pete slipped up. I told him it was too risky getting involved with someone, even if it were only to get close to the girl."

Mickey's stomach dropped and the queasiness intensified. Her vision blurred and she blinked to keep the room in focus. Doubt had crept in about Pete's role in Becca's disappearance, but now there was no hiding from the truth. Pete had Becca, and she had to pull herself together. She had to find Becca.

She had to keep the woman talking so she could come up with a plan. "How did you get into my apartment?"

The footsteps came closer and her body tensed. "Pete gave me your spare key. How sweet of you two to decide to take the next step in your relationship. It's too bad you didn't ask for the key back when you broke up with him."

A sharp clink ricocheted beside her and the spare key bounced on the table. She'd been so excited when they'd exchanged keys. It had been the first time she'd ever taken that step and it had cemented their relationship in her mind. Things had progressed quickly for them, but they both had believed their meeting was fate.

What a mistake that had been.

Even when the excitement of their whirlwind romance had died down and Pete's temper had flared, she had told herself everyone had flaws. Maybe Suzi was right, maybe she'd kept him around too long because it was better than being alone. Now the decision to make him a part of her life might cost her everything.

The gun came back to rest against her head and she sucked in a sharp breath. "Breaking up with him really set him off, you know. He hates when people make decisions for him, especially women. He might have even spared poor Becca if you'd kept on screwing him." Moist lips rested against her ear and she choked back a sob. "He said you were an excellent lay."

Mickey gripped the edge of the table until her knuckles turned white. Fury burned the blood flowing through her veins, heating her from the inside out. Every muscle in her body screamed to turn around and knock the bitch on her ass, but she couldn't act yet. She needed to be smart.

The barrel twisted against her head, winding her hair into a painful knot. "Now I have to make sure you don't ruin everything. You said Pete didn't say anything, but he had to have slipped up at some point. You two spent months together. I don't see any other way to make sure all the loose ends are tied up before we leave town."

"Please don't kill me." Mickey hated the frantic sound of her voice. "Pete didn't say anything. I don't know a damn thing."

"I wish I could believe you, but your time's up."

Mickey squeezed her eyes shut. At least it'd be quick. A soft rattling sound followed by muffled curses came from the door. Her eyes flew open and her heart clutched in a vise. She glanced at the clock.

Shit. Lydia's home.

Her heart pounded in her ears. She held her breath and bit into her bottom lip as her focus returned to her purse. The rattling stopped and the door creaked open.

"Who's there?" The gun left her skull. Now was the time to act. She jutted her elbow backward and slammed it into the soft stomach of the woman behind her. The woman grunted and stumbled backward, staggering to stay on her feet.

"Get out of here, Lydia! Now."

The door slammed shut. Mickey's arm shot out and her hand plunged into her bag. Her fingers found the hard handle of her taser and she pulled it out. Turning on the balls of her feet, she lunged at the woman, tackling her to the ground. A primal scream tore from Mickey's mouth and the gun fell to the floor. The woman twisted around, but not before Mickey saw a flash of sapphire eyes and the hard lines of her face.

Long bleach-blond hair trailed down the woman's back as she stretched out, reaching for the gun. Mickey's reach was longer, and she swatted the gun away. Mickey's arms wrapped around the woman's waist and she pulled her back. Keeping one arm in place as the woman clawed her way forward, she pressed the taser to the back of the woman's neck and pulled the trigger. Yellow sparks jumped out and the woman convulsed beneath her before falling limply to the floor.

Mickey jumped to her feet and grabbed her phone. She turned toward the gun on the floor. She didn't know how long the woman would be down and couldn't risk her waking up and grabbing the gun. Reaching down, she grabbed the butt of the gun and then ran toward her room. She couldn't risk running into her assailant's partner downstairs. Her fingers trembled as she unlocked her phone and pressed send. Agent Grassi's number flashed across her screen before she pressed it to her ear.

Come on. Answer the damn phone.

Her heart raced as she waited for him to answer. She closed and locked her bedroom door, and then sat on the floor with the gun pointed at the door. If the bitch came after her again, she'd be ready.

"Agent Grassi."

"Someone's trying to kill me! I need you to come to my apartment, or call the police, something. Just get someone here fast." Her voice trembled and she whispered into the phone as she squeezed it between her shoulder and ear.

"Who is this?"

"It's Mickey." She sucked in a deep breath to calm her shaking nerves. "Please come here. She jumped me in my apartment and put a gun to my head." Her words tumbled out faster and her beating heart slapped harder against her chest.

"Okay, calm down." His voice softened but his breath

turned ragged, as if he were running. "Where are you now?"

"In my bedroom. I knocked her out with my taser and ran to my room. I have her gun in case she comes in here." A slight tremor rippled through her hands and she squeezed the butt of the gun to steady them. She couldn't let fear stop her from protecting herself if need be.

"You're still in the apartment? Where's the woman who broke in?" The panic in Graham's voice made her blood pressure spike.

"She's passed out on the kitchen floor. I don't know how long she'll stay down. I didn't know what to do. I thought she was going to kill me, but then my roommate came home." Her breaths hitched and sharp, shallow gasps wedged in her throat. "Oh my God, Lydia. I told her to run. What if she comes in and gets hurt?"

"I'm going to hang up and call the police. Keep your phone right beside you. I'll call you right back. I'm close by, but I might need backup and I want them on their way."

"Okay. Hurry." She shifted the gun in one hand and held the phone in the other. Her gaze locked on the screen and she willed it to ring. Agent Grassi couldn't do anything until he got there, but it made her more confident just having him on the phone.

Seconds stretched out like hours. She kept her body as still as possible, her ears tuned into every shift and groan of the old apartment. Her phone vibrated in her hand, and she swallowed back tears of relief as Agent Grassi's number popped up on the screen.

"Hello?" The word came out on the release of a pent-up breath.

"The police are on their way. Your roommate called them."

A million scenarios played in her head of Lydia getting caught in the middle of this mess. Becca was missing. She didn't need Lydia getting hurt because of her too. She couldn't live with herself.

"She's across the street at a coffee shop waiting for the cops. She's fine, and she did the right thing by getting the hell out of there and calling the police." An irritated sigh sounded through the phone. "You should have gotten out of there, too."

Irritation intertwined with her fear. "She said someone was waiting downstairs. I didn't want to get away from one psychopath just to run into another," she hissed through clenched teeth.

"I should be there before the police, so hold tight. Have you heard any activity?"

"I haven't heard anything. But my door's closed, and the kitchen is down the hall. I don't know if I'd hear her if she moved around."

"If she woke up and planned on coming after you, there'd be no reason for her to try and be quiet. You'd know."

Great, just what I wanted to hear.

Her heart stopped beating for a second and she held her breath. She strained her ear toward the door. "I don't hear anything."

"Good. I'm turning the corner right now. I'll be there in a couple of minutes."

"Be careful. She has long blond hair and I don't know if she had any other weapons on her." The guy might be a dick, but she didn't want him to get hurt.

"I'll be fine," he said with another annoying laugh. "I'm going to hang up now. I'm the first one here, and I need both hands."

Panic tore through her. She didn't want to get off the phone. As stupid as it sounded, he was her lifeline right now. "Why do you need both hands?"

A beat passed before he said, "In case I need my gun.

Keep your phone close in case you need it. Do you know how to use a gun?"

"Point and shoot?"

"Good enough. Hang tight."

The call disconnected and she laid her phone face up on her lap. She wrapped both of her hands around the grip of the gun and kept her eyes locked on the door. The front door banged open and a muffled yell floated down the hall. Adrenaline sparked from her nerve endings, causing her teeth to clatter and her foot to bounce up and down on the shaggy rug. Graham was here, but it didn't mean she was safe yet.

Heavy footsteps barreled toward her. "Mickey, I'm here," he called out.

The vise of fear squeezing her lungs loosened, but her frayed nerves stayed on high alert. She kept the gun trained on the door.

Bam!

Another door slammed open. The sudden burst of noise made her jump.

Bam!

And another. This one closer and louder. Probably the bathroom door right next to her room. Her grip tightened around the gun. *Please, Lord, let that be Graham*

Bam!

Her door burst open, wood splintering from the doorframe, and Graham swung into her room. His legs stood firm, his feet planted on the ground. Both arms stretched out in front of him and a gun, much like the one she held, was aimed at her. His eyes darted around the room, and he walked in slowly.

She stood. "What the hell is your problem? You could have knocked, or just opened the damn door. You scared the shit out of me."

His intense gray eyes hardened and his jaw tightened. "Are you alone in here?"

"Yes, dammit." She lifted her hands in frustration. "Who do you think would be in here?"

Graham dropped the gun to his side, his gaze never leaving hers. "I don't know. But there sure as hell isn't anyone out there."

Chapter Six

She must think he was a damn idiot.

He'd rushed over here, broken down the door, and found absolutely nothing wrong. And why had she called him instead of the police? It didn't make any sense. The weight of his gun hung heavy in his hand as it dangled at his side. He studied Mickey. Red blotches dotted her porcelain skin and her dark pupils overpowered her irises. Her hands shook, causing the gun to bounce in her too-tight grip. He walked over to her dresser and yanked a T-shirt from the top drawer. With the soft cotton cupped in his hand, he eased the gun from hands and her arms dropped to her sides. The last thing he needed was for her to accidentally pull the trigger.

Maybe it wouldn't be an accident.

She eyed him wearily. "What do you mean nobody's out there?"

He held the gun away from his body. He needed to have it checked for prints, and he didn't want to contaminate what they might find. His brows rose at the question. "I mean the only person in this apartment is you."

Mickey shook her head and the corners of her mouth dipped down in a frown. "That doesn't make sense. She's got to be here somewhere. I used my taser on her. Wouldn't the stun keep her off her feet for a while?"

"It depends on how powerful the taser is. Have you ever used it before?"

"No. My dad bought it for me when I moved into the city after college. I always assumed it'd keep someone off their feet for a while, at least enough time to get away."

Graham bit back a smart-ass retort. He couldn't let his irritation show. He needed to keep her calm so she could give him some damn answers. Pushing aside her ignorance of a weapon she owned, a weapon she could hurt someone with if she didn't know what the hell she was doing, he said, "I've checked the entire apartment. I don't even see a sign of a struggle in the kitchen where you claimed she was passed out on the floor."

If the fire from her hard stare could have burned him, he'd need a paramedic. A small vein running down her forehead bulged. "Where I claimed? Do you think I made it up?"

He lifted his shoulders. "I honestly don't know."

Her jaw tightened; she jumped to her feet and pushed past him.

Great job keeping her calm.

He jammed his gun into the smooth leather of the holster on his belt. Cool metal pressed against a tiny spot of skin above his waistband, sending a shiver up his spine. His eyes did a quick scan of her bedroom. The room was small, with just enough space for a double bed and an armoire tucked in the corner. A soft pink bedspread with some sort of gray swirls covered the bed, not like he could see much of it. Clothes lay everywhere, their discarded hangers thrown carelessly on the floor. The woman was a slob.

Turning on his heel, he walked out of the room and found

Mickey in the kitchen. The top of the table was as cluttered as her room. Mickey's arms swiped the papers from side to side, uncovering bits of wood from underneath. Paper rustled as she picked up magazines and loose newspaper pages and shook them in the air.

"What are you doing?" he asked as he watched with annoyance.

"My key. I can't find my key." She didn't stop shifting through the clutter as she spoke. "She threw it on the table, but it's not here."

Graham walked to the counter and set down the gun he'd taken from her, making sure it stayed nestled in the shirt. "How did she get a key to your apartment?" His mind raced as he continued to watch her. No matter how much he wanted to believe the redheaded knockout with the killer body had nothing to do with the case, he couldn't ignore all the glaringly obvious signs that told him otherwise.

Mickey dropped to her hands and knees and her head disappeared under the table, giving him an excellent view of her ass. His jaw dropped and he groaned out his frustration. "She had my spare key. She said Pete gave it to her."

"Convenient."

Her body jerked and the top of her head slammed against the table. "Sonofabitch!" She crawled out from underneath the table and rubbed the top of her head, tousling the strands of her already messy hair.

This was the first time he'd seen her hair down, and his fingers itched to tame the wild wisps around her face. He crossed his ankles as he leaned against the counter and plunged his hands in his pockets to keep from doing something stupid.

She scrambled to her feet and crossed her arms over her chest, pushing her cleavage up toward the scoop neck of her tank top. He fought to keep his eyes on her face. Her eyes narrowed into slits. "Do you think I made this whole story up?"

"I don't know." His gaze stayed locked on her and he tried to keep his facial expression passive.

Her jaw tightened. "What could I possibly gain by calling you, asking for you to help me, and making up a story about a woman breaking into my house and trying to kill me?"

"Why'd you call me and not 911?"

She blew a long, slow breath out of her mouth and sank down into one of the chairs at the table. "After you left earlier, I went to Suzi's and tried to talk to her."

"What did she say?"

Moisture clouded over her tawny eyes and her shoulders dropped. "She's pissed I brought Pete into Becca's life, and then told me to leave. On my way home, I knew I had to do whatever I could to find her. There has to be something Pete said over the past four months that could help. So, when I got home, I planned to call you. I put your number in my phone, but the woman pressed a gun to my head before I could press send."

"When you got away from her, you just called the number that was already there?"

"Yes. It's not like it was a friend or something. You're FBI. I figured calling you would be just as good as calling the cops."

He nodded, taking in her words, but didn't speak.

Her eyes widened. "You don't believe me."

"I'm trying to figure this all out. What did this woman say to you?" He wanted to sit down beside her, but he needed to keep his distance. His mind wouldn't be focused on separating fact from fiction if he was consumed with figuring out what she did to smell so damn good all the time.

Mickey rested her elbows on the table and rubbed her temples, her eyes closed as her slender fingers massaged the spot. Graham took the opportunity to let his gaze roam from the top of her vibrant red hair, down the smooth lines of her bare arms, over to the healthy curve of her breasts under her shirt. Her eyes flew open and their gazes locked.

Lust pooled in his gut and his chest tightened. A sexy blush engulfed her high cheekbones, and she quickly glanced away. "Umm...she said she needed to tie up loose ends before she and Pete left town." Her fingers picked at the crumbled newspaper lying on the table and she avoided his gaze.

Her words snapped his mind back to focus. "Why would you be a loose end? You told me you didn't know what Pete was up to."

"I don't!" Her fingers traveled from her temples to her hair and she fisted it in her hands before pushing herself up from the table. She faced him, a finger pointed at his chest. "I called you for help, and you're treating me like criminal."

"Then why was someone threatening your life to keep you quiet?"

If anyone had been here at all.

Tears spilled over her long lashes and ran down her face. She let them fall and dropped her hand to her side. "I don't know," she whispered.

He sighed and a war twisted inside him. Nothing about Mickey added up, but he couldn't look past the nagging voice in the back of his head yelling at him to trust her.

Knock, knock, knock

Graham glanced up at the police officer pounding on the doorframe. He nodded a silent greeting and the police officer pressed his lips into a thin line. A second officer stood beside him, his hand on the butt of the gun in his holster.

"We were called in to investigate a possibly dangerous situation at this residence," the older cop with the cool green eyes said.

"I'm Special Agent Graham Grassi with the FBI. Miss

O'Shay"—he nodded toward Mickey, who stood in front of him, her back to the door—"called me directly."

The younger cop with his hand on his gun glanced around the apartment. "Where's the intruder? The roommate is downstairs and is a bit of a mess."

Mickey whirled around. "Lydia's downstairs?"

The older cop nodded. "She was told to wait downstairs until we allowed her access. We were unaware the threat had been taken care of." One eyebrow raised, he stared at Graham.

"The woman in question was gone by the time I got here." He dipped his chin toward Mickey. "You're going to want to take her statement. I'll talk to you when you're finished."

Ignoring the sparks shooting from Mickey's stare, he grabbed his phone from his pocket and walked into the hallway. He turned his back to the door to the apartment and called Eric.

"Hey. Did you find something?" Eric asked after he answered on the second ring.

"More like something found me," Graham said.

"Huh?"

"I was on my way to talk to the family of the first girl who went missing, who just happens to live in the west loop close to both Miss O'Shay and the Stanleys, when I got a frantic call from Miss O'Shay." He glanced over his shoulder. Fear and confusion played out on Mickey's face as she talked to the cops. "She claims someone broke in and tried to kill her."

Eric cleared his throat on the other end of the line. "Claims?"

Graham squeezed his eyes shut and rubbed a hand over the deep creases in his forehead. "When I got here, she had locked herself in her room and had a gun in her hands, but no one else was here. She says she used a taser on the back of a woman's neck in her kitchen, but there's no woman passed out on the floor."

"Did you check the setting on the taser?"

"I didn't get that far. The cops showed up. Besides, even if the cartridge confirms she shot it, it doesn't mean she used it against an intruder. I did grab the gun she claims the woman pressed to her head. We can try to get prints and I'll look up the registration number." He dropped his hand and paced back and forth in the small hallway. "Her roommate called the police when she tried to get in and Mickey yelled at her to get out."

"Did you talk to the roommate? Did she see anything?"

Annoyance flared. He should have waited to call Eric, but he'd wanted some insight. "Again, I haven't gotten that far. She's downstairs. I'll talk to her while the cops take Mickey's statement."

"Good plan." Eric coughed and phlegm rattled in his throat. "Did Miss O'Shay see what the woman looked like?"

"Oh my God, dude, I got here ten minutes ago. All she said was the woman had blond hair." He took a breath and collected himself. His nerves were on edge with this case. He didn't need to snap and take it out on his partner. "I just wanted to give you a heads up."

"Okay. Let me know when you find out more." A beat passed before he added, "I think you're right about one of us needing to go to Mexico. I haven't found Pete's place in Chicago, but I found a house near Playa Del Carmen listed under the name Paula Montgomery."

Graham stopped moving and searched his memory for that name. It didn't ring a bell. "Who's Paula Montgomery?"

"Paula is the name of Pete Bogart's stepsister and Montgomery is his grandmother's maiden name. We need to check it out."

A low whistle whizzed between his teeth. "He buried that pretty good. How did you figure it out?"

"I'm that good," Eric said with a smile in his voice before he turned serious. "I'll go alone if you want to stay in Chicago."

Beads of sweat broke out on the base of his neck as flashbacks of the plane plummeting toward the ground assaulted him. He couldn't let it paralyze him. He needed to get back on the horse...or the plane. "How about you head there tomorrow and if you need me to meet you, I'll book a flight as soon as I conduct interviews with the family? We don't have shit to go on in Chicago. Maybe the leads in Mexico will prove more lucrative."

"We've got Miss O'Shay. She might be the only lead we need."

A brick dropped in the pit of his stomach. Eric might be right. "It shouldn't be long before we find out. I'll call you later."

He clicked off, put his phone in his pocket, and started down the stairs. If Mickey's roommate was waiting outside, he wanted to talk to her before she saw Mickey. He opened the door and blinked several times so his eyes could adjust to the evening light. It didn't take long. It never got too dark in the city.

Only a few people lingered on the sidewalk, and it didn't take him long to spot Mickey's roommate. He'd never seen her before, but there was no mistaking the petite woman with raven hair wringing her hands. Her wide eyes stared at the front door to the building and he slowed his gait, approaching her slowly.

"Excuse me, are you Miss O'Shay's roommate?"

The woman jumped and her head moved a fraction of an inch to face him. "Yes. Who are you? Is Mickey okay?" Her breaths came out in quick spurts, her words as fast as lightning.

"I'm Special Agent Graham Grassi with the FBI."

Her wide eyes narrowed before they scanned him from head to toe. "How do I know if you're really FBI? And why would you be here? I called the police."

He pulled his badge and ID from his pocket and held it out for her. She studied it, and then gazed back up at him. "Okay, so you're FBI. Where's Mickey?"

"She's inside giving her statement to the police. I'm sure they'll clear you to go up and see her soon."

She put a hand on her heart and her shoulders dropped. "Oh, thank God."

"What's your name?" Mickey had mentioned it, but he couldn't remember.

"Lydia. So, Mickey's not hurt? What happened in there?"

He put his ID back in his pocket and pulled out the pen and notepad that were as much a part of him as his right arm. "I was hoping you'd be able to tell me."

Lydia shook her head and not one hair fell out of place. "I don't understand. Didn't you talk to Mickey?"

He nodded. "Yes, but I think you might be able to shed a little more light on the situation."

Lydia lifted her gaze up to the second-story window. The streetlight behind them shone down on her, showing off her furrowed brow. "I don't understand. Mickey yelled at me to leave as soon as I cracked the door open, and I knew something was wrong. But I didn't see anything."

Graham turned and followed Lydia's gaze to Mickey's apartment window. Another lead with nowhere to go, another story without an ending to clear Mickey's name. She didn't know it yet, but another nail had just been hammered in her coffin.

Chapter Seven

"We can't stay here tonight," Lydia said.

Her dark eyes glanced over at Graham, who stood in the corner of the kitchen, talking on his phone. "G.I. Joe over there busted the door. And even if we could get it to close properly, that woman still has a copy of the key."

Mickey sank deep into the soft cushions of the couch, wishing she could disappear. At least for the night. Exhaustion weighed her down. "She won't come back tonight. That'd be stupid. And I'm too tired to pack my stuff up and figure out where to go."

Lydia crossed the room and sat beside her. "Come with me to my parents' house."

Mickey's eyes drifted shut. She didn't have the energy to keep them open anymore. Not after the day she'd had. She'd spent the last hour giving her statement to the police and then rehashing everything again with Agent Grassi. But the more she'd talked, the more he stared at her with those intense, distrusting eyes. It didn't help that Lydia hadn't actually seen anything. At least Lydia didn't think she was lying.

"You should listen to her," Graham said.

Her muscles tightened and her eyes flew open. He stood over her, so close she could smell the lingering sweat that had soaked through his shirt earlier. "Why do you care? And why are you still here?"

His eye twitched, but his features remained calm. "I was talking to my partner about our next move. Talking to you is important in finding Becca and the other girls. The fact that this woman said they were tying up loose ends before leaving town is crucial. If Pete's still in town, so are the girls."

"I thought you didn't believe me."

"I said I didn't know what to believe."

She snorted and pulled herself up from the comfortable cushions that cradled her in their softness. "Whatever. I don't care what you think. I just want you to do your job and find Becca."

His lip hitched up in the annoyingly sexy half smile that made her blood hum. But it didn't matter how the scruff on his chin highlighted his strong jaw or if his shirt showed off all the definition that lay beneath it. He was off limits the minute he had questioned her about her whereabouts like she was a suspect in her own goddaughter's disappearance.

"We agree on something then," he said. "That's why you're going with your friend to her parents for the night while I stay here. I don't think the woman who attacked you will be back tonight, but if she is, I want to see her for myself."

In one day, Graham had gone from the sexy mystery man who saved her life to a major pain in her ass. No way she would let him tell her what to do, especially after the way he'd treated her all day.

"I'm not going anywhere. If you want to stay, good. Then Lydia could leave and be out of harm's way without worrying about me." She stood and looked down at Lydia. "You go. I have G.I. Joe with me for the night. I'll be fine."

Graham snorted out a laugh. "G.I. Joe?"

Mickey's lips curved into a tight smile and she batted her lashes at him. "Yep. My hero."

"I don't want to leave you here. You've had a rough couple of days." Lydia reached up and grabbed her hand.

"And all I want to do is fall into my bed and go to sleep. I'll be fine. Graham's here." She plastered on the same smile she used at work—the one that hid the irritation dying to scream from her pores. The last thing she wanted was to spend more time with Graham, but she wanted to keep Lydia and her family safe. If someone was following her, what would stop her from leading them to the doorsteps of her best friend's parents' house? As much as she hated to admit it, the safest place for her was with Graham.

Lydia arched one finely shaped eyebrow. "Graham?"

"Agent Grassi." Graham chuckled behind her and she gritted her teeth. "Now go pack your bag and get out of here so I can go to sleep."

Lydia gave her one last pleading look before getting up and heading to her bedroom. Mickey turned to face Graham and planted her fists on her hips. "You could've asked if I was okay with you staying here. You can't tell me what to do, and then think I'm all right with you making yourself at home in my apartment. It doesn't work that way."

Graham took one step toward her, bringing him way too close in the small space. "How does it work then, darling?"

She swallowed hard and stood her ground. "I don't care what you think of me, you will treat me with respect. And you won't call me 'darling.' You don't get to waltz in here and dictate what I do. I've done nothing wrong, and I won't stand for being treated like a criminal. If you want to stay here tonight, fine. You can sleep on the couch. Pillows and blankets are in the hall closet. I'm going to bed."

Turning away from him, she walked to her bedroom and

closed the door. She pulled off her clothes and threw them in the corner of the room before grabbing a large T-shirt from her drawer. The soft material bunched in her hands. She hadn't showered at all today, but it would be too much work right now. Besides, maybe Graham would keep his distance if the sweat from her workout still hung in the air around her. He might not trust her, but if he was half as attracted to her as she was to him, she had to do whatever she could to keep space between them.

Yanking the old Cubs shirt over her head, she pulled the long strands of her hair out from under the shirt and climbed into bed. The mattress dipped low beneath her weight and she pulled the down blanket around herself. She shifted, trying to find a comfortable position. Her muscles relaxed, but the tension in the back of her neck remained. She closed her eyes, willing sleep to come, but images of Becca played on repeat in her mind. Tears sprang to her eyes and leaked down onto her pillow. They had to find her. Failure wasn't an option. She just prayed that when they did, it wouldn't be too late. Holding on to that prayer, sleep finally came and gave her a short reprieve from the nightmare of her life.

. . .

Mickey bolted up in bed, a cold sweat clinging to her brow.

Her room was dark, except for the tiny sliver of moonlight seeping in through a slit in her curtains. She pulled her blanket over her chest and her eyes scanned the room. Her heart raced and she tried to steady her shaky nerves. The rapid banging of her pulse beat through her eardrums. Something had woken her. A noise? No. That wasn't it. She had to get out of here, though.

Her gaze flew to her nightstand, and she reached down and grabbed her taser. She'd been too tired to be afraid of staying in her apartment for the night, but she wasn't stupid. The taser had been switched to a higher setting, and she'd made sure it was within reach before she went to sleep. If someone came back for her tonight, she'd be ready. And this time, the person wouldn't be walking out of here.

The floorboards of the old apartment shifted. She held her breath and strained to hear anything happening outside her bedroom door.

Nothing.

Blood thundered in her ears, drowning out everything around her. Taking a deep breath, she swung her legs over the side of her bed and stood. Cold air blasted out of the vent above her and a shiver tore through her. The hairs on her arm stood on end, but she wasn't sure if it was from the cold or fear.

Her bare feet padded across the carpet and her hand rested on the doorknob. If someone was out there, she'd rather be on the defensive. She wasn't going to lie in her bed and wait for someone to kill her. Something, or someone, had woken her up. Taking a deep breath, she turned the handle and stepped out into the dark hall. Not even the moonlight lit a path for her, and she blinked to adjust her eyes to the total darkness.

The plush carpet absorbed the sound of her tiptoeing down the hall. Her hands wrapped around the taser and she pointed it straight in front of her. The hallway seemed to stretch on forever, and her heart beat harder with every step.

A soft creak came from the direction of the kitchen. She stopped, squeezed her eyes shut, and gathered all of her courage. *You can do this. Don't be a victim. Take control.* She took two long strides to the end of the hallway, whipped around the corner, and sucked in a breath as a dark figure in the kitchen turned toward her. Her finger shook against the trigger of the taser.

"Holy shit, Mickey. What the hell are you doing?"

"Something woke me up," she said as she released a pent-up breath. She dropped her arms to her sides and relief washed over her.

"And you didn't think if a threat was in your apartment the FBI agent would take care of it?" He grabbed a glass from the cabinet and filled it with water before facing her again.

No curtains hung from the kitchen window, and moonlight streamed in and danced across the tiled floor. Graham stood in front of the sink. Dark circles hung low under his eyes, but that wasn't what caused her pulse to pick up. Graham Grassi, Mr. G. I. Joe himself, stood in her kitchen with bare feet and his white dress shirt unbuttoned to reveal his smooth, muscular chest.

She met his gaze head on. "For all I knew, you fell asleep and got caught with your pants down. It seems I was partially right since you're walking around my home half naked." She had to hold on to her annoyance to keep from drooling over his washboard abs.

Even with his face slightly hidden in the shadows, there was no mistaking the spark of humor in his eyes. He shrugged and the muscles in his shoulders bunched together. "I wanted to make myself a little more comfortable before I went to sleep. It seems I'm not the only one," he said, dipping his chin low in her direction.

She glanced down and heat erupted in her like a volcano. The T-shirt she'd thrown on barely skimmed the top of her thighs and her nipples pressed against the flimsy cotton of the ancient shirt. Thank God it was dark. It'd be harder for him to see how red her face grew when she was embarrassed. Swallowing down her humiliation, she met his gaze once again. "I'm in my own home. I can dress however I like."

He cocked his head to the side. "I didn't know there was a dress code for guests. You should have warned me of that before you stormed off to bed earlier."

Anger flared inside her, but it was hard to stay focused when all she wanted to do was run her fingers down the hard board of his stomach. My God. How many hours a day did the man work out to get such chiseled abs? She couldn't tear her eyes off them.

"Do you like what you see?" He took a step toward her, and she took one back.

Her eyes snapped to his and her face tingled. "I don't know what you're talking about." She crossed her arms in front of her chest and instantly regretted it. Instead of hiding her breasts, the material clung more firmly against them. She took another step toward the hall and dropped her arms back to her sides. "I'm going back to bed."

"I didn't mean to wake you. I wanted a drink of water before I went to sleep."

She glanced at the clock and raised her brows. "You're just now going to sleep? It's almost three."

Graham lifted the glass to his lips and took a long sip. "I had work to do."

"Did you find anything?"

He shook his head. "I can't discuss the case with you, Mickey."

"But you said earlier it was important to talk to me." She ground her teeth together. It couldn't hurt to tell her what he'd found out. Hell, it might even help him. No one knew Pete and Becca like she did.

"I needed to talk to you about what happened tonight, and you gave me some interesting insight. Beyond that, the only thing we can discuss is any information about Pete that you think might be helpful in finding him."

"I don't know what else—"

Bang!

Mickey jumped and threw herself at Graham. His strong

arms circled around her back and pressed her tightly against his hard body. His lips pressed against her ear. "Shh...you're fine. It was a car backfiring."

She closed her eyes and pressed her forehead against his chest. The unsteady rhythm of her heart had as much to do with being so close to him as it did the damn car that scared her to death. Small hairs tickled her skin and she took a deep breath, inhaling an intoxicating blend of spiced cloves and coffee. She lifted her chin and found Graham's eyes, dark with desire, shining down on her.

Her hair fell across her face, and his knuckles brushed it back, before his hand traveled to the back of her neck. His fingers slid through her matted hair and rested at the back of her head. His other hand pressed against the small of her back, molding her into him. Tingling sensations danced in her belly and her nipples grew hard as they rested against his skin. She bit into her bottom lip. Maybe she should stop this before it started, but the comfort he offered was tempting as hell.

Graham made the decision for her. He leaned down and pressed his lips to hers. A soft moan purred from her throat and she melted into him. She parted her lips and his tongue invaded her mouth. His tongue slid steadily over hers and the taste of him filled her senses. Her arms circled around his neck and Graham's hands dropped to her ass. His palms settled on her bare cheeks exposed by her thong, branding her skin. Her eyes flew open.

She pulled back and pushed against his chest. What the hell was she doing? Agent Graham Grassi was the last man she should be kissing right now. Hell, she could barely tolerate the man. She struggled to get enough air in her lungs and calm the desire crashing over her.

Graham's hands covered hers as they lingered on his chest. "What's wrong?" His breath came out as ragged as hers.

She shook her head and kept her gaze locked on the floor. If she stared up at his sculpted jaw or broad shoulders, she wouldn't stand a chance. "I know what you think of me," she whispered.

Graham dropped his hands to his sides and took a step away from her. The distance was small, but it spoke volumes. She glanced up, and he rubbed a hand across his face. "I'm sorry. I shouldn't have kissed you."

"I shouldn't have thrown myself at you because a car backfired," she said with a smile, trying to ease the awkwardness.

He chuckled. "I don't blame you for being jumpy. We both need some sleep."

She nodded and turned toward her room. This day had gone from bad to worse to monumentally embarrassing. She wanted it to be over.

"And Mickey?"

She spun back toward him and her mouth went dry. She cleared her throat. "Yes?"

His lips hitched up on the corner. "Don't let those backfiring cars scare you tonight. She had a key, remember? No need to make a bunch of noise to break back in."

She rolled her eyes and fought to suppress a laugh. "That doesn't make me feel better, G.I. Joe." Turning back around, she walked toward her door. Realization struck her like lightning and she whipped around to face him. "Graham, did you guys go to Pete's apartment today?"

"Shit," Graham said. "No. We haven't been able to find where he lives. Do you know where he lives?"

A grin spread across her mouth. "Even better. I've a copy of his key."

Chapter Eight

"You're not coming with me." Graham fixed his most intimidating stare on Mickey, which was hard as hell to do when she stood in front of him with her explosion of red hair raining down her shoulders and hands fisted on her hips.

"I don't see how you have a choice. I have the key and I know where the apartment is."

Dammit, she was right. He'd called the owner of the apartment complex Pete lived in to get his permission to enter the premises, but no one had answered. Not that he was surprised. It was close to four in the morning. No sane person would answer their phone right now unless they worked in law enforcement or had children to worry about.

"Just give me the key and let me call in backup. I'll make a call to secure a warrant and pray like hell it comes in quickly."

They'd run Pete's name all day yesterday and hadn't found anything listed under his name, or any combination of names associated with him. Besides the house in Mexico, they had dick to go on. Mickey's involvement in all of this was still pretty sketchy, but if she was willing to lead him to Pete's apartment, he had to jump on the opportunity.

"I'm the one he gave a key to. If he didn't want me inside, he should have taken it back. There's nothing stopping me, an angry ex-girlfriend, from snooping around his place."

"And contaminating evidence we might find to catch him?" Lord, the woman was infuriating. She didn't understand how she could ruin everything by being such a stubborn pain in his ass.

Or maybe she did understand.

Mickey pressed her lips together and returned his intimidating stare with one of her own. He hated to admit it, but hers was better.

He sighed. They'd wasted enough time arguing. "Let's go. My car's parked in a garage a couple blocks over."

"We can walk. His apartment is closer than the garage." She looked at her broken door and winced. "What should I do with the door? I can't even shut it all the way, let alone lock it."

"I'll make a call and have someone stand watch until the guy comes to fix it. You said he'd be here soon, right?"

"Yeah." She glanced around the apartment. "Okay. There's nothing much for anyone to take, and I want to get to Pete's in case we find something to get Becca back. I don't want to waste time."

"If you're worried about it, you can stay here while I check out the apartment."

If looks could kill, he'd be flat on the floor. "Never mind. It was only a suggestion. Let's go."

He closed the door as best he could, and then followed Mickey down the stairs. He sent off a quick text to Eric, requesting a man stationed at Mickey's door, and then put his phone back in his pocket. He stepped outside and a light mist sprayed down on him. Gray clouds filled the early morning sky, and people huddled under umbrellas as they hurried past. The sun hadn't even risen and people were already on their way to work. Or maybe on their way home from the bar. He glanced at Mickey. "Do you still want to walk?"

She smirked at him and the small mole above her mouth lifted. "Afraid of a little water?"

"No, but I'm not the one wearing white." His eyes scanned the long line of her body and his chest tightened.

Mickey's chin dropped, taking in the color of her T-shirt, and a crimson blush crept up her chest and consumed her entire face. He smiled. Damn, she was cute when she was embarrassed.

She hunched her shoulders forward and took off walking, her long legs carrying her quickly down the sidewalk. "I guess we better walk fast then," she called over her shoulder.

Graham couldn't help the smile that took over his mouth. He followed closely behind her, weaving in between people they passed on the way down the block. The light mist formed into tiny droplets that coursed down his face. He didn't mind. A little bit of water was better than the suffocating humidity from yesterday.

Mickey stopped short in front of him and the toe of his shoe came down on her heel. She lurched forward and he reached out and wrapped his arms around her waist to steady her. She fell back against him. The subtle curve of her spine and the rounded shape of her ass molded to his body. He sucked in a sharp breath through his nose. Heat poured through his veins and need pulsed deep inside him.

The drops of rain grew larger as they fell from the sky. He bunched the wet material of her shirt in his hands and his knuckles brushed against the smooth flesh hidden underneath. Her body tensed. The smell of rain mixed with the damn scent of strawberries that clung to her tempted him to draw her closer. He leaned down and buried his nose in her hair.

She spun around and faced him. "What are you doing?"

His hands released her shirt and he gripped her hips. "I'm... I don't know."

Anger darkened the color of her eyes. "You sniffed my hair. Why?"

He avoided her pointed stare, but he couldn't pull himself away from her. "I'm sorry. I wasn't thinking."

"Obviously not." She pointed at the old brick building in front of them. "Do you want to go in, or stand in the rain and keep smelling me?"

He dropped his hands from her hips but didn't step away. Heat vibrated between them, mixing with the rain as if he were standing in the middle of a damn jungle. He glanced around. People continued to pass by them, oblivious to the battle warring inside him.

Was Mickey oblivious, too? Did she know how bad he wanted her?

Of course she does, you idiot. She just caught you sniffing her hair.

He finally took a step back. Flirting with Mickey was a big mistake. Not only was it taking his mind off the case, but she could be playing off his obvious attraction to her to keep him from putting the pieces of her involvement with Pete together. He had to get his shit together, and quick.

"Lead the way," he said, extending an open palm toward the building.

The smirk from earlier came back on her face, and he fought every impulse not to kiss it off.

Pete's building was older than Mickey's, even though it was only a block away. And if he were a block from Mickey, he had lived close to all three of the girls he had taken in the last month. He hunted close to home. Pulling his phone out, he brought up Eric's number. His thumbs flew over his screen as he wrote out Pete's address.

Here's his address. Find out who it's listed under.

Mickey held the door to the building open for him, and then turned to the only apartment on the first floor.

"Did you come here a lot?" he asked as she pushed open the door and he followed her inside.

"No. He'd just moved to town when we met, and he said he needed to furnish the place. When he was in town, he spent a lot of time at my apartment." She spun the key in her hands.

"He didn't get far," he said, scanning the room. "How did you two meet?"

She snorted out a sad laugh and walked by him. "We ran into each other at a grocery store. Literally. We were both looking through the produce and our carts smashed into each other."

He glanced to the right at the kitchen. The room was so small, not even a table could fit on the thin strip of dingy tiles. "Did he speak to you first? Who asked who out?"

"Why does it matter?" she snapped. "I started a relationship with a nice man. I didn't knowingly invite a monster into my life."

He faced her with raised brows before continuing his quick appraisal of the apartment. A dirty green recliner sat in the middle of the otherwise empty living room. Dust hung heavy in the air and cobwebs cluttered the corners of the walls. Pieces of paper littered the time-warped wooden floor. He bent down and picked up a couple pieces of notebook paper crumbled beneath his shoe. Names and dates scrawled across the pages. They'd have to search every single one.

"I'm surprised he gave you a key. There's not much in here. Is this what it looked like when you came here with Pete?"

She shrugged. "Pretty much. I think the only reason he

gave me a key is because I gave him a copy of mine. He didn't make a big deal about it."

Footsteps echoed behind him, and he turned as Mickey disappeared around a corner. He stood to follow her. The last thing he needed was for her to hide, or worse, destroy, an important piece of evidence. The floorboards creaked under his weight as he took a few long strides down the narrow hallway. Mickey disappeared into a room at the end of the hallway, but a closed door on his right grabbed his attention. His hand curved around the handle, but when he tried to turn it, it wouldn't budge.

"Mickey, what's in here?"

She stuck her head out of the doorway. "'I don't know. I've never been in there."

"Do you know where the key is? It's locked."

She shook her head. "No, but the locks look the same as the ones in my apartment. You can turn the lock with the edge of a credit card."

He grabbed his wallet from his back pocket and Mickey disappeared again.

What was she looking at in there? Should he follow her before he opened the locked door?

Curiosity and a strong gut instinct won out. He grabbed a credit card and the corner squeezed into the small slot on the door handle. Turning the card slowly, he turned the lock and opened the door. His eyes darted around the room and a low whistle vibrated through his lips.

He stepped into the room and grabbed his phone. He turned on the camera and took pictures of the far wall. Pictures scattered the cracked beige surface from floor to ceiling. He snapped pictures of every inch and then sent them all to Eric. Leaning closer, he studied each of them. The smiling face of Becca stared back at him. Some of her with her mom, others with Mickey.

The other two girls littered the wall as well, and he clenched his hands into fists. The pervert had been stalking them all for months. Pictures of each of the girls leaving school, playing on a playground, and walking around the city were posted for the bastard's pleasure. Pete had captured photos of the girls with their mothers, friends, and other close family members.

He hadn't dated anyone close to the other girls, but both of the mothers interviewed yesterday recognized Pete. Both of them were horrified to discover he had taken their daughters. Pete had become a casual neighbor, showing up at places they had frequented and starting friendly conversations while waiting in line or passing on the sidewalk. Neither woman knew his real name, but he had always been quick with a smile or a piece of candy for their daughters.

The sick bastard had slowly earned their trust from a distance before luring them away.

And they weren't the only girls up there. He'd bet money some of them matched the names on the papers he'd found.

His blood boiled and muddled his brain. But one question stood out in his mind. Why was it different with Becca? Pete had gotten to know Becca on a personal level, through Mickey. That couldn't be a coincidence. Had he targeted Mickey to get close to Becca? Or was his gut wrong, and Mickey was involved in this disgusting mess? One thing was certain, he needed to stop letting his attraction to her creep up and steal his focus. Not only was it stupid, it could cost these girls their lives.

A sharp gasp sounded behind him, and he spun around and faced Mickey's wide eyes. She lifted her shaking hand and covered her mouth, her gaze fixed on the wall of pictures. "Oh my God."

He studied her as her eyes darted over the wall. "Looks like we found his hideout. Too bad there's not a big sign pointing to where he ran to next."

All the color drained from her face and moisture filled her eyes. "This is the most disturbing thing I've ever seen."

He squinted and kept the muscles in his face relaxed. Had she gone pale because of the disturbing images, or was she feeling guilty for knowing where Pete was? Maybe she had willingly brought him here because she knew Pete would be long gone, and there'd be nothing left to show him where to look next.

Her gaze drifted from the picture to his face and she dropped her hand from her mouth. Her jaw hardened and the moisture left her eyes and fire replaced it. "Stop looking at me like that."

He tilted his head to the side and fixed a bored stare on her. "Like what?"

She threw her hands in the air. "Like I'm a criminal." She gestured toward the wall. "Do you honestly believe I had something to do with this?" Her voice broke and she bit down on her lip and turned her head.

"I think we have plenty to secure a warrant once we figure out who owns the apartment. We should leave before we ruin more evidence than we already have."

Her mouth dropped open and he walked past her toward the door. He ignored the nagging guilt in the pit of his stomach. He had to keep a wall up between them until he figured her out. His phone vibrated against his thigh and he pulled it out. A text message from Eric scrolled across the screen along with the picture of a blond woman with cold blue eyes.

"Does the name Connie Difico mean anything to you?" He turned and watched her reaction to the name Eric had just sent him.

Mickey shook her head and her hair swirled around her, stirring up the dust in the air. "No."

He crossed the room and held his phone in front of her face. "Does she look familiar?"

If possible, her face became even more pale. Fear flashed in the irises of her eyes as she stared at the screen and her chin quivered. "That's the woman who tried to kill me. Did the police find her?" Her voice shook and rose an octave with every word.

"This is the woman who was in your apartment last night?" He flipped the phone toward him and studied the picture again. She couldn't be older than twenty-five.

"Yes. I told you I didn't make it up." She pointed at the phone. "I know that's her."

"The police don't have her, Mickey. But we're standing in her apartment."

Chapter Nine

Panic clawed at her throat and she glanced around the apartment, her feet moving toward the door. Her hand pressed against the back of her head where the gun had been lodged last night. "We need to get out of here. She might come back."

Graham lowered the phone to his side and shook his head. "She won't come here. If Pete gave you a key, he'd do so knowing you wouldn't run into her. He probably used her name so he'd be harder to find. He made some mistakes with you, but he's not stupid."

She dropped her hand from her head and narrowed her eyes at him. Fury replaced the panic consuming her body and she clenched her hands into fists. "What do you mean he made a mistake with me? Because he couldn't cut off the loose end, or because he dated me in the first place?"

Graham's chest expanded as he drew in a large breath. "I mean because he gave you his real name and let his guard down with you. Most of what he told you was a lie, but some truth could have spilled out. You claim you were unaware of his true intentions, but something had to have slipped."

Heat rushed into her cheeks. "There's that word again. *Claimed*. Like I'm making everything up, like I was part of this big plan to kidnap my goddaughter and sell her for sex. Do you hear what an ass you sound like right now? I've known Becca for eight years, and Suzi since grade school. Why would I decide to help some sick bastard I'd only met a few months ago take her? I love her."

He tunneled his hand through his hair and sank down into the dirty recliner in the center of the living room. "You're right. That does seem odd. But look at this from my side. Pete is a criminal who has been on the inside of a human trafficking ring for years. He's successfully moved to Chicago from Mexico, has taken three girls from this neighborhood, and has God knows how many girls moving here from Playa Del Carmen. Why would he tell you who he really is? Why risk the entire operation to get you in bed?"

His words halted her anger and made her mind spin. She had been so wrapped up in her own turmoil she hadn't stopped to wonder why she looked so damn guilty to a trained FBI agent. Her heart slammed against her ribcage. He made a valid point, but there had to be a reason. And if he couldn't figure it out, then she had to.

She walked across the room and rested her backside on the ledge of the bay window looking out into the gloomy morning. The rain still fell in quiet drizzles and cars littered the street. Her gaze stayed fixed on the world outside and she said, "I don't have an answer for you. Believe me, I wish I did. When I think about all the time I spent with him, and how badly he deceived me, I want to curl into a ball and never get up." She turned her head to face him. "But that's not a choice. That won't help Becca."

Graham didn't respond; he just held her gaze. Something softened in his eyes, even if only a little. It made the pressure in her chest ease a tiny bit.

"We should go," he said.

She nodded. "I need to get ready for work. I have an early flight."

The corners of his eyes dropped in concern. "Are you going to be okay? It's a little soon to go back to work, isn't it?"

She widened her eyes. He was a walking contradiction, and she couldn't keep up with his constant change of attitude toward her. How was it possible to go from suspecting her of a disgusting crime to being concerned about her well-being so quickly? Regardless of his sincerity, or lack thereof, he was giving her emotional whiplash.

"I'll be fine. The two other flight attendants who were on the plane will be with me, and it's a short flight to Detroit. I'll be home this evening." She straightened and walked toward the door, mentally slapping herself. She didn't need to tell him all of this. He wasn't her friend. Hell, he was about as far from a friend as she had. Even if there was this strange invisible string that connected her to him. She needed to figure out how to cut him loose and leave him behind. She couldn't waste more time figuring out if she wanted to slap him or kiss him.

The chair squeaked behind her and his footsteps fell heavily against the wooden planks. A strong hand came down on her shoulder, branding her skin with its heat, and she spun around to face him. "You were brave as hell that day. I never got the chance to tell you."

"Thanks." Heat crept into her cheeks again, but this time it was because of the way his warm breath caressed her skin. She tilted her head as she stared up at his strong jaw. "What are the chances we were both on that plane when a hijacker tried to crash it?"

The gray in his eyes darkened to coal and he glanced down.

"What?" she asked. Her pulse picked up.

"Nothing. We need to get going." His shoulder brushed against her and he walked toward the door.

She reached out and grabbed his arm, pulling him to a stop. "Who was the man who tried to crash the plane?"

He cleared his throat and pulled his arm from her grasp. "Some crazy guy with an ax to grind."

He knows something.

Snippets of information shifted around her mind until they clicked into place. She held up her palm to stop him from leaving. "Wait a minute. You said earlier Pete was moving girls up from Playa Del Carmen. How do you know that if you just found out his name yesterday? How do you know so much about the human trafficking ring he runs? Were you chasing him in Mexico?"

His body stiffened and clenched muscles molded against his shirt. "I'm not discussing my investigation with you."

"Then tell me why you were on that plane." She spoke each word through clenched teeth.

"Why does it matter? It happened, I took in the bad guy, and it's over. Move on." He yanked open the front door and glanced back at her. "Now let's go."

The floor swayed beneath her and her knees buckled. She leaned against the wall to steady herself. It all made sense. The man on the plane knew Pete, and he happened to be on her flight. That's why no one had known an FBI agent was on the plane to begin with. He was following the hijacker.

No wonder she was on the top of their list of suspects. She had been in contact with not one, but two men in the investigation. Even she could admit it was one hell of a coincidence. But how could she prove them wrong?

Her hand slid into her front pocket of her denim shorts and wrapped around a small piece of paper. What she'd found might not give her any answers, but it could be a start.

She couldn't let Agent Grassi shut her out. She'd have to do this on her own. Becca's life, and hers, depended on it.

• • •

Mickey took a deep breath to settle her shaky nerves. It didn't help. She stared at her reflection in the bathroom mirror at O'Hare airport. A strong, confident woman stared back at her. It didn't matter that dark circles hung low under her eyes or her hands trembled slightly at her sides. All the passengers on board to Detroit would see was a competent flight attendant doing her job.

Righting the collar of her white button-down shirt, she stood tall. She smoothed down her hair and made sure the pins held the bun at the nape of her neck in place. She was as ready as she'd ever be. Time to get this over with.

Her heels clicked on the white linoleum floor as she hurried to the plane. Her normally long stride was cut short by the tight A-line skirt that hugged tightly to her curves. She rounded the corner toward the gate and relief loosened the knot in her stomach. Allison and Vanessa stood together with forced smiles, their hands clasped together. Mickey hurried toward them and threw her arms around them, pulling them close to her.

"How are you guys holding up?" she asked Allison. She pulled back and took in the dilated pupils in their widened eyes. She grabbed onto each of their hands and squeezed. "This is going to be fine. As soon as we get back into our routines, everything else will fade away."

Tears filled Allison's velvety brown eyes. "I heard about Becca in the news. Are you sure you can handle this right now?"

Mickey's shoulders dropped forward. She'd hoped neither Allison nor Vanessa had found out about her missing goddaughter. She could only handle one crisis at a time. Getting back on the Boeing 747 staring at her from outside the large window would be hard enough. She'd fall apart if she had to talk about Becca right now, too.

"I'm fine, and they're going to find Becca. I know it." She put as much false enthusiasm in her voice as she could muster. The truth was, Becca had been missing for over twenty-four hours now. The more time that passed by, the slimmer the chances of finding her.

"How's Suzi?" Allison asked. "My heart breaks for her. I can't imagine how scared she is right now."

Mickey bit back pain that threatened to pull her under. Besides Suzi and Lydia, Allison was her closest friend. They'd taken jobs at the same airline together after college when they couldn't land a job in their field of study, and after flying all over the world together over the last five years, they knew almost everything about each other. It made sense Allison would want to know how Suzi was.

"She's as good as can be expected." She couldn't bring herself to admit Suzi thought she played a role in Becca's abduction. Suzi had been on her mind all day, and she wanted to reach out, but fear of Suzi's accusations kept her from making the call.

Allison folded her arms in front of her and rubbed her hands up and down her arms. "It's been one hell of a week. First the plane and then Becca. Let's hope it's not true what they say about bad things happening in threes."

Mickey's blood turned cold. She couldn't handle anything else in her life going wrong. But if she didn't find a way to clear her name, her entire life might be the third thing to go to shit in this scenario. But it was a price she'd gladly pay if it meant Becca came home safely.

Vanessa leaned in closer and lowered her voice. "Have either of you talked to Captain Fuller?"

Mickey and Allison both shook their heads.

"I went to visit him and his wife at the hospital. He told me the hunky FBI agent who saved us went to see him. He asked him a lot of questions about what routes he usually flew and the crew he worked with. He wanted to know if Fuller had ever seen anything suspicious on one of his flights to Cancun."

"More suspicious than a man stabbing him and stealing his plane?" Allison asked with a snort.

Vanessa cringed and her face went white.

"Sorry," Allison said and rubbed a hand down Vanessa's arm.

"It's okay. But anyway, Fuller said it seemed like he was fishing for information about someone who worked for the airline."

The knot in Mickey's stomach tightened again. He'd been fishing for information about her. What did he think he'd accomplish by asking an airline captain about his crew? Sure, Fuller knew her well. She almost always flew with the same crew. But he didn't know much about her personal life.

She tried to keep the quiver out of her voice when she asked, "Did Fuller say why he was being asked all of these questions? Did he know what the guy was after?"

Vanessa glanced around and nodded as the captain and co-pilot of their flight walked by. She waited until they were out of earshot to answer. "He thinks it had something to do with human trafficking."

Mickey's saliva caught in the back of her suddenly dry throat. She covered her mouth and coughed. Allison grabbed a bottle of water from the black tote hanging from her arm and handed it to her. "Thanks," she said as she unscrewed the cap and chugged half the bottle. Her nerve endings sparked with electricity and she swore a sign on her forehead read, *I slept with a pedophile.* But even if she did, no one could judge her as harshly as she judged herself.

"Are you all right?" Vanessa asked. "I know it's upsetting to think about someone involved with that on one of our flights."

Mickey pressed her lips together and shook her head.

"It probably happens more than we realize," Allison said, her voice thick and low. "You can never let your guard down these days. You never know what kind of creeps are lurking around under your nose."

Vanessa shivered. "I'll have my eyes open from now on. If a guy like that can get on a plane, and then try to crash it, what other sickos are we serving every day?"

Mickey bit into her tongue to stop from saying anything. What Allison and Vanessa said was true, but it was a lesson she'd already learned. Even if it was too little too late.

People drifted to the gate and sat down to wait until boarding began. The door to the walkway opened, signaling it was time for her to board the plane and start preparing the cabin. Her chest tightened and she glanced at her friends. Fear lurked behind their false bravado, but they straightened their spines and hardened the lines on their faces.

"Are you guys ready?" she asked.

They both nodded.

Mickey turned on her black heels, stepped through the door, and walked toward the plane. The last time she'd done this, her life had been normal. It had been just another day, just another flight. But now everything was different. The last plane she'd been on had almost crashed into the ground. She never imagined she'd prefer that nightmare to the one she was currently living. At least on the plane she'd had a brave knight to help her take down the villain.

Now she had no one fighting in her corner, and the monster was a whole hell of a lot scarier. He knew everything about her, and he held the most precious thing in her life in his hands.

As she stepped onto the plane and took in the familiar sight, relief washed over her.

She could do this.

She could get through this flight, and the next one. And then she would do what she needed to do to find the sonofabitch and push a dagger through his heart.

She had no other options.

Chapter Ten

His damp clothes clung to him like a second skin. Cold air blasted down from the vents in the elevator and a shiver ran down his spine.

All he wanted was a hot shower and change of clothes. If the old man pressed against the corner of the elevator was any indication of how he smelled in his day-old clothes, a shower couldn't come fast enough.

The elevator stopped at his floor, he nodded to the old man, and walked to his apartment. Fatigue pulled at him. He hadn't gotten much sleep last night, not with all the notes he had to pour over, and then the memory of Mickey's soft lips on his. After he'd left her at her apartment earlier this morning, he hadn't had time to stop at home. He had too much to do and not enough time to do it.

He'd talked to the mothers of two of the missing girls. The notes in their files had been extensive, but he wanted to see things for himself. Now he needed to talk to Suzi Stanley again, but he had to take a small break to fuel up and regroup. The best way to do that was with a quick bite to eat after washing the grime from his tired body. His stomach growled, reminding him he hadn't eaten all day.

Stepping into his apartment, all the tension of the past two days eased away. He sighed, rubbing a hand over the rough whiskers on his chin. His gaze flitted around his familiar surroundings, and all he wanted to do was sink into the brown leather couch and shut his eyes for a few hours.

But there was no time to rest. His long strides took him past the kitchen and living room and into the bathroom. He opened the glass door of the shower and turned the nozzle. Hot water sprayed down, trickling down his forearm, and steam clogged the small room. He shook the water from his arm before he pulled it out of the shower and peeled his wet shirt off his chest. He threw it in the corner where it landed with a loud *plop*. Stepping out of his pants and boxer briefs, he sighed as he added them to the mound on the floor, and then stepped into the shower.

Warm drops of water pelted him from the large showerhead mounted on the ceiling. He quickly lathered shampoo in his hair and soap on his body. The water sprayed down and the suds swirled around the drain before disappearing. He leaned a forearm against the marble wall and let the water pelt the back of his neck.

One minute…just one minute to close my eyes and let the weight lift from my shoulders.

One minute stretched into two and the warm, wet air erased the tightness in his muscles. He allowed himself the small luxury of closing his eyes and blew out a long, slow breath.

Ring, ring, ring

And just like that, all the tension snapped back in his muscles like a rubber band stretched to its limit. He yanked the nozzle, turning off the water, and jumped out of the shower. Drops of water dotted the tiled floor, forming small puddles. He reached for a white towel and wrapped it around his waist before he grabbed his phone from the pocket of his discarded pants.

"Agent Grassi." The interruption of his short moment of peace soured his mood, turning his words hostile.

"It's Harper. I want to know your progress on the Bogart case."

Graham swallowed down his irritation. He didn't need to be reminded he'd messed up in Austin by Harper micromanaging him. Harper's constant checking in and refusal to offer extra support only fueled his desire to close this case.

"I'm about to check on Becca Stanley's mother. I didn't get a chance to speak with her very long yesterday. I'm also waiting for a warrant to come through on Pete Bogart's apartment." The towel slipped low on his hips as he walked into his bedroom and pulled a pair of pressed steel gray trousers and a baby blue button-down shirt out of his closet. He glanced toward his discarded gym shorts and T-shirt from a few days ago. He'd much rather throw those back on and call it quits for the day, but it was only four p.m. He still had plenty of hours left to track down Pete, and the FBI preferred their agents to look a little more put together than dirty shorts and a ratty Aerosmith T-shirt.

"You mean a warrant for the apartment you already entered without permission?" The calmness of Harper's voice made the words he spoke harsher somehow. The hairs on the back of Graham's neck rose.

"I tried to speak with the building manager before I entered but couldn't get through. When we touched base this morning, he was more than willing to let me back into the apartment. Before that, I was let into the apartment by a friend of the suspect who was given a key. There was no forced entry. Nothing illegal was done to get onto the premises."

A harsh laugh vibrated through the phone. "You're right. Technically you did nothing illegal, and that's the only reason you aren't being taken off this case. You've already been warned to toe the line, and having a person of interest let you into the apartment of the man who kidnapped three girls is treading dangerous waters, Grassi."

He ground his teeth together. Eric must have told him Mickey was the one who'd let him inside. He'd deal with his partner's big mouth later. Now, he concentrated on Harper's harsh words. He wasn't telling him anything he didn't already know. Instead of arguing, he said, "Yes, sir."

"Now, let's discuss your involvement with Miss O'Shay. I understand you stayed the night at her apartment last night."

He pushed his teeth together harder until pain shot through his jaw. "That's right." The towel dropped to the floor and he activated speaker phone before setting the phone on the deep blue comforter covering his bed. He wasn't going to give Harper more information than what he asked for.

"Do you think that was a wise move? Or the best use of your time when you should have been following leads and tracking Bogart? Do I need to remind you of the agency's policy in regards to getting involved with someone connected to one of your cases?" Harper's voice rose a notch with every word. Graham could imagine him sitting at his desk, his face growing red with anger.

He rubbed the back of his neck and blew out a tight breath. Of course he thought it was a wise move or he wouldn't have done it. Okay, so kissing Mickey in her kitchen was a bonehead move, but it was a mistake he wouldn't make again. She might be hot, but she wasn't worth risking his career. Harper was a jackass, but he needed to keep his temper in check.

"Yes, on both counts. She claimed someone broke in and tried to kill her, and I wanted to be there in case the person came back. As it turns out, the woman who broke in is the same woman who leased Pete Bogart's apartment." His voice was low as he slid the shirt over his arms and buttoned the small white buttons before yanking on his pants and grabbing a pair of socks. The soft mattress dipped beneath his weight and he crossed his ankle over his knee and jammed the soft cotton on his foot.

"Does that surprise you?" Harper asked with amusement.

Graham froze with one sock halfway on his foot, the white tip dangling toward the floor. "What do you mean?"

"Miss O'Shay is a suspected accomplice. If she's smart, she'd want to divert attention from herself. Regardless of the depth of her involvement, she had a relationship with Bogart. By claiming someone who has a connection with Bogart broke into her apartment and tried to kill her, she's shifting suspicion onto someone else."

Sonofabitch.

It had entered his mind Mickey might have other reasons for letting him into Pete's apartment, but he'd assumed it was because there was no risk of Pete getting caught. Mickey wanting him to find the connection between Connie Difico and the woman from her apartment never crossed his mind.

He squeezed his eyes shut and the image of her pale face and worried eyes branded his brain. He'd bet money she hadn't known the woman who'd tried to kill her also leased her ex-boyfriend's apartment. Spending so much time with Mickey over the last day might not have been the wisest move, but it had eased his suspicions about her relationship with Pete.

If only he could trust his instincts.

"With all due respect, sir, I don't think Miss O'Shay was aware of whose name the apartment was listed under. Nor was she aware of what we'd find once we got there."

"You sound awfully confident. Does that mean you

figured out why Bogart broke all the rules with Miss O'Shay?"

A sliver of doubt crept into the back of his mind. After what had happened in Austin, his career would be over if he messed this case up, too. Not to mention God knows how many girls would be lost forever. He had to stay focused on the task and stick to the facts. He jammed the rest of his sock on his foot. "Not yet."

"Well, you better figure it out soon. Stop wasting your time and get some answers."

"Another agent on the case could really help, sir. Eric's in Mexico following a lead on a property he found and I have my hands full with interviews. If I could have someone running names and digging into backgrounds at the office, it could speed everything up."

Harper's short laugh made him want to reach through the phone and punch him in the face. Asking for help hadn't been easy, but dammit, he needed it. Hell, the missing girls needed it. "You have all the resources you need to get this done. If you don't agree, I'll find someone else to do the job."

The line went dead. Shit. Doing his job was hard enough, but doing it with a pissed off boss and his only help in another country made it nearly impossible. Harper had a reason to be pissed at him, but Harper allowing his feelings toward Graham to affect his current case was unacceptable. They should be throwing everything they had at this case, not letting past issues get in the way of the job.

Pushing himself off the edge of the bed, he walked back into the living room and grabbed his laptop. It hummed to life as he turned it on. He didn't have time to go into the office to run the names he'd uncovered…mainly Connie Difico. And Eric was on a flight to Cancun so he couldn't do much right now. But he could start a search on his home computer while he ran to Suzi Stanley's.

He pulled up the software he needed to run a standard

search and typed in Connie's name. The cursor spun in a circle as it got to work. These things could take time, which was one of the reasons he hated doing them. While the search ran, he grabbed his phone and emailed himself the picture Eric had sent him earlier. Chances were Connie Difico wasn't the woman's real name. They might have more luck running a facial recognition search. If she was in the system, she'd pop up pretty quickly.

Dammit, what was the other name he needed to dig up?

The sharp hunger pain in the pit of his stomach stole his attention. He set the laptop on the glass coffee table and headed for the kitchen. His mind spun and he searched his memory while he grabbed a protein bar and bottle of water from the fridge. It wasn't much of a meal, but it would hold him over until he could get something more substantial.

The wrapper crinkled as he pulled it down and bit into the hard chocolate bar. He closed his eyes on a low moan. He must be starving if the low-calorie bar tasted this damn good.

His eyes shot open and he hurried over to his laptop. He had to look up the stepsister Eric had mentioned. The initial search on Pete had shown he was an only child whose parents divorced when he was young. He had lived with his mother until she'd died in a car accident when he was a teenager. He had then gone to live with his father, who had never remarried. But Eric had mentioned a house in Mexico that belonged to Pete and was listed under his stepsister's first name.

Graham had been so excited about finding a property to check out, he hadn't even asked how Eric figured out Paula's connection to Pete. He had seen no record of her. His best guess was Pete's father had a serious relationship with a woman who had a daughter, but the two never were officially married. He shook his head. Eric really was a genius with this stuff.

Glancing at the clock, he grabbed his phone and opened

his text messages. Eric would land soon. He could wait to get the information he wanted until then. Hell, it'd probably take him longer to find it himself.

What is the full name of Pete Bogart's stepsister?

He set the phone down and brought the bottle of water to his lips. His gaze scanned the computer screen as he debated whether he should venture out to talk to Becca's mother tonight or not. Forming his own impressions of her was important, but nothing ground-breaking would come from a conversation with her. The police, and Eric, had already spoken with her at length.

Since he had no choice but to spread his attention in multiple directions, it was important he stuck with the lead that gave him the best chance at catching a break. Even if it meant sitting in front of a computer for the rest of the night. Sinking into the warm leather sofa, he leaned his head back and settled in for a long night doing grunt work.

Ping.

He sat straight and stared at the picture on his screen. A match on the facial recognition search. Leaning forward, he studied the picture and let out a low whistle.

Well I'll be damned.

Graham pressed the print button in the corner and the machine behind him chugged to life. His small apartment didn't have an office, so he walked back into the kitchen and stood in front of the printer on the granite countertop. The machine spit out a piece of paper and he held it close to his face to get a better look at the girl in the picture.

He'd been right. Connie Difico was not the real name of the woman who was currently leasing Pete Bogart's apartment and who tried to kill Mickey. Her name was Chelsea Adams; she'd been missing for the last twelve years.

And the apartment Pete had lived at wasn't the only property listed under her name.

Chapter Eleven

She crinkled the small piece of paper in her hand. She should have told Graham about the address she'd found in Pete's bedroom, but there was no way he would have let her go with him. Hell, he'd probably be convinced she knew what he'd find at the address, and she'd kept it from him just long enough to make sure Pete got away. The man was infuriating. His eyes had been cold as steel when he'd looked at her today, as if every word out of her mouth was a lie.

She was tired of it. After mulling it over all day, she had no doubt she was right. She needed to do something to clear her name, and if she could find Becca while she did it, even better. Graham had other leads to track down anyway, including working on a warrant for Pete's apartment. If she found anything worth mentioning, she'd call him. Besides, he hadn't given her much of a chance to tell him. He'd practically run away from her after dropping her off at her apartment earlier. He couldn't get away from her fast enough.

Except when he was kissing her in her apartment and smelling her hair in the rain. Her pulse kicked into high gear. He had some nerve accusing her of helping kidnap her goddaughter for sex-trafficking one minute and then knocking her off her feet with a simple touch the next. She hated the way her body responded to him. What she hated even more was how badly she wished they could have seen where that kiss led.

Stop it. Get Graham out of your head. He thinks the worst of you, and you need to prove him wrong and find Becca. Finding Becca is the only thing that matters.

She put the address into her GPS and then wadded up the piece of paper before she threw it on the floor on the passenger's side of her car. Her hands tightened around the steering wheel and she concentrated on the instructions as she drove through the city. The rain poured down in sheets from the dark sky and the traffic backed up on the slippery highway. Glares from the streetlights bounced off the slick roads, making it difficult to see.

Her phone trilled on the seat beside her and Lydia's name popped up on the touchscreen on the dashboard. She pressed the button on the steering wheel to turn on her Bluetooth.

"Hey, Lydia, what's up?"

"I'm just checking in. Did they catch the woman who broke in? How was your flight?"

Despite the unease boiling in her stomach, she couldn't help but chuckle. "Slow down a little."

Lydia released a loud breath. "Sorry. I've been worried sick about you. I don't know why you insisted on going to work today. No one would have blamed you for taking the day off. Hell, if I were you I'd take the whole month off."

"I need to keep my mind occupied. Sitting around and stewing over what's happened won't help anything."

"What about the fact someone tried to kill you? You shouldn't have stayed in the apartment last night. I couldn't sleep from worrying about what could happen to you."

Mickey's heart lurched. "I should have called you earlier. I'm sorry. My mind's been all over the place today. I took Agent Grassi to Pete's apartment before I went to work, and now I'm trying to find something. If you want to go back to the apartment, I had the locks changed this morning, but it's still a little creepy being in there." She'd spared just enough time going back to their apartment to check the locks herself before taking off again.

"I think I'll stay with my parents until that woman is caught."

Red brake lights flashed in front of her. Her heart slammed into her chest. "Shit!"

She swerved to the side of the road. Water sprayed under her tires until she hydroplaned on a river of water on the shoulder. Her hands clutched the steering wheel and her pulse thundered through her ears. Lydia's voice broke through the hum of panic rampaging through her skull. "What happened?"

Mickey's knuckles threatened to break through her skin as her grip tightened and her elbows locked. She turned the wheel left, and then right, trying to even out the car as it slid toward the side of the highway. As soon as the tires bounced back down on the road, she pulled over on the side of the highway, hit the brakes, and gasped for breath. Turning her hazards on, she fell back in her seat.

"Stupid car in front of me almost got me killed. I'm fine, but damn. I need to get off the highway."

"Where are you going?"

"I found an address written down in Pete's bedroom. I want to see where it is." Checking her mirrors for traffic, Mickey eased back onto the road. GPS showed she needed to get off at the next exit toward Old Town. Thank God. She hated driving so fast in the rain.

A beat passed before Lydia said, "I don't think that's a

good idea. You should leave this to the police."

Turning off the highway, she blew out a sigh of relief. Her grip on the steering wheel relaxed, but her muscles remained tense. "I can't. They've been trying to find Pete and Becca for over thirty-six hours, and time's running out. Let them run down the leads they have. I need to do this. For Becca and Suzi. Suzi...she blames me." Emotion clogged her throat.

"You didn't know Pete was going to take Becca, or anyone else. You can't blame yourself. And Suzi's upset right now. She's scared to death and needs to lash out." The sympathy in Lydia's voice threatened to tear down the thin wall she'd built to keep her emotions at bay.

Mickey's eyes burned with unshed tears, but she refused to let them fall. "I let him in, Lydia. I was blind to who he is. How could I not have seen it?"

She shook her head, marveling at her own stupidity. Nausea rose from the pit of her stomach, just like it did every time she imagined all of the time she'd spent with Pete. All of the nights she'd spent with him, the plans they'd made for the future. It'd all been a lie, a trap to get his hands on the most important person in her life. Bile burned her esophagus as it rose up her throat, and she swallowed it down. She couldn't dwell on this now. She had to focus on the directions the GPS spewed.

"I'm not going to argue about this over the phone. Why don't you meet me for a drink?" The rain pounding on the hood of her car and the whoosh of the windshield wipers almost drowned out Lydia's plea.

"I have to do this. I can't sit around and let everyone else try to find Becca. Especially when Agent Asshole thinks I had something to do with it. You're not going to talk me out of it, but if you want to stay on the phone while I figure out where the hell I'm going, then fine."

Nothing but heavy breathing came through the speakers.

Every shred of her focus stayed on the voice from her GPS telling her where to turn. The city lights whirled by her and traffic blared its angry horns. She shut it out of her mind as she weaved through the city streets.

"I just passed St. Michael's church." She glanced around, but not many pedestrians littered the tree-lined sidewalks in the storm.

"You're in Old Town?"

"Yeah. I turned off Eugenie Street onto Cleveland Avenue." White numbers on mailboxes announced the house numbers. She found the one she wanted and slid her car next to the curb across the street. "The address I have is for an old house. It looks old enough to have been here before the Chicago fire burned this part of the city to the ground. There's an SUV parked in the driveway. Should I knock on the door?"

"Are you crazy?" Lydia's screech pierced her eardrums. "If the house is connected to Pete, nothing good is going on inside. Call Agent Grassi!"

She bit into the side of her cheek as she considered her options. "I don't know. I'm here now. I could go up and see what's going on before I waste his time. I could get Becca out if she's in there."

"With what? Your charm? You're a flight attendant, not a cop."

Ignoring Lydia, she dimmed her headlights and surveyed the area around her. Her gaze locked on the old Victorian house. The door opened and a blond woman stepped out of the house and walked toward the SUV. Mickey slid down low in her seat. "Oh my God, it's her. Connie Difico is at the house. Pete has to be in there."

"Who's Connie Difico?"

"The woman who broke into our apartment." Her pulse beat wildly in her ears, blocking out whatever Lydia was saying. She rubbed her sweat-slicked palms on her thighs, leaving tiny marks of perspiration on her dark blue skirt.

Connie threw a suitcase into the SUV and walked up the stairs to the porch. She opened the door and stepped back inside. Mickey scanned the front of the house as she weighed her options. Hostas and ferns lined the sidewalk and filled in the space in front of the dark gray porch. The yard was small, but well maintained.

The front door swung open again, but this time a hulking man with broad shoulders and a face hidden by a black hoodie stepped out with Connie. His massive frame dwarfed her, but the determination in her stride showed who was in charge. Connie climbed into the passenger side of the SUV, the man jumped into the driver's seat, and they peeled out of the driveway without a moment's hesitation.

"She left with a man. She put a suitcase in the car. I wonder if they're gone for good, or if they'll come back soon." Mickey searched for a sign of someone else in the house, but there was none. No lights shone through the windows, no shadows danced across the yard.

"It's time to stop acting like an idiot and get out of there."

She sighed and closed her eyes, trying to figure out the best move to make. She could call Graham and tell him she'd found Connie, but a sliver of resistance nagged at her gut. He still believed she wasn't being honest with him. She'd come to this house with hopes to find Becca, and to find something to convince him she was a victim in this whole thing. Not an accomplice. Besides, she had no idea how much time she had before Connie and the man came back. If she waited for Graham to come to check things out, she could miss her chance to find Becca.

"I need to get a closer look at the house."

"No, you don't. You need to call the authorities. These people are dangerous, and you're only going to get yourself killed if you get out of your car and try to save the day."

A shiver of fear raced up her spine. She couldn't argue with her friend. Lydia was right. It would be dangerous and stupid to go up to a house where a woman that had tried to kill her lived. But she didn't care. Wherever Becca was, she was more afraid and more alone than Mickey had ever been. She had to act...now.

"Sorry, but I have to go. I'll call you later."

"Mick—"

Mickey ended the call. Add guilt to the kaleidoscope of emotions twirling through her mind. Unclasping her seatbelt and stepping out of the car, she pushed Lydia's frantic voice from her brain and crossed the street to the house.

The soft melody of crickets sang into the night and her heels slapped against the brick pathway to the front porch. The rain no longer came down in sheets, but the drizzle left over from the storm spat down on her and coated her. Goosebumps prickled over her skin as she approached the looming old Victorian. Green, a shade darker than the painted siding, outlined the windows and the scalloped peaks of the roof. The trim appeared to grow darker as it slid down the side of the house, until it bled into the dark gray of the porch, almost as if tears were falling into a dark abyss.

A prickle of fear puckered on her neck and she glanced around. Not a person in sight. Lights shone from the windows of the neighboring houses, but no shadows flitted across the closed shades.

Mickey stepped onto the front porch and the semi-rotted wood sagged beneath her weight. Her gaze darted around and indecision froze her feet to the ground. Did she walk in and pray no one had been left to watch the house? Should she ring the bell, and then pretend as if she was lost if someone answered?

Ring the bell.

Gathering her courage, she pressed the yellow-stained bell on the side of the door. Nervous energy zipped through her and she wiggled her toes in an effort to get it the hell out of her. She strained her ears for any indication someone was coming to the door. Nothing but the call of the crickets filled her ears.

Two small windows separated by a metal bar nestled in the middle of the door. Mickey stood on her tiptoes and peered into the dark house.

Nothing.

She needed to get a better look inside. Her trembling fingers circled the knob, but it didn't budge when she tried to turn it.

Dammit.

Mickey hurried down the porch stairs and searched for other windows to look into. The foliage was thick around the front of the porch, and wet vines brushed against her ankles as she rushed around the side of the house. At least she hoped they were vines. She didn't focus on it as she searched for a way to see inside the house. Blinds or curtains or God knows what covered all of the windows at her level. Her heels sunk into the soft, moist grass and tendrils of wet hair slipped from the bun at the nape of her neck. She let the limp strands linger on her cheek and concentrated on the overgrown shrubs hiding the side of the house.

Shifting a wayward branch, a beam of moonlight bounced off glass on the bottom of the house. A window. She shimmied through the branches and the jagged twigs scraped against her leg. She rested a palm on the peeling paint of the siding to steady herself, and then dropped to her knees to look into the window. She wiped the caked-on dirt off the glass with the hem of her skirt and leaned in close. Thick block glass clouded her view, but she narrowed her gaze to center the objects in her line of vision.

And her blood turned cold.

Dirty cots lined one wall of the dingy basement. She couldn't make out the rough outline of the objects littered around the room, but one piece called to her and there was no denying what it was or who it belonged to. A bright pink backpack with a glittery, black embroidered *B* on the front pocket.

Becca was here.

Hope surged inside Mickey and adrenaline coursed through her veins. She burst through the wedge of shrubs. The sharp edges scraped across her flesh, but she surged on. She had to get inside. She broke free of the gnarled weeds and ran toward the front of the house. One heel sunk into a patch of mud and she struggled to pull her foot from the glue-like goo.

She pulled, grunting as she stumbled forward and out of her shoe. She shot her arms in front of her as she fell, but her palms slid on the slick blades of grass and her face smashed against the ground. Pain punctured her nose, but she jumped to her feet, pulled off her other shoe, and ran up the steps to the porch. Splinters scraped against her bare feet and she pushed on the door handle. The ancient wood of the doorframe buckled, and she summoned all the strength she had for one more push.

The door swung open and Mickey stumbled forward but managed to keep her balance. She charged into the house and the stench of rotting food and garbage slammed into her nostrils. She coughed and fought the overwhelming urge to gag. Darkness enveloped her. One tiny shaft of moonlight flitted through the slit of the open door. But that's all she needed.

Blinking to adjust to the dark, she followed the shaft of moonlight down the hallway and into the kitchen. The outline of days' worth of dishes sat in the sink. Pizza boxes and empty take-out containers took over the counter. A door stood open and Mickey glanced down the wooden stairs that led to the basement. She sucked in a deep breath and cringed as the stale, rotten air entered her lungs. She could do this. She had to do this. Becca could be down there. She flicked the light on for the stairwell and the coolness of the top step seeped into her foot. She descended the stairs and pulled in a deep breath.

Dear God, please let Becca be down here and no one else… Otherwise she'd likely just served herself up on a silver platter to the enemy.

Chapter Twelve

Tension wound all the muscles in his body as tight as a coiled spring. The cool leather of the steering wheel bit into his calloused hands.

The lights of the city flew by in a haze as he sped across town. Pete had been a genius about covering his tracks, but he had dropped the ball with Connie Difico. Not only had he rented his apartment with her name, but Graham had also just uncovered a house in Old Town she was renting as well. And that's not all he'd unearthed about Pete's accomplice.

Graham called the precinct in Old Town to give them a heads up on his arrival, but they wouldn't help with a search until his warrant came through. After what he'd uncovered in Pete's apartment, he had little doubt the warrant would be his in no time.

Pushing the voice command button on his steering wheel, he called Eric's number. A few clicks sounded through his speakers before the line started ringing.

"Hey. I finally got a cab out of the damn airport," Eric said. "Did you get the name I sent you? Find anything new?"

"Yeah, thanks. I've got a search going for Paula Williams now. I also ran Connie Difico's name through the database. Turns out that's not her real name." The sheets of rain slowed to a heavy drizzle as he made his way across town. "Her name's Chelsea Adams and she went missing twelve years ago. Looked like a runaway."

"Why did they assume runaway?" Eric asked.

Graham blinked and tried to erase the image of the preteen girl with the sad blue eyes that were too big for her face and the bow shaped mouth set in a permanent frown. "She had a rough home life. Raised by a single mother with no idea who her father was. Her mom bounced around a lot. They lived on the south end of the city. The girl took off after the mother moved in with a new boyfriend. The boyfriend didn't seem concerned, claimed she was an ungrateful brat."

"What about her mom?"

"Says the girl was jealous and figured she'd come home eventually. She never did."

Eric's low whistle rattled his speakers. "Do you think she was taken?"

He shrugged and his eyes stayed focused on the road ahead. Water sprayed on his windshield and his wipers worked to keep up. "Either that, or they found her on the street and brought her in to the sex-trafficking ring. She's from Chicago, so if they wanted to move their sex ring here, it makes sense to bring in a local. Even if she hasn't lived here in a while."

"It's another connection. What about Mickey? Do you think she was telling the truth about the woman breaking into her apartment and trying to kill her?"

"The more I discover about Connie, the more I believe Mickey. I can't trust her completely until we find out why Pete slipped up with her and Becca. It doesn't make any sense."

His grip on the steering wheel tightened. Partly from

his thoughts about Mickey, partly from the glare of the rain bouncing from the blacktop. "I also don't think Pete would use two different women to deal with the girls he takes. It'd be too risky."

"True," Eric agreed. "Not to mention it makes more sense for a runaway abused by her traffickers to be used to help her captors. As sick as it sounds, most victims of sex-trafficking are chained to their abusers for life. A girl like Mickey, it's hard to imagine how she'd end up in a mess like this."

"Let's hope she can stay out of it from now on. Harper gave me shit for going into Pete's apartment with her. Why did you tell him before I had a chance to explain my actions to him? I knew it was crossing a line, but dammit, time's running out to find these girls."

A heavy sigh sounded through the phone. "I'm sorry. You've been on Harper's shit list for a while, and going into Pete's apartment the way you did definitely didn't help the situation. I understand your motives, but Harper has to play by the rules. I'll call him later and try to smooth it out."

Graham pressed his lips together to hide his irritation. "I don't need you fighting my battles."

"We're partners. This is our battle."

"I have to call him anyway. I found another address listed under Connie Difico's name. I'm on my way there right now."

"Do not go into the house," Eric warned, his parental tone once again raising Graham's ire.

"I'm not an idiot. I called to secure a warrant, which should come through any minute, and I let the locals know I needed backup to work the scene. I want to be there and ready to go in as soon as I get the go ahead. Harper needs to know I have all my bases covered."

"Dude, this could be huge. Do you want me to catch a flight back to Chicago so we can check it out?"

"We don't have time. I have to get in there now." He

turned onto Cleveland Avenue and scanned the houses for the number he had scrawled on a piece of paper. "Besides, you need to look for Pete in Mexico. See if he has anything going on in his house down there. We need to track down every lead we find."

"Be careful."

"I will. I just wanted to catch you up. I'll get a hold of you later if I find something." He clicked off the line and slowed down.

There you are, you big ugly sonofabitch.

His nerves danced with anticipation. The house called to him to come inside for a closer look. The missing girls could be on the other side of those walls and he had to sit in his car and twiddle his damn thumbs. Bureaucratic bullshit and red tape were the bane of his existence. Young lives were on the line, but he couldn't act until some judge crossed all the T's and dotted all the I's. Sometimes it didn't make sense to wait.

A streetlight flickered, casting shadows across the lawn and slicing through the air. The full moon beamed down plenty of light for him to study the layout of the house and the yard, even through the fuzz of rain. His car idled in its spot and he watched and he waited. Nothing stood out as being out of the ordinary. The old house, albeit a bit creepy for his tastes, was located in a respectable neighborhood in a nice part of town. The yards were cared for and the houses well maintained.

Nothing about the scene in front of him screamed for help. Nothing alerted the neighbors that children were being kept inside. He slapped his hands against the steering wheel. He didn't need the house to tell him anything. His gut told him something wasn't right inside this house, and it wouldn't be long before he discovered the truth.

He glanced at the clock. How long would he be forced to wait here? He might as well call Harper and get it over with.

He dialed his boss's number, pressed the phone to his ear, and kept his gaze locked on the house he'd come to search.

"What have you got for me, Grassi?"

Graham winced at Harper's sharp tone, but let it slide off his back. He didn't have time to worry about the strain between him and his boss. "I wanted to fill you in on a recent development in the Bogart case."

"I just got off the phone with Agent Short. He told me about the house. Has something else happened, or are you just calling to tell me what I'm already aware of?"

Graham ground the tip of his shoe into the floor. He'd told Eric he would call Harper. He couldn't believe Eric would go behind his back…again…and call their boss first. "I apologize, sir. I was unaware he contacted you."

"Maybe you two need to get on the same page. If you did, Bogart might be behind bars already."

Graham bit into the tip of his tongue to keep from asking what Harper meant. He and Eric had always worked well together, even when they didn't agree on how to handle every aspect of their cases. "Again, I apologize. I'll talk to Eric about us being clearer with our intentions in the future."

"Do that. I don't like being dragged into problems."

Now he and Eric had problems? Harper's words made no sense, but he was wise enough not to question his meaning. "I understand, sir. If you've already been briefed, I don't need to bother you. Once the warrant goes through and backup arrives, we'll enter the premises and lock the place down. I'll keep you informed of our findings."

Harper grunted his opinion and hung up the phone.

Graham pulled the phone from his ear and stared at it. He needed to call Eric and find out what the hell was going on, and what Eric had told Harper about the case, but he couldn't get into that now. He needed to focus on the task at hand and be ready to act the moment he was given the go ahead. Whatever petty shit Eric had brought up to Harper didn't matter. At least not right now.

He narrowed his gaze at the phone and willed the damn thing to ring. His chest tightened and he held his breath, but the generic background mocked him. Screw it. He had to move. A tiny peek around the perimeter of the house wouldn't hurt. He'd keep his hands in his pockets the whole time.

Graham stepped out of the car and resisted the urge to slam it closed. No cars loitered in the driveway, but that didn't mean the house was empty. Hunching his shoulders against the constant drizzle, he crossed the empty street. He crept along the shadows, out of range from the flicking streetlight. He turned on the flashlight on his phone and pointed it at the ground. With all the greenery around the house, there were bound to be snakes. He hated snakes.

He hugged the side of the house and found nothing out of place except a pair of woman's shoes lying in a pile of mud. A tall privacy fence blocked the backyard from his view, but no toys littered any part of the yard he searched. Water sloshed against his heavy footsteps, but the cool night air couldn't chase away the warmth stirring in his blood as adrenaline spiked inside him.

He rounded the corner of the house and crouched behind the shrubs for cover. The front porch beckoned to him. A quick look would prepare him for when it was time to enter the house. He glanced around to make sure no nosy neighbors had noticed him skulking around and ran toward the porch.

The stairs creaked from his weight and he stopped and sucked in a breath. Against the backdrop of crickets and rain, the quiet creak was loud. He hurried into the safety of the shadows and the splintered wood of the doorframe caught his eye. His fingers itched to run along the broken wood, but he kept one hand in the pocket of his pants and the other tightly wrapped around the phone. He couldn't afford to contaminate the scene, and he hadn't had the forethought to bring a pair of gloves with him from the car.

The leaves rustled along with a gust of wind. The sudden breeze swirled onto the porch, kicking around some trash and causing the door to swing open an inch. Graham pressed his back against the worn paint of the wall beside the door. He slid his phone into his pocket and placed his palm on the butt of his gun. If someone was coming outside, he'd be ready.

Nothing happened.

A whoosh of air left his lungs and he sagged against the wall. He peered around the door and his gaze landed on the broken latch.

Well that's interesting.

He crouched in front of the door and studied the busted latch. Someone had wanted to get inside pretty badly. Or someone had wanted out.

"Oh my God! Help!" A woman's shrill shrieks of panic erupted through the narrow opening of the door.

Graham shot to his feet. Removing his hand from his gun, he grabbed his phone and called 911.

"This is Special Agent Graham Grassi. I need backup at 7225 Cleveland Avenue. Distressing calls for help were heard from inside a suspected crime scene. I'm going in."

He hung up, plunged his phone back in his pocket, and grabbed his gun from the holster at his side. The familiar weight of the weapon brought a sense of calm to his frayed nerves. He pushed the front door open with his foot and entered the house with the gun pointed in front of him.

"Special Agent Graham Grassi entering the house. If anyone's in here, please come out with your hands up."

He waited a beat and listened. The subtle groans and shifts of the floorboards were all that answered his announcement. He took a step further into the house and swung his gun into a room at his side. No one was there. Shafts of moonlight bounced inside from the open door and illuminated the living room. Or what he assumed was a living room. Two folding chairs and a rusted metal table sat to one side of the room, a small tube television sat on the other side. He slowly put one foot in front of the other as he pressed farther into the room. Dammit, he'd heard a call for help. He was certain. Where the hell had it come from?

Thump, thump, crash!

He whirled around and faced the way he'd entered the room. He quickened his pace and retraced his steps to the hall. He kept his gun trained in front of him and stepped into a thick wall of stale air in the kitchen. The urge to cover his nose and mouth were overpowering, but he concentrated on the open door on the far side of the kitchen.

He surveyed the kitchen and gave a brief thanks to God for not having to spend another second in there. A dim light lifted toward him from the bottom of the stairs. He pointed his gun down the darkened stairway. "I'm coming down and I'm armed. If you have any weapons, drop them to the floor."

Graham groaned at how stupid he sounded. If someone had set a trap for him, they wouldn't willingly lay down their weapons because he told them to—especially when they had the advantage. The light in the basement was small, but it was better than the dark pit he looked into. Maybe he should wait for backup.

"Graham? Is that you?" The fear and pain in Mickey's voice carried to him. He'd have recognized her voice anywhere. He hadn't been able to get it—or her whiskey eyes—out of his head since they'd met.

Shit. What the hell is she doing here?

"Mickey? Are you okay?" He turned slightly so his back wasn't exposed to an unexpected assailant.

"The light went out when I was coming downstairs. I

tripped and fell. I hurt my ankle a little and I think a bat flew into my hair."

If he wasn't so pissed she was here, and on edge about entering a suspected crime scene without backup, he would have laughed. "Is anyone else down there with you?"

The light he'd trained his eyes on twisted, leaving only darkness in his sight for a moment. "No." The word came out on a rush of disappointment.

"Are you sure?"

"Yes."

He could barely make out the word over her tears.

"I saw Becca's backpack through a window. I thought she'd be down here."

"Calm down. I'm coming downstairs now. Lift your light so I can see where the hell I'm going."

The light lifted and illuminated the rotting stairs he wished like hell he didn't have to step on. He lowered one foot at a time, taking care not to place too much weight on one step. He didn't need to end up in a heap at the bottom of the steps with Mickey.

He tightened his grip on the gun. His suspicions had died down over Mickey's involvement with the sex-trafficking ring, but that didn't mean he was right. If his gut was wrong, the outcome would be a lot worse than it had been in Austin.

This time, he'd be the one dead.

Chapter Thirteen

Heavy footsteps pounded the stairs toward her. The vibrations from the shaky wood shook her nerves. Mickey pulled herself to a sitting position on the dirt floor and kept the light from her phone pointed on the steps. "Graham?" She whispered his name and the word echoed around the empty room.

Black shoes came into view and her taut muscles relaxed... but only a little. No way she'd completely relax while inside this house. Graham's broad shoulders filled the archway and tears of relief slid into the corners of her eyes.

Until she spotted the gun.

"Holy shit," she screamed, scrambling backward like a skittering crab. "Why are you pointing a gun at me?"

Graham lowered the gun, but his finger stayed close to the trigger. Too close for her comfort. He stopped at the base of the stairs, his muscles bunched together like a jungle cat ready to pounce on its prey. "I told you I had a gun."

"And I told you I was the only person down here." Anger quickly replaced her fear and she jumped to her feet. She placed too much weight on her right foot and winced, but was too pissed to stop and acknowledge the pain. "Did you think I lied? Big bad Mickey lured you here so she could take care of you once and for all?"

"I didn't know what to think." He shifted the gun to one hand and shoved the other hand through his dirty blond hair.

Good God, the man was infuriating. She swept a hand in front of her and gestured around the basement. "As you can see, it's just me. We missed them." Her voice caught and she struggled to keep her composure.

Graham stepped into the room and ran his long fingers along the wall. He flipped a switch and flickering lights poured from low-hanging lightbulbs. Not that it helped much. The light from her phone offered much more light than the barely lit bulb above her head. "I need to make sure no one else is down here. It's not safe for you to be in here. Hell, it's not safe for me."

Mickey straightened her shoulders and faced him. She refused to let him browbeat her into more guilt and fear than she already had. Hell, even if he shoved it down her throat, her body was already filled to the brim with exhausting emotion. She'd been through more in the last forty-eight hours than any human should be forced to endure.

But it still wasn't as bad as what Becca was dealing with. "I found this address in Pete's apartment and wanted to see what it was. I didn't want to bother you, and Lord knows I didn't need to hand you anything else to use against me."

The strobing light beat down on his face and the fury in his eyes had her taking a step backward. "Are you kidding me? It took me hours to find this address. And I'm still not supposed to be inside. I'm waiting for a warrant so we can use whatever we find in this hell hole as evidence if we catch the bastard we're looking for. If you had told me the address, I could have gotten the ball rolling a whole hell of a lot faster."

A vein throbbed above his eyebrow and blared a

warning to Mickey. His temper was slipping, and his slow and controlled tone was far more intimidating than if he'd screamed at her. She tucked her bottom lip into her teeth and her gaze darted around the shabby room. Her breath caught on the ball wedged in her throat.

Oh my God. What did I do? He could have caught them before they'd left.

She took another step backward and the back of her knees folded against something hard. The unexpected movement had her sitting down on a cot. The old hinges squeaked, but the hard board of a mattress didn't budge. She grazed her fingers against the torn and tattered blanket on top of the cot and her heart splintered in two.

"I'm sorry. I...I didn't think about that. I just thought...I wanted..." Sobs tore through her words and rocked her body. She wanted to be strong, helpful. She didn't want to be the reason two sex-traffickers had escaped. "When Connie and the other guy left with a suitcase and I saw Becca's backpack, I had to act. Instinct took over. But you're right. I should have called you or the police. I shouldn't have—"

"What did you say?" The urgency in his voice had her finally meeting his eye.

"I should have called the police."

He shook his head. "Not that. The part about Connie and a guy."

"Oh. I was sitting in my car watching the house when Connie carried a suitcase to the car, and then she left with a guy. A big guy in a black hoodie. I thought maybe they'd left the girls alone for a minute."

"How long ago was this?"

She shrugged. "Not long. Maybe twenty minutes."

"Shit. I missed them by minutes. Dammit, I need to call this in and get the police searching for them right away. What kind of car did they drive?"

"A black SUV. An Escalade I think."

Graham pulled out his phone and pressed a number. "Yeah. It's Grassi. I've got a witness who saw Connie Difico and an unknown male accomplice in a black hoodie drive away from 7225 Cleveland Avenue twenty minutes ago in what's likely a black Cadillac Escalade. I want everyone looking for that car, and I need backup here five minutes ago."

He ended the call and stood in front of her. "This is good. We could get them. They don't have a lot of time on us, and if it weren't for you, we wouldn't know when they'd left. But that doesn't mean the house is clear. I need to go through every room and make sure no one else is here."

Mickey staggered to her feet. "I'll go with you. I'm not staying down here by myself."

"How about I start down here and then we can argue about where you'll go once I move upstairs."

She glanced around the room. "Graham, no one else is in the basement."

"You're probably right. But I need to check anyway."

He turned his phone light on, the thin beam of light joining with hers, and stepped away from her. The lack of his body next to hers made her all too aware of the untold horrors of where she sat, and she hurried to follow behind him.

"The ceiling's low, so watch your head." Graham lowered his head and crept into the black ink of the basement. "Stay close."

She reached out and grabbed his hand. His strong grip steadied her and calmed the anxiety bouncing between her organs. She ducked and the damp wood brushed against the top of her head, snagging frayed strands of her hair. Her gaze followed the light and her stomach muscles clenched. A jacket laid bunched in one corner of the room, a dirty tennis shoe in another. They followed along the walls of the small basement and then turned back toward where they'd started. Five dirty cots lined the back wall. The tattered blankets on the beds were no more than glorified sheets filled with holes.

"What are the buckets for?" She pointed at two five-gallon buckets set up in the corner. The heavy scent of ammonia and feces made her question moot, but she hoped beyond reason they weren't what she assumed.

"Makeshift bathrooms." His voice was hard and he tightened his grip on her hand.

She dug her heels into the ground and dropped his hand. Bending at the waist, she hugged her middle and took deep breaths to fight against the nausea swimming in her stomach. It only made it worse as the air-clogging stench filtered into her mouth. "I…I can't do this. I'm going to be sick."

A gentle hand pressed against her back, circling between her shoulder blades. "Do you want to wait outside? You shouldn't be down here anyway. It's not safe."

"No. I don't want to be by myself. And if there's something here that could help, we need to find it now. Enough time has been wasted because of me." She straightened and pinched the bridge of her nose. She evened out her breaths but couldn't stop her heart from beating against her ribcage. She couldn't stop the quiver in her limbs or the hole of despair in her soul from growing bigger and bigger. "Even though I can't deny what a sick monster Pete is any longer, actually seeing where Becca and those other girls have been locked up like animals makes the picture so much clearer. So much worse. It's a lot to take in."

"We can go upstairs. No one is down here, and this area will be swept over by professionals once they get here. You witnessing the nightmare Becca's been forced to endure won't solve anything. Besides, I still need to clear the rest of the house."

Red beady eyes lit up in the darkness and streaked across the dirty floor, flittering over her naked toe. Tiny claws poked into her skin and coarse fur brushed against her ankle. Her breath hitched in her throat and she stumbled backward until she pressed up against something hard. "Oh my God. A rat just ran over my foot." She shook her foot, as if the rat still lingered on it and a shudder of disgust rippled through her. She glanced behind her, taking in the empty rows of an oak bookcase.

"I think you'll live." Graham stepped beside her and skimmed his hands along the shelves still supporting her weight. "Why do they have a bookcase down here?"

He lifted the light to examine the empty dust-filled shelves and something caught her eye. She lifted her finger, pointing to the small scrap of paper trapped on the edge of the bookcase. Only one corner was visible, the rest of the paper seemingly hidden behind the case. "What's that?" She reached out to pull it out, but it wouldn't budge from behind the heavy wood.

"I don't know, but don't tear it." Lifting the phone closer, Graham leaned forward. He traced a finger along the edge of the bookcase. "Take my phone. I'm going to move it out and see if I can get it."

She grabbed the phone and took a step back to give him some room. He studied the bookcase for a minute, and then used his fingertips to shimmy the side from the wall. Little by little, inch by inch, he moved it forward. The paper floated to the ground and she crouched down and picked it up. Carefully, she unfolded it.

Help

The large letters were barely visible on the wrinkled paper, as if whatever was used to write with barely contained enough ink to get the message out. Her heart froze in her chest. Fogginess clouded her vision and her knees buckled beneath her.

"I got you," Graham murmured in her ear as he wrapped his arms around her waist and held her against him. "Take it easy."

Her mind couldn't find any words, so she pressed the note in the palm of his hand.

He lifted it in front of his eyes. "Shit."

"Becca wrote this note." Confidence filled her voice even as disbelief stole the function of her muscles.

Graham lifted the paper close to his face and narrowed his eyes as he studied it. "Are you sure?"

"Absolutely. She always adds a little flourish to the bottom of her p's." Mickey used her pinky to point it out and couldn't help the sad smile from forming on her lips. "You see the swirl? That has Becca written all over it. She's a smart girl. She wouldn't have stuck this behind a bookcase for no reason."

Graham didn't need any more convincing. "I need to move this out more. It doesn't look like there's a wall behind it. Can you stand?"

Finding a cry for help from Becca filled Mickey with new determination. If the backpack hadn't been enough proof Becca had been here, her note was. "I'm fine. Do what you need to do." Drawing herself up, she straightened her spine and stiffened her resolve. She couldn't be weak right now. "Do you need help?"

Graham pulled at the bookcase and wisps of air streamed in from behind it. His muscles bunched as he maneuvered the heavy bookcase forward. "Let me see the light." He grabbed the phone and shined the small beam into the large space he'd created. "It looks like there's quite a bit of space behind this thing. I can't see the back. There isn't a wall or anything back here."

She sucked in a breath. "Oh my God. Do you know what

this is?"

"Obviously not." He snorted.

"Graham, we're in Old Town." Excitement battled with the constant blanket of fear that had covered her all night. Under any different circumstance, excitement would have won out. Not tonight. But she still couldn't stop her words from tumbling out a little too quickly.

He turned to look at her, his brow lifted. "So?"

"This could be a tunnel from the Underground Railroad." Her voice grew louder with every word. She lifted herself on to her toes to see above Graham's head and smacked her head on the ceiling. "Ouch."

His mouth drew down, causing wrinkles to ripple on his chin. "That's crazy. No way that's what this is. It's probably a pit they dug to hide girls."

She shook her head and wonder laced through her voice. "I'd bet my paycheck this house was here before the fire. This part of town was heavily used to transport slaves from the South. The city was a hub of activity, and a lot of the different routes through Illinois came here."

"I never knew that."

"I'm not surprised, most people don't. My dad's a huge history nerd, so we used to come to Old Town when I was a kid and he'd point out different areas of importance during the Civil War. Even places that aren't standing anymore. Most of the houses that were a part of the Underground Railroad burned down, but there are a few left. This has to be one of them."

He rubbed the tips of his fingers over his chin. "If you're right, this would be the perfect house to set up a human trafficking operation. They'd be able to move the girls in and out of the house without drawing any attention to themselves. Hell, no one would even have to know girls were in the house at all."

"In a seriously disturbed way, it's genius," she said. "They must have taken the girls with them. Where would it lead?"

He nodded and studied the space he'd uncovered behind the bookcase. He glanced back at her and raised his brow. "There's only one way to find out."

Chapter Fourteen

"I need to make a call before we go in there." Every muscle in his body screamed at him to dive down the rabbit hole and screw protocol. But he needed to do this right. He couldn't afford another fuck up.

He glanced down at his phone and a moment of hesitation kept him from dialing Eric's number. Would Eric call Harper and feed him a line of bullshit? He hated not having complete trust in his partner. But he had to call someone. He'd already called for backup from the local police department...twice. Eric was his best option right now. Hell, Eric had never given him a reason not to trust him before. And if he called Eric to let him know he'd covered his bases, it might tame the tingling shred of guilt gnawing into his conscience telling him to wait for backup and keep Mickey away from the crime scene.

Hitting the send button with his thumb, he brought the phone to his ear and waited for his partner to pick up. One, two, three rings sounded in his ear before Eric's voicemail picked up. Not enough rings for the phone to take him to voicemail on its own. Eric had declined the call. Maybe he was busy with the case and couldn't be disturbed. That would make the most sense.

"Hey, man. I found something interesting in the house. I'm waiting for backup, but I have to check this out now. I'll fill you in later." He clicked off his phone and faced Mickey. "How's your battery? It'd suck to be wandering around in there with no light."

She glanced down at the screen. "Not great. Thirty-one percent. It should be fine. What about you?"

"Sixty-four percent." He flicked his thumb across the screen and clicked on his flashlight. "Ready?"

Mickey nodded and took one step behind the bookcase. A door slammed and Mickey whipped around, her hands gripped his shirt, her eyes wide. Heavy footsteps made the floorboards above their heads shudder. Dirt drifted down and Mickey swiped it off the matted strands of her still-damp hair. "Someone's here."

Graham lifted a finger to his lips and tilted his ear toward the ceiling.

"Chicago Police Department. We have a warrant to search this house, and backup was requested by Agent Grassi."

"Backup's here." His gaze stayed glued to the ceiling and indecision warred within him. He should alert the Chicago PD to what he'd found and help them clear the rest of the house. They'd be pissed if they discovered Mickey with him, her fingerprints marking up their crime scene. But he was in the mouth of the tunnel and the girls could be on the other end.

Besides, Mickey would throw a fit if he tried to get her out now. He dropped his gaze to ask Mickey if she wanted to wait upstairs, but she'd already disappeared into the pit behind the bookcase.

Shit.

He turned sideways to squeeze into the dark space in front of him. He lifted the phone and shuddered. The light washed over the sides of the stone walls that stood on either side of him and his head brushed against the ceiling. "Mickey?"

"I'm right in front of you. I didn't want to wait. Come on."

He quickened his step to catch up to her. "I hope you're not claustrophobic," he said in her ear. She slowed her pace and her body pressed against his.

"This is my worst nightmare come to life. Is it getting tighter? I think the walls are getting closer together." Her words tumbled out of her mouth along with her ragged breaths. "I should have waited for you to go first."

"Too late now." He fought the urge to stop and comfort her and pushed her forward. They needed to get to the end of this damn tunnel. If there was any chance of finding whoever wrote that note, they needed to hurry. "Actually, I think it's getting wider the farther we go."

"God, I hope so."

Dust rose in the air with every step he took, filling his lungs and coating his throat. Sweat trickled down his back and his shirt clung to his skin. The heat was unbearable. He concentrated on putting one foot in front of the other. Time passed slowly, but he didn't check his phone to see how long they'd been down there. It'd probably depress him.

Shrill squeaks and low whistles vibrated through the walls. Bats. Mickey stopped moving and he crashed into her back. He strained his ears, trying to recognize the sound. "I think we're almost to the end. Nothing would echo back here if the walls continued to stay so narrow. It must open up soon."

"Glad to hear it, but I don't want to know what's making that noise."

Cool air whipped down the narrow corridor, blasting

him in the face and combatting the heat. He sucked in a deep breath and savored the sudden reprieve. His pace quickened and the walls spread farther and farther apart until the ceiling opened up a couple of feet. Mickey stepped into the opening and turned in a wide circle. He lifted the light and sucked in a breath. "Holy shit."

Mickey stepped up beside him, her light joining his as they surveyed the area in front of them. "What is this place?"

He stepped through the archway and walked into a large, open area. Three tunnels, each slightly larger than the one they came from, led in three different directions. Old tracks led down each tunnel, like an abandoned mine. He turned toward Mickey, lifting the light to see her face. "Do you remember when a bunch of buildings downtown experienced flooding in their basements and they didn't know why?"

"That was over twenty years ago," Mickey said as her eyes darted around the deserted space. "I remember my dad being annoyed by it, but I was too young to care."

"Same here. I was eight, but I remember my parents bitching about it. Do you remember what caused the floods?"

"No. I don't think anyone ever told me."

"The Chicago river flooded, and the water breached a bunch of old utility tunnels most people forgot were even under the city, tunnels that had been shut down in the late fifties." He stepped toward the opening of one of the narrow tunnels and crouched down to study the tracks. "I'm guessing these are some of those tunnels. They were built in the early 1900s so carts could carry out the debris dug out to install telephone lines. I'm surprised the one from the house ran into these. They must have connected them somehow."

Mickey crouched down beside him. "How many tunnels are there?"

He shrugged. "I don't know, but I'm sure there are miles and miles of track laid down here."

"We'll never find them." Her voice trembled.

He stood and studied the tracks of the other two tunnels with his light. "I can't tell which track they used. At least not with this shitty light. If I come back down with better equipment, I might find footprints or something to lead me to them."

"Can you get equipment tonight?"

"Let's head back the way we came and I'll call my partner when we get back to the house. We'll figure out the best plan to lay out to my boss. He has to get on board after this."

• • •

Graham stepped back into the basement, and his sudden appearance had the two officers downstairs lifting their weapons in his direction. He held both hands in the air and dipped his head in greeting. "I'm Special Agent Grassi. I'm going to grab my badge slowly."

The guns trained on him didn't make him break a sweat, but they had Mickey trembling close behind him. He reached into the pocket of his pants and pulled out his badge, lifting it high for the officers to inspect. The closest officer took a couple steps forward, studied his badge, and nodded his acceptance.

Graham reached behind him until his hand found Mickey's. He wove his fingers between hers and led her out from behind the tunnel and next to him.

"I'm Officer Fisher," the young man who'd studied his badge said. "We've cleared the house and are combing through for fingerprints, paper trails, and anything else we can bag for evidence." A smile touched his face and his gaze flickered to Mickey. Jealousy burned Graham's veins and he cleared his throat to gain the man's attention. "Sorry, but who'd you find?"

"This is Ms. O'Shay. If you'll excuse me, I need to get her upstairs. I'll be back down after I fill my lieutenant in on what I've found." He made a beeline for the stairs and pulled Mickey along behind him.

Controlled chaos greeted them at the top of the stairs. Curious glances slid their way, but Graham ignored them as he passed through the kitchen, through the hallway, and escaped out the front door. The moon still shone bright and the rain had passed. A sprinkling of stars littered the sky and humidity hung in the air like a blanket. Graham briefly wished for the coolness of the tunnels to chase away the suffocating heat.

"You need to go inside and work. I'll go home." Mickey's small voice floated through the quiet night. Red and blue lights twirled through the dark sky and highlighted the paleness of her face.

"You need a minute to calm down. The adrenaline's leaving your body." He led her to the porch step and sat down beside her.

"We have to find them." Her breaths came out in short gasps and her chest rose and fell rapidly. "We have to find Becca."

Not knowing how else to comfort her, he wrapped his arm around her shoulder and pulled her close. Her body shook and he rubbed his hand up and down her arm. "I'll figure it out. This isn't my first rodeo. I've taken down bastards like this before, and I plan on doing it again. I won't give up."

"I just…it's all…I can't." A sob broke free and her words become a jumbled mess. Tears streamed down her cheeks, mixing with the dust that had clung to her face from the tunnels.

"Hey, everything's going to be fine." Her hair had fallen from the messy bun she'd worn earlier, and he ran his hand through her matted mane. Clumps of dirt and dried sweat mangled the long strands. Pressure built in his chest as he held her in his arms. Tonight had been tough for him, but he'd been through worse. It was part of the job. Processing it was part of his training. But Mickey hadn't been prepared for what she'd found. For the first time, he was absolutely sure she had no part in any of this.

Her tears fell unhindered as she faced him. The usual fire in her eyes had been replaced with a hopelessness that split his heart in two. "How will it be fine with people like that in the world? I never thought this stuff happened here, it was somebody else's problem. But being down in the basement and knowing what they made those poor girls do... I don't want to live in a world where that's okay."

"Look at me," he said as he cupped both of her cheeks in his palms. His thumbs moved over her cheeks, wiping away her tears. "What they're doing is not okay. That's why I do what I do. I stop them and I make things right. I'm sorry you had to go through this tonight, but now you know this shit happens. A lot more than you think."

"How do you do it?"

The side of his mouth lifted. "I'm saving lives. I'm making a difference. And you can too."

She laughed, but it bordered on a hysterical snort. "How?"

"Keep your eyes open. Look for things that don't make sense, situations that leave you with a bad feeling. Especially while you're working. You never know when you'll be able to help."

A shaking breath blew through her parted lips, warming his face. "Okay. Does it make me a horrible person if I just want to forget about it for tonight?"

He pulled away and dropped his hands from her face. "Not at all. Let me call my boss and fill him in on what we found. Then we'll get you home."

Mickey rested her elbow on her knee and then dropped her cheek to her hand. "I can get myself home. They need you here."

"I've been working for twenty straight hours. I need some sleep." He leaned forward and pressed his lips to the smooth skin on her forehead and then called his boss.

Graham bit back a sigh and waited for his boss to answer the phone.

"Did you find the girls?" Even at this late hour, fatigue didn't lace through Harper's gruff voice.

"No, but we did find tunnels leading from the house."

"Did you find Bogart or Difico?"

Graham bit into his cheek. "No, sir."

"Is this conversation of the utmost importance, or can it wait until morning?"

Graham wanted to argue that anything to do with this case was of the utmost importance, but he'd rather wait until morning to have this conversation. He needed a decent night's sleep to regain his composure and put his thoughts in order. And he needed to get Mickey the hell out of here. "The morning's fine."

"Good. Come to my office first thing."

The call disconnected before Graham could reply. He stood and extended a hand to Mickey. She curled her fingers around his and he helped her to her feet. The warmth of her hand heated his blood. He glanced at her as they crossed the yard and pride swelled inside him. She was a tough cookie. He'd been attracted to her from the beginning, but now she'd earned his respect and trust. That was one hell of a combination.

Mickey yanked on his hand, halting his progress toward his car. "Wait, I need my shoes."

He dropped his gaze to her bare feet and winced. He'd forgotten she didn't have any shoes on. Dirt stained the tops of them, but at least it hid the dried blood from where the rat had scratched her. "Were those your shoes I found in the yard?"

"At the corner of the house, in front of the shrubs? Probably. One got stuck in the mud, so I took the other one off and left it outside so it wouldn't slow me down."

A soft chuckle tickled his throat. She was one of a kind. "Hold on a second." He dropped her hand and his body screamed in protest at the lack of her warmth. He walked toward the spot she'd mentioned and his gaze scanned the long blades of grass until he found her heels.

He jogged back to her and handed her the shoes. "There you go. Now get in your car and follow me to my place. I'll sleep on the couch and you can take the bed."

"What? No, I want to go home." Exhaustion made her words come out heavy.

He reached over and captured her hand again. "Listen to me. You just experienced something no one should ever have to. You shouldn't be alone tonight."

Her body sagged and a yawn tore from her mouth. She widened her eyes as they locked with his. "That's really sweet, but I'll be fine, really. I desperately want my own bed."

She shifted her gaze to face their cars parked on the street and he studied her profile. Her shoulders drooped forward and her eyes closed, as if needing privacy to fight an internal battle. She'd been through enough tonight, she didn't need him arguing with her. But dammit, her apartment wasn't safe and who knew what terrors would come for her in the night. He couldn't stand the thought of her dealing with it all alone.

"Mickey, I don't want to scare you, but Connie's still out there. We have her face and her name now, but who knows how long it will take to track her down. She might come after you again. You might have had your locks changed, but that doesn't mean your apartment is safe."

Her hand tightened in his. "So much has happened tonight, I didn't even think about that." She opened her eyes and faced him once more. Her chin lifted and a hard glint sparked in her irises. "You believe me?"

Guilt pressed down on his chest like a weight. Mickey had been through hell the last couple of days, and he'd only added to her problems. "Yes. About all of it."

Tears filled her eyes and she drew in a wobbly breath. Shaking her head, she said, "You're right. Staying at my place isn't a smart move."

He squeezed her hand before letting it go and reaching for his keys. "Good. Do you want to ride with me? Driving might not be the best idea right now."

Taking a deep breath, Mickey squared her shoulders and shook her head. "I'll need my car to get to work tomorrow. Just don't drive too crazy, and I should be able to keep up."

Excitement ran through him at the thought of Mickey sleeping in his apartment, but he pushed it away. She needed a safe place to stay for the night, and nothing more. At least that's what he told himself as they walked toward their cars. The memory of her touch burned his skin. He had a fifteen-minute car ride to get his head on straight. Even if he believed Mickey was innocent, she was still off limits. He suppressed a groan.

Nightmares of what they'd found tonight wouldn't be the only thing keeping him awake.

Chapter Fifteen

Graham opened the door to his apartment and ushered her inside, his hand pressed to the small of her back. Exhaustion weighed down every muscle in her body.

She needed a shower and she needed sleep, but fear lingered in the forefront of her mind. No doubt ghosts waited to greet her as soon as she closed her eyes. Images of Becca, cold and afraid, waiting for someone to help her. She blinked the thoughts away. At least for the moment. She glanced around. His apartment was small, but nice. Granite countertops and gleaming hard wood floors enticed her forward, and she traced a finger along the smooth surface of the counter that jutted out from the wall, separating the kitchen from the living room.

"Why don't you have a seat, and I'll make us something to eat?" Graham nodded toward the backless stools in front of the granite peninsula.

"I'm not hungry." Food was the last thing on her mind, even if she hadn't eaten in hours.

"Sit down anyway. I'm starving, and you need to unwind

a little before you go to sleep. Trust me, if you don't try to let some of what happened tonight leak from your mind, it will just make things worse."

His gentle tone prodded her to sit down on the stool. Mickey settled her elbows on the hard surface and held her head up with her palms. Her gaze followed him around the kitchen as he grabbed leftover lasagna from the refrigerator and heated it up. Despite her earlier refusal, he grabbed two plates and slid the warm food under her nose and then took a seat beside her.

The combination of garlic and oregano was too tempting to resist, and she grabbed a forkful of food and took a bite. "This is really good."

"I'll let my mom know you think so. She tries to make sure my freezer's always stocked with something to heat up."

A smile touched her mouth. "That's nice. I wish my parents lived close enough to do that. Not like I'm home much anyway."

"They don't live in Chicago?"

Mickey shook her head. "No. They live a few hours away. Close enough to visit when I get a chance, but not close enough to supply food on a regular basis. I moved here when I started working for the airline."

"How long have you been a flight attendant?" Graham stood and grabbed two bottles of water, setting one by each of their plates, and sat back down.

The food sank to the pit of her stomach and mixed with the fear that had taken residence there. Mickey dropped her fork and stared at him. "Really? That's what we're going to talk about right now? I don't think I can sit here and pretend like I didn't just walk away from a living hell." She hated the way her voice shook, but she couldn't stop it. The dam was about to burst, and she didn't care.

Graham set his fork down and twisted to face her. He

cupped her cheek with his hand, and she closed her eyes and leaned into his warmth. A tear slid down her cheek, and Graham used the pad of his thumb to wipe it away.

"I know this is hard, but the best thing you can do for yourself right now is try and think about something else. Just for five minutes. Give yourself a small break so you can get your head on straight."

Opening her eyes, she sucked in a deep breath and focused on the tiny specks of aqua in his gray eyes. She could do this. Blinking away the moisture on her lashes, she said, "I've been a flight attendant for six years. I studied political science in college, and when I couldn't find a job my friend and I decided to work for the same airline for a few years. We figured it'd be a good opportunity to see the world before we settled down with our careers. We fell in love with flying, and haven't thought about quitting yet."

Graham nodded, the side of his mouth hitched up in a half smile, and he dropped his hand from her face. A rush of cold air slid against her now-bare cheek, and she wished like hell for his touch again. He kept his gaze locked on hers, as if he understood she needed that connection to cling to in order to stay calm. "It's good to do what you love. Makes a tough job easier."

"Does loving your job make it easier to deal with the horrors you see every day?"

"It will never be easy to see what I see, but it does make it easier to keep showing up. I can't imagine doing anything else."

"When does it become too much? When do you get to the point where you've seen too much, witnessed too many bad things?" She couldn't help but ask the question. Graham might think talking about her job and other mundane things could help her keep it together, but nothing would. What she needed was his calm reassurance that he was going to find

Becca.

Graham shifted in his seat and glanced down at his half-eaten pasta. Silence lingered between them, and she sensed something brewing inside him. Something he wasn't willing to share. She wanted to press him, but she was desperately trying to keep her head above water in a lake of her own emotional turmoil. Whether it was fair or not, she couldn't handle some else's baggage right now.

Clearing his throat, Graham lifted his gaze to hers once more and shrugged. "The day it becomes too much is the day I need to find a new job."

The raw pain in his beautiful gray orbs nearly knocked her off her stool. The ache in her heart grew, but this time it wasn't because of Becca. She ached for him and whatever secrets he'd buried inside. She placed her hand on top of his on the counter, and Graham twisted his wrist so his palm faced up. Their fingers linked, and a rush of heat flooded her body.

"I'm sorry you're in the middle of all this, and I'm even more sorry I made things worse by not trusting you," he whispered.

Relief had her leaning forward and resting her head against his hard chest. He'd told her before they'd left the house in Old Town he believed her, but hearing it again was like salve on a burn. She could stop fighting so damn hard to prove her innocence and concentrate solely on finding Becca.

"Thank you." His dirty shirt muffled her words, and she glanced up, her chin still resting against his collarbone. His warm breath slid across her forehead, and he skimmed her arm with his free hand. He was so damn close that the rapid beating of his heart echoed against her.

She leaned back and the gentle touch of his long fingers against her stopped. He lifted his hand and tipped her chin up with his index finger. His eyes searched hers, as if waiting for some sort of signal or answer to an unasked question. Her pulse picked up and she moistened her lips, preparing for what she hoped was to come.

Graham's mouth pressed down on hers, and she wrapped her arms around his neck. For a split second the nightmare of the last few days fled her mind, and she focused on the feel of the warm-blooded man in front of her. But the moment ended, and Graham pulled away. Reality crashed back down on her, and she glanced down. Her mud-caked feet and streaked skirt stared back at her, and humiliation heated her cheeks. No wonder Graham only wanted to give her a small peck on the lips. She had to look like death, and no doubt didn't smell much better.

"Umm...could I grab a shower? I don't want to sleep before I wash away the filth of the day."

Graham shot to his feet, and the legs of his stool scraped against the hard wood. "Absolutely," he said, his voice coming out thick and sexy as hell. "Everything you need is in the bathroom. I'm going to clean up the kitchen really quick. Do you want something to sleep in?"

"A shirt would be great. I need to wash my clothes, too. I have to work in the morning."

Graham nodded and grabbed the dishes, clearing them before placing them in the sink. "No problem. I'll take care of it."

"Thanks." Mickey stood and turned to search for the bathroom. Two doors occupied the wall on the opposite side of the living room. She swept her gaze around the tidy living space. Nothing out of place except an opened laptop on the coffee table surrounded by scattered papers and files.

All the blood drained from her face as she stared at the computer screen. She lifted a finger and pointed at the screen. "Who's that?"

Graham stepped up beside her. "Who?"

Her gaze never left the computer. "Who's the woman on the screen?"

Graham turned toward the computer and tilted his head to the side. "Paula Williams. Her mom used to live with Pete's father. Why?" He narrowed his gaze at her.

"She looks exactly like Becca, only about fifteen years older."

Graham stepped around the sofa and stopped in front of the coffee table. He shuffled around the papers and pulled out a picture. His eyes squinted at the corners and then widened as he glanced up at her. "You're right. The coloring, the face shape, even the way the hair curls at the ends. My God, they could be mother and daughter...or sisters."

The back of the sofa pressed into her abdomen as she leaned forward to get a better look at the screen. "She looks more like her than Suzi does, and Becca looks a lot like her mother." Her eyes scanned the information listed beside the picture. "She lives in Mexico?"

Graham bent down and closed the laptop. "Mickey, I told you, I can't discuss the investigation with you."

She planted her balled fists on her hips. "Even after everything we've been through tonight?" Her chin quivered, making her words tremble. His continuing to shut her out hurt more than she wanted to admit.

The corners of his mouth dipped down in a small frown and he walked over to her. He laid a hand on her shoulder and met her gaze. His eyes weren't so intense this close. The gray not so unrelenting. "Even after tonight. Grab a shower. It's been a long night."

A beat passed before she gave in. "Fine." She turned and walked toward the bathroom. She'd weaseled her way into enough of the investigation and needed to leave it to Graham. But as she stepped into the hot spray and rinsed the dirt and sweat out of her hair, one thing kept circling in her mind...the address beside Paula's picture on the computer screen.

Casa Del Mar 500, Playa Del Carmen.

What an easy address to remember.

• • •

Darkness surrounded her. Her hands reached out and brushed up against the cold stone of the walls that encased her on either side. She tried to turn in a circle, but the walls moved in, wedging her between them. Her heels dug into the dirt floor and she used all of her body weight to try to push the wall back.

It didn't work.

Panic gripped her heart and she clawed at the stone. A fingernail snapped and she yelped in pain and sucked on the wounded finger. A bright light shone from the distance and she turned her shoulders to the side to shimmy down the damp tunnel. She reached toward the light, but the more she walked the farther away the light moved.

"Help!" A shrill voice pierced the air.

She turned her head to the side. Who was that? Was someone down here with her? "Who's there?" Her voice bounced back at her and echoed off the walls.

"Why did you leave me with them?" The small voice sounded like a child's and a shiver of fear ran down her spine. Becca?

"I'm trying to find you," she called out. She squinted and searched the distant light, but nothing appeared.

The walls pressed in closer, stealing the breath from her lungs. The smooth stone turned jagged as it pushed into her tender flesh. She tried to take a breath but the walls pushed in farther. She reached for the light, for the voice, but complete blackness surrounded her yet again.

"Mickey...Mickey! Wake up."

An urgent voice penetrated through the walls. Light pressure pressed against her arms and her muscles tightened. Her body twisted and turned, her feet peddled through the air but didn't touch anything. Her eyes flew open and Graham's furrowed brow and concerned eyes stared back at her.

She gasped for air and pushed a sheet of hair from her face. The damp strands stuck to her hand, and she shook them off as she sat up. Tears clouded her vision, and she glanced around the dark room. Her lungs burned, but she couldn't seem to fill them fast enough. Graham tucked her hair behind her ears and gathered her close against his hard chest.

"I was in a tunnel and the walls closed in." Her words came out quick, her voice thick with tears. "I heard a voice, but I couldn't get to it. I couldn't save her. The walls were crushing me, killing me."

"You were having a nightmare. It's okay. Everything's fine." His fingers grazed her spine, bunching the material of her shirt.

She sunk into him, letting the slow motion of his fingers calm her. Sweat clung to her hairline, but she let it linger, focusing only on the slow movement of the tips of his fingers up and down her spine. Up and down, up and down.

Her back stiffened and she sat up straight on the bed. She wasn't wearing a bra. She crossed her arms over her chest and looked down. What the hell was she wearing? A large white T-shirt hung loosely on her, but her exposed nipples somehow managed to press tightly against the soft material. Heat scorched her cheeks.

"You're shaking. Are you cold?"

"No, I'm not cold. I just can't get my nightmare out of my head. The little girl's voice will haunt me for the rest of my life." Goosebumps lined her arms and a chill tore through her body.

"I've had my fair share of nightmares. They can be brutal."

She dropped her gaze and her eyes landed on Graham's naked chest. She cleared her throat and forced her eyes up to his face. "How do you get over them?"

His arm came around and pressed against her back, pushing her close to the hard muscles of his chest. "Some of them never go away. The others drift away on their own."

She rested her head against his breastbone. "I'll never be able to sleep." Her heart beat a steady rhythm, matching Graham's under her cheek.

Graham pulled away and lifted her chin with his thumb. "You're stronger than you think."

His touch branded her skin and she swallowed hard. Her tongue swiped across her lips, her eyes never leaving his. "Do you think so?"

A soft chuckle rumbled from his throat and he leaned closer, his warm breath caressing her skin. "I think a lot of things about you, Red."

She smiled up at him. "You can't get more creative than Red?"

A lazy grin spread across his face. "You can't get more creative than G.I. Joe?"

She shrugged and the T-shirt rose a little on her thighs. Graham's hand traveled from her chin to cup the back of her neck. "Do you want me to show you what I think of you, Red?"

Oh, boy.

She gulped and nodded. She wanted him to take her mind far away from the nightmare that still lingered in her brain. His warm body pressed against hers and chased the chill from her skin. His free hand wrapped around the small of her back and bunched the shirt up even higher. She closed her eyes and the horror from moments before vanished like a fine mist floating out to sea.

It wasn't real. Graham was real…this moment was real. And dammit, she needed something to make her feel good for just one minute of this rotten day. She took a deep breath as he lowered his lips to hers. Electricity zipped through her veins.

Oh, freaking boy.

Chapter Sixteen

All the blood rushed from his head as his lips pressed against Mickey's. Her lips were soft, her mouth eager for his. He threaded his fingers through her hair and his tongue parted her lips. He licked into her mouth and she moaned, going lax against him.

"Lie down," he said in a hoarse whisper.

She obeyed. Her long legs entwined with his as he lay down beside her, and he ran a hand up one smooth calve and tightened his grip on her firm thigh. She didn't protest, only arched her back and pulled him back down to her mouth. He rested on his elbows as he leaned over her, his tongue once again invading her mouth. His fingers itched to ride higher on her thigh and past the T-shirt she wore, but he didn't want to move too fast.

Mickey's hand snaked around the back of his neck, her other wrapped around his shoulders, pulling him on top of her. Her firm breasts, unhindered by a bra, pressed against his chest. His leg parted hers and nestled close to her center. His hand came up from her thigh and the tips of his fingers rode up the curve of her hip and skimmed over the soft skin on her side. Little by little, inch by inch, he trailed them over her ribs and under the tender flesh of her breast. He lifted his thumb and let the pad rub gently over her nipple. Desire surged through him as a soft moan of pleasure slipped from her mouth.

She sucked in a sharp breath and her hand roamed up and down his back. Each stroke of her slender fingers on his bare skin heightened his desire for her, and dammit, all she touched was his back. He throbbed beneath his boxer briefs, his member pressed firmly against her stomach. His thumb and index finger came together on her nipple, pinching and teasing until it became a hard nub.

"God, Graham. That feels so good." Her words floated on a purr and she squirmed under him, bringing him closer to the warm spot between her legs. His blood burned hot, fueling him on.

His mouth left hers and trailed kisses along her jawline and up to her ear. He nibbled on the lobe and then said, "I told you there's a lot of things I think about you. And this is something I haven't stopped thinking about since I kissed you in your kitchen."

He lifted his face and gazed down at her. Damn, she was beautiful. Lust sparked in her whiskey-colored eyes, but she bit into her bottom lip the way she did when she was unsure. Funny how he'd picked up on that after only a couple of days with her.

His muscles tensed. Shit. He'd only known her a couple of days, and most of that time he'd suspected her of being an accomplice to a sex-trafficker. Now, instead of comforting her after a nightmare, he had his boner pressed to her stomach and his hand up her shirt. Not to mention she was still connected to the case. He couldn't risk compromising this case by becoming involved with her.

At least not yet.

He lifted his hand from her breast and cradled her cheek. She leaned into him, her eyes never leaving his. "How about we slow this down?"

The lust in her eyes dimmed and her brow furrowed. "Is everything okay?" she asked.

Rolling off her, he propped his head in his fist. He weighed his words. If he mentioned a conflict of interest with sleeping with her now, she'd fly off the hinges and think he still doubted her. No need to tempt that. "You tell me. You've had one hell of a day. Are you sure you're ready for this? I mean, we don't know each other very well."

A blush as red as her swollen lips flooded her face. She tried to turn away from him, but he refused to let her. Her gaze drifted slowly up to his. "I'm not the kind of girl who sleeps around."

Shit. He never considered she'd come to that conclusion. "Honey, I didn't think you were. But I don't want you to do something you'll regret. Especially with me." A shiver of awareness coursed through him. Somehow in the past few days, Mickey had become important to him. He didn't want to mess up a chance of a future with her, or his job, because they acted on impulse. As much as he wanted to sleep with her, he wanted her to know he respected her more.

She took a deep breath, and he suppressed a groan when the motion made her breasts mold against her shirt. "You're right. This," she waved a hand between them, "wouldn't be right. At least not tonight."

Graham leaned forward and pressed a kiss to her forehead. "I want to get to know you better, Mickey. Away from all the craziness of the past two days. Let's do this right."

She nodded and a strand of hair fell across her face. He brushed it back and turned to climb out of the bed. A warm touch on his arm stopped him, and he turned to face her.

"Will you stay in here with me? I don't want to be alone... not after what happened tonight."

The lines around her eyes deepened and her teeth tucked into her lip again. His body still burned for her. Sleeping in the same bed, with her so close, would be pure torture. But he couldn't say no. He wanted to be there for her and show her he meant what he'd said.

Climbing back into the bed, he nestled in behind her. His arm wrapped around her middle and he pulled her tight to him. Her hair tickled his nose, and the scent of strawberries assaulted his senses. "Go to sleep," he said in her ear.

She relaxed against him and her breathing slowed until the steady rhythm of sleep took her under. He glanced at the clock over her shoulder. Three a.m. Sleep was the last thing on his mind.

"Graham, where are my clothes?" Mickey whispered into his ear.

"Hmm? What's going on?" He reached out to pull her back into his arms, but she backed away with a small laugh.

"Stop it. I've got to get to work, but I can't find my clothes."

His eyes drifted open. Mickey stood beside the bed, her hair pinned back in a neat bun at the nape of her neck. Sun shone through the curtains on the opposite side of the room, and he swore she looked like an angel with the early light streaming behind her. "What time is it?"

"It's six. I really need to get dressed." She pulled the T-shirt away from her body. "This isn't exactly work appropriate."

He rubbed the sleep out of his eyes and sat up. The blanket fell to his lap, and Mickey's gaze drifted to his chest.

"I washed your uniform after you came to bed last night. I hung them up beside the dryer so they wouldn't wrinkle."

She leaned forward and pressed a quick kiss to his lips. "Thanks. I'm going to change and head out. I'll talk to you soon."

His groin tightened as he watched her hips sway, the white T-shirt barely skimming the tops of her thighs. He deserved a medal for stopping things last night, and then still sleeping with her curled up beside him for the rest of the night. He glanced at the clock and groaned. Harper wouldn't be in the office until nine a.m. He didn't want to wait to talk to him about what had happened last night. He also needed to book a flight to Mexico so he could talk to Paula Williams.

Mickey was right—she looked an awful lot like Becca Stanley. Paula might be the missing piece of the puzzle he'd been searching for.

• • •

Graham's heart beat against his chest like a heavy drum.

This was so foreign to him. Harper had always been a stern boss. Hell, Graham respected him for his no bullshit approach on handling situations, but he'd never encountered the stubborn pain in the ass attitude Harper constantly threw at him on this case. It was as if Harper didn't want him to succeed. He didn't know how to deal with it.

Stepping out of his car, he looked around the quiet neighborhood. Shade trees lined the street, small cages encasing the bottoms of their skinny trunks. Traffic was light, but older couples walking their dogs littered the sidewalks. He nodded hello, taking in the attractions around him. A few restaurants and an abandoned movie theater sat nestled in with the townhouses and office buildings. Birds singing out in the early morning mingled with the snippets of conversation and yaps of little dogs.

Graham buried one hand in the pocket of his chinos while the other held a file at his side. His dress shoes tapped against the sidewalk, and he blew out a long breath as he walked up the steps to the front door of a townhouse.

Harper's going to kill me.

After Mickey had left, he'd been lucky enough to find a flight to Cancun leaving midmorning. He didn't have time to dick around, waiting for Harper to get into the office. He'd called in and wasn't surprised his boss wasn't there. Then he'd tried Harper's cell phone, but was sent straight to voicemail. So, he decided to come straight to his residence. He was already in hot water. What would a little more heat do?

He hated the slight tremor in his hand as he lifted it and knocked on the bright red door. Weakness could not be shown, at least not right now. There was no doubt in his mind he was on the right track, and he needed Harper to finally see it, too. He couldn't convince Harper if he showed weakness.

An eternity passed and his entire career flashed before his eyes before the door opened and Harper stared at him with the look of death in his eyes. "What the hell do you think you're doing?"

"You wanted to see me first thing this morning, but I don't have time to meet with you once you get to the office. I have a plane to catch. I figured you'd rather speak to me before I left the country."

"So you came to my house? Are you insane?" Harper's face grew red and a vein in his forehead bulged.

Graham bit into his cheek and stood his ground. He lifted the file in the air. He'd printed off the pictures he'd taken of the house last night to add to it before coming to see Harper, along with the picture of Paula Williams. "I brought some evidence to show you. I think it might change your mind about how I've handled the case."

Harper waved his hand through the air as if swatting away an annoying gnat. "Do you think I haven't seen it? And everything you have in your file is circumstantial at best. Mere speculation and garbage at worst."

His fingers curled around the edge of the thin file and he ground his teeth together. "Sir, I respectfully disagree with you. And there's new evidence I added late last night."

A heavy sigh lifted Harper's broad shoulders and he pinched the bridge of his nose. "Don't you understand? We can't use anything you found in that house. You didn't wait for the warrant. Looking at it won't do a damn thing except piss me off."

"I had a damn good reason to go into the house before the warrant came through last night. A woman cried out for help. Any judge would agree with me and take everything we found last night into consideration."

"Watch yourself, Grassi. You've been skating on thin ice for a while. I'd hate for you to fall through. I'm not sure you'd ever resurface."

Graham thrust the file toward him. Harper hadn't even seen the photos from last night yet, and he didn't know about Paula. "If you'd just—"

"Enough." Harper leaned forward and shook a bony finger in Graham's face. "I'm not the only one who thinks you're pulling on the wrong thread. Either you come up with something fast, or I'm taking you off the case. The lives of three young girls are at stake, and I'm not going to let your mistakes lead them to their graves. Now get to work."

Numbness crept into his limbs and he turned to walk down the stairs. Before his legs complied, he threw the file at Harper's feet. What the hell was going on? He'd never been treated this way before. And someone else thought he was messing up? A million questions danced on the tip of his tongue, but he swallowed them down.

"Grassi."

He stopped at the bottom of the stoop and turned his head to face his boss. The deep lines of Harper's face seemed even more severe with the morning light streaming directly on him. His intimidating presence dominated the doorframe. "Yes?"

"You have one week. If you can't find me something concrete, you're done." The door slammed shut and Graham flinched.

It took all the self-control he had not to storm back up to the door and give Harper a piece of his mind, but he couldn't waste his time, or his breath. A glance at his watch showed him he only had an hour before he needed to be at the airport. A quick thrill raced through his veins. Maybe he'd get lucky and Mickey would be working his flight.

Oh shit, Mickey. He groaned as he walked to his car. He hadn't even asked her how her first flight back had gone. And now she would be working the same flight that had almost gotten her killed. She'd never believe he wanted to see where things could go between them if he didn't even remember to ask her the most basic questions. Pushing it to the back of his mind, he grabbed his phone from his pocket and called Eric.

"Hey, man," Eric answered on the third ring.

"I hope you've missed me, because you'll be seeing my ugly mug soon." He pressed the phone between his ear and his shoulder as he put the car in drive and headed home. He had just enough time to pack and make it to the airport for a stiff drink before boarding his plane.

"I guess Harper wasn't impressed with the house you found last night?"

Graham snorted. "That's an understatement."

"Did you show him the pictures you sent me?" Eric's voice held a hint of disbelief.

"He wouldn't even look at them. He's not convinced my

search was legal," he said with a slight shake of his head, even though Eric couldn't see him. "I threw them at his feet when I left. Hopefully he'll stop being a stubborn ass and at least flip through them."

Eric let out a low, long whistle. "Damn. You've got balls."

"Drastic times call for drastic measures, right? And our backs are against the wall here. Harper gave us one week, and if we don't find the girls or Bogart, he's pulling us off the case. Well, me at least."

"You go, I go."

"I might be getting pulled off more than just the case." A gnawing sense of dread settled in the pit of his stomach. He'd worked his ass off to get where he was. Getting it all taken away would kill him. "Did you find anything at the house yesterday?"

"No. But I'm casing the place today. Gonna try to talk to some neighbors, canvas the neighborhood. Maybe we'll get lucky."

"Let's hope so. My flight takes off in a couple of hours and I'm heading straight to Paula Williams' house." He turned into the parking garage and slid into an empty spot.

"Do you want me to meet you at the airport and go with you?"

"Nah, stay where you are. Try to find Pete. I'll touch base after I speak to Paula." He said goodbye and then disconnected before making his way to his apartment.

He had one week to find a sex-trafficker, three kidnapped girls, and save his career. A cold sweat broke out on the back of his neck. He would need a lot more than luck on his side to pull this off.

Chapter Seventeen

Oh God. What the hell was she doing? She should turn around. She should get in the cab waiting for her and never look back.

Mickey glanced over her shoulder as she walked up the concrete sidewalk to the two-story white stucco house. The cab she'd taken from Playa Del Carmen sat idling on the curb. She'd paid him a ridiculous amount of money to bring her to the address that had circled in her mind since she'd first seen it, and then wait for her to finish whatever the hell she was doing to take her back to her hotel. Turning back toward the house, she drew in a long breath and slowly made her way to the large wooden door.

The sound of waves crashing against the shore roared from behind the house and the large palms on the trees beside her swayed in the breeze. Beads of sweat formed at her hairline. Mexico in August was brutal. Unless she was parked in front of a pool or lounging on the beach, she preferred to escape the miserable Chicago winters for the warm Mexican sun. At this time of year, it was just trading one warm, humid day for an even hotter warm, humid day. Even this late in the afternoon, standing outside sucked the air from her lungs.

Her thoughts bounced around in her head. Nerves danced around in her stomach to the tune of the mariachi music she couldn't get out of her head. She didn't know what she would say to Paula if she answered the door. Hell, she hadn't decided to come here until after her second margarita.

Who was she kidding? She could lie to Vanessa and Allison all day about why she wanted to stay in Playa Del Carmen instead of Cancun. They didn't even question her when she'd said she wanted to stay away from the craziness of the Cancun streets, and stay somewhere a little quieter. Not like Playa Del Carmen was much quieter these days. But she couldn't lie to herself, not any longer. Casa Del Mar 500 had played on repeat in her mind, and she needed to see Paula Williams for herself.

Her hand trembled as she made a fist and knocked on the door. Three loud, decisive knocks. She studied the front of the house as she waited for someone to answer. Two cars sat under the large balcony that jutted out from the second story, a sort of makeshift portico. Bamboo stairs wound around the side of the house, connecting the small patio to the second story. Thatched roofs adorned the doors that led out to the balcony above her, and white Romanesque columns stood tall between the two stories and gave the impression of a grand manor.

The door creaked open and Mickey snapped her attention back to the reason she was here. A sliver of light inked out into the twilight and a petite woman with wide blue eyes and a small oval face peeked out at her, half hidden by the door. Confusion creased the fine lines at the corner of her mouth.

"Can I help you?"

Mickey's jaw dropped. This is what Becca would look like as an adult… "Hi, my name is Mickey O'Shay." She extended a hand to Paula, who opened the door wider and offered a firm handshake.

Paula had pulled her ash blond hair off her face in a high ponytail, showing off her smooth, tan skin. Her denim shorts and floral tank top hung loosely on her small frame. Her hand lingered on the door handle, as if unsure whether she wanted to shut the door in Mickey's face or not. She tilted her head to the side. "Do I know you?"

"No, I don't think you do. But we both know Pete, and I'd like to know if I'm the only woman he's lied to and ripped her world to shreds."

All the color drained from Paula's face, leaving behind a scared woman with a haunted look in her eyes. A woman who looked like nothing more than a girl. "I have nothing to say about Pete," she said as she tried to close the door.

Mickey placed her palm on the solid wood, refusing to be dismissed so easily. "Please. I don't want to upset you, but he took my goddaughter. I need answers."

The pressure of the door on Mickey's hand stopped and she grabbed her phone and pulled up a picture of Becca. She turned the screen toward Paula. "This is Becca. She's only eight years old and Pete took her Sunday morning. She's been with him for almost three days." Mickey's voice broke and her throat clogged with tears.

Paula sighed, turned from the door, and walked into the expansive house. "Come in," she said over her shoulder.

More columns stood proudly in the foyer, holding up the catwalk that ran along the width of the room. Wooden stairs wound their way up the stone wall, almost as if suspended in air, to the second floor. Mickey's footsteps rang loud against the travertine tiled floor, echoing off the high ceilings as she walked into the great room. A fan spun lazily in the middle of the ceiling, circulating the cool air that blew from the air conditioner.

Mickey stayed quiet as she followed Paula into the great room, her mind searching for the right words. Being blunt, and a little rude, had gotten her in the door, but might not keep her here. She didn't know how much Paula knew about Pete's recent activities, or if she could even trust whatever Paula told her. But she had to take a chance, and she needed to figure out the best approach to get Paula to open up to a complete stranger.

A tall man with olive skin and slicked-back black hair stood from a white suede couch. He held a tumbler of something golden in his hand, and he swayed the glass back and forth as he watched her with interest.

"Were we expecting company?" His brown eyes never left Mickey.

Paula walked up beside him and leaned into him, and his arm automatically wrapped around her small shoulders.

"She said Pete took her goddaughter. She has some questions." The friendliness from earlier had left, and her voice held a sharp hint of something. Fear? "This is my husband, Jose."

"Hola. And your name is?" The velvet of his eyes melted away, replaced with a hard edge that made the brown almost black.

She swallowed hard. "Mickey O'Shay."

"And you're from?"

"Chicago."

One dark brow lifted. "You flew all the way down here to Mexico to ask Paula questions about the man who has made her life a living hell since she was nine years old? How did you find her?"

She could picture Paula at nine; she would look just like Becca did today. Pieces of the puzzle clicked into place with rapid speed and clarity.

"I know I shouldn't be here," she said, ignoring the

question, "but I need to find my goddaughter. Time's running out, I can feel it, and you might be the only one who can help find her."

Paula used her hands to brace herself as she sunk into the couch. Jose sat next to her with his back ramrod straight, his hands locked on Paula's. Mickey shuffled her feet and her gaze flicked around the room.

"Please sit," Paula said. Mickey took a seat across from Paula in an armchair that matched the sofa. The suede material was smooth against the backs of her legs and she fought the urge to run her fingers along the supple suede. "How could I possibly help you?"

Mickey cringed at the note of defeat in Paula's voice, as if the mere thought of Pete was too much for her to handle. She shrugged and clasped her hands on her lap. "I don't know. All I know is Pete lied to me and used me for four months in order to earn the trust of my goddaughter. No one knows where he is, or why he picked me to break his pattern. But I think you have the answer."

"What do you mean by breaking his pattern?" Jose asked, leaning forward slightly.

Mickey met his gaze. "He took three girls all within weeks of each other, but Becca is the only one who actually knew him. I'm the only person he gave his real name to, who he had a relationship with."

"That's horrible," Paula said, shaking her head. "But why would you think I have any answers? I haven't spoken to him in years."

"Look at this picture again. Please." She held out her phone. Jose grabbed it and lifted it in front of him and Paula.

Paula gasped. "She looks just like me."

"My God. That's uncanny," Jose said. "That's your goddaughter?"

"Yes, that's Becca." Her throat closed up around the

words and her voice came out in a small squeak. "It can't be a coincidence you look so much like her."

Paula closed her eyes as Jose handed back her phone. His arm held her against him and he whispered something in her ear as tears fell down her face. She nodded, and then opened her eyes. This time determination lurked behind the sapphire blue. She drew in a deep breath and then said, "No, you're probably right. It's not a coincidence."

Jose's fingers grazed up and down the side of her arm. "Are you sure you're okay? You don't have to tell her anything." His accent thickened when he spoke softly to Paula.

"Yes. I do." She cleared her throat and then swiped her tongue over her top lip. Her gaze stayed fixed on her lap. "My mom met Pete's dad when I was very young. They fell in love and moved in together quickly. Robert was always good to me. It was a happy life. A simple and happy life. I knew he had a son, but Robert hardly ever talked about him. His son lived with Robert's ex-wife, and they had a pretty toxic relationship. It's the reason he never married my mom."

"Did that bother your mom? That her boyfriend had a son she never met and he wouldn't marry her because of past mistakes?" The answer didn't matter, but Mickey was curious.

"No, at least I don't think so. Life was good just as it was… until Pete came to live with us." Paula stopped speaking and grabbed the crystal glass from Jose. Tilting her head back, she swallowed the rest of the drink and then handed it back. "I was nine, and excited to have a big brother. Nervous, but excited. But it didn't last. It didn't take long for Pete to show me the kind of person he really was."

A small shudder made Paula's body shake. Jose placed a large hand on the back of her neck and leaned in close. Mickey shifted in her chair and glanced away, feeling like an intruder. She had brought this into their house, but she had to. Paula could be the key to finding Becca.

Paula shared her story, ending by saying, "I cried and kicked and tried to scream, but he covered my mouth with his hand and pressed me against the bed. He was fifteen."

Shock and disgust made all the words in Mickey's head disappear. She'd known it'd be bad, but not this. Her stomach muscles clenched and she fought the urge to run out of the house. She didn't want to hear anymore. Didn't want to know everything this poor woman endured at such a young age.

"I'm so sorry, Paula." The words were small and so damn insignificant. Forcing herself to continue, she asked, "How long did this go on?"

Paula snorted. "It's never really stopped. I'd threaten to tell on him and he'd laugh at me...just laugh and tell me no one would believe me. He said Robert would leave us and my mom and I would be tossed on the street. I believed him for a while, and every night I'd pray he wouldn't come in my room. After a year, things got worse. He started...like I said it was worse. I finally told my mom."

"Did she believe you?" Mickey asked in a whisper.

"Yes, and so did Robert. Pete had been having other issues, but they were horrified when I told them what he'd been doing to me. Robert begged my mom to let him handle it, and she agreed. She thought he could get through to him." Paula's voice shook and she bit into her top lip. "He couldn't."

Jose stood and linked his fingers behind his head as he paced back and forth behind the couch. Mickey's gaze followed him as she asked, "How long did you stay in the house with him?"

"For another year. My mom even slept in my room with me, but he'd always find a way to get me alone. Nothing stopped him. Robert continued to beg my mom not to call the authorities, it would ruin the rest of his life, so we left. We were both crushed to lose Robert, but at that point I think my mom had fallen out of love with him."

Mickey refocused on Paula. "So then it stopped?"

Paula's small mouth curved into a half smile and she shook her head. "Like I said, it's never really stopped. He always found us. No matter how far away we moved or where we went, he'd show up. My mom would report it, but no one ever saw him so nothing could be done. I've spent my entire life looking over my shoulder, holding my breath, waiting for him to show up. To ruin the life I'd built by tormenting me. He's smart, and we both know if he ever touched me again I'd call the police in a heartbeat. But he likes to get inside my head, to remind me any way he can of the past."

She glanced up at Jose and caught his hand as he walked behind her. "And then I met Jose. He's the first person to make me feel safe, protected. We decided to move to Mexico a few years ago and get a fresh start. I'll never forget what Pete did to me, but at least I can sleep at night knowing he'll never find me again."

A weight dropped in Mickey's stomach. A beat of silence passed and she hated herself for what she was about to do, for shattering Paula's illusion of safety. "Um, do you know he's been spending time in Playa Del Carmen?"

Paula's head whipped around to Jose, but his wide eyes searched Mickey's. His brow furrowed and Paula's muffled sobs tore Mickey's heart in two. "How do you know? Where is he? I'll kill him if he comes near her." A flash of hate sparked in his eyes, and Mickey believed him. Hell, she'd help him.

A heaviness fell over Mickey the minute she walked out of Paula's house. She climbed into the waiting cab and sunk into the tough material of the worn seat. She pressed a hand to her stomach to quell the bile from sloshing around. She'd brought Pete into Becca's life, and there was no telling what horrors awaited her if Mickey couldn't find her.

Her mind spun in a million different directions, leaving

her dizzy. She leaned her head against the seat and her gaze focused on the palm trees flitting past her window as the cab sped along toward her hotel. The constant flash of green leaves and brown trunks only made her dizziness worse.

How could she not have seen who Pete really was? How had she let his easy smile and quick wit slip through her defenses? My God, she'd let him in her bed. The bile moved from her stomach and up her throat. She pressed her hand to her mouth to keep it from escaping. The last thing she needed was for her cab driver to toss her out for making a mess.

Pressure built in her chest and tears built in her eyes. She squeezed her eyes shut and tried as hard as she could to block it all out. To block out the pain, and the guilt, and the utter revulsion of what she'd done. Instead, she closed her eyes and she pictured Becca. If they couldn't find her goddaughter, Mickey would never be able to forgive herself.

Chapter Eighteen

Anger simmered through his veins as he sat on the stool at the small hotel bar. His day had gone from bad to worse. First his conversation with Harper, then he'd landed in Cancun to find out Eric still hadn't found anything more about Pete, and then there was the call he'd had twenty minutes ago. That call was the one that had set his blood to boil.

He leaned against the wall at the end of the bar and trained his eyes on the open doorway leading into the lobby. Music and laughter spilled in from the street, only increasing his irritation. The boutique hotel he'd booked boasted a great beachfront location right off the busy pedestrian street in Playa Del Carmen, but offered little else in terms of luxuries. Including a good bartender. The young Mexican was too busy flirting with tipsy tourists to worry about refilling his beer.

Just as well.

He sighed and pushed his empty glass across the slick bar. Crossing his arms, he drummed his fingers against his bicep as he waited. As the time ticked by, frustration mixed with anger and swirled inside him like a hurricane coming to shore until his gaze landed on the one person who was about to walk right into the eye of the storm.

Mickey.

His blood pumped wildly in his veins and pressure built in his chest. He wanted to march up to her, pull her to his room, and yell at her for being such an idiot. But something about the way her shoulders hunched forward and the contorted features of her face stopped him. He sat, frozen to his seat, unsure of how to approach her. How could someone stir up so many emotions in him at one damn time? As if his mind and his heart were in constant battle over the best way to handle her.

With his gaze fixed on Mickey, he sat up on his stool. Even though he wanted to strangle her, the low plunge of her dress drew his eyes to her breasts. He groaned. Maybe this wasn't a good idea. He should talk to her once he calmed down. With his nerves screaming at him and his mind racing, he was bound to do something he'd regret.

Or would he?

He straightened his legs and then stood just as Mickey turned his way. Their eyes met across the room, and her long legs stopped short. He raised his brows in her direction and her mouth twitched at the corners as she pressed her lips into a firm line. She dropped her gaze to the ground and weaved in between the small groups of people loitering in the lobby, through the bar, and stopped in front of him. Without her heels on, the top of her head reached past his nose.

His jaw tightened and he curled his hands into fists at his sides. His thumbnails dug into his palms to keep him from reaching out and pulling her into his arms.

Her eyes were wide as she stared at him with her head cocked to the side. "How did you know I was here?"

"I work for the FBI, Mickey. It wasn't too hard."

Her cheeks sunk in, as if she were biting on the inside of

her mouth. "That's a complete invasion of privacy."

"Is it? Interesting coming from a woman who just showed up at a complete stranger's house and asked her personal questions pertaining to a federal investigation." Graham threw his hands in the air. "Really, Mickey, what the hell were you thinking?"

Color stained her cheeks. "I was getting answers. Answers I need to find Becca. To figure out why Pete used me."

"That's my job. You need to stay away and let me do it."

Fire flashed in her eyes. "How is my asking questions getting in the way of you doing your job?"

Graham sucked in a long breath through his nose. "Did you ever think Paula would be so upset after talking to you she wouldn't want to talk to anyone else? That it would be too painful to go over everything again so quickly after just discussing it?"

"I guess I didn't think of that," Mickey said with a grimace.

"No, you didn't. Because you didn't think at all." His voice rose higher than he intended, and a few heads turned their way. "Dammit, Mickey. Every time I turn around I find you in the middle of this investigation. You aren't helping me. You're only making my job ten times harder than it already is."

God, she's gorgeous when she's pissed.

"I came all the way here to see her, and she refused. Now I have to try again tomorrow, and that's more time wasted." He ran a hand through his hair and then let it drop to his side. "Can you understand how your actions screwed me?"

"I'm sorry, okay," she said and threw her hands in the air. "I can't help it. Knowing Becca's somewhere with that pervert is eating me alive. She's alone and scared as hell and probably wondering why in the hell I would let this guy into our lives. I can't stand around and wait for answers. If I see a way I can do something, I have to do it."

Tears stained her skin and he kicked himself for his temper. She deserved it, but he shouldn't have been so harsh. This case was taking its toll on him, and he didn't have a personal stake in it like she did.

She crossed her arms in front of her, accidentally pulling down the silky fabric of her dress. The creamy flesh of the top of her breasts peeked out from the low neckline and his groin tightened. With her anger splayed brightly on her cheeks and her thick red hair in a riot of loose curls around her shoulders, she was like a sexy temptress daring him to touch her.

He couldn't resist.

Graham reached out and grazed his fingertips over her arm. Her muscles relaxed at his touch and the anger melted from her features. The flames in her golden irises now matched the lust in his gut. He pulled her close and let his hand linger at the small of her back.

"I know this is hard on you, but you have to listen to me. Please, let me handle this investigation. I want to find Becca, and the other girls, as badly as you do. And I will. I'm damn good at my job, but you have to let me do it."

She leaned her head against his shoulder and the moisture on her face seeped into his shirt. "Paula looked so much like Becca. I couldn't believe it when I opened the door."

He rubbed circles around her spine. "What did she say about Pete?"

Mickey's body shuddered against him. "He's obsessed with her. Always has been. She's had to live her whole life watching over her shoulder. And the things he did to her..." Her voice trailed off, but she didn't have to finish the thought for him to understand.

He glanced around at the growing crowd in the hotel bar. Voices rang loud and tourists pressed against the bar for another drink. "Let's go up to my room and talk."

She pulled back and glanced up through dark lashes. "I don't want to talk. Not right now. I just want you to take my mind off everything for a little bit."

Indecision warred within him. Common sense had prevailed last night, but not by much. Getting involved with Mickey right now was wrong. But one look at the pain swimming in her amber eyes and all logic melted into a puddle of goo.

He leaned down and pressed his lips to hers. He pulled back and studied her. "Are you sure?"

She nodded and the need in her eyes had the power to bring him to his knees.

Turning toward the lobby, he kept his hand on her back and led her to the elevators. Desire throbbed through him with every beat of his heart, faster and stronger with every step. Screw taking their time and waiting until they got Pete behind bars. He wanted her now.

Two giggling girls stepped out of the elevator, and he ushered Mickey inside. The silver door slid shut, leaving them alone in isolation, the noise of the hotel and crowded streets long behind them. Her reflection stared back at him everywhere his eyes landed. His hand slid from the small of her back to the side of her waist and tightened on her hip. He gazed down at her, and fire burned like hot coals in her eyes.

"Dammit," he growled. His blood burned hot in his veins and he needed a taste of her. "I can't wait to have you."

He leaned forward and pressed the emergency stop button on the elevator before he grabbed the back of her head and brought his lips to hers. His fingers roamed through the silky tresses until her hair rained like wildfire around her face. Her legs parted as his knee pressed between them and he pushed forward, trapping her against the wall of mirrors behind her. He released her hair and used the tips of his fingers to trace the outline of her face. Her full lips parted, and he swept the pad of his thumb over them.

Mickey arched up on her toes, nipping at his thumb.

He drew back his hand and a husky laugh vibrated from his throat. "I should have known you wouldn't be a submissive wallflower. But I might need to tame that wild streak of yours."

She lifted an eyebrow. "I'd like to see you try."

He was more than up for the challenge. He grabbed her wrists and pinned them high above her head and her breath hitched in her throat. He pressed his mouth to her ear and nibbled the lobe, before pressing hot kisses down the side of her neck. The hem of her dress rose high on her thigh, and he shifted her wrists to one hand, while the other dropped to her side. White flesh peeked out, stark against the floral material. He leaned forward, his body pressed into hers, his lips lingering on the hollow dent between on the base of her neck. His lips traveled down as he leaned forward and cupped her sleek calve in the palm of his hand, and then grazed the subtle curve up to the inside of her knee, over the back of her thigh, and stopped when he reached the soft flesh not covered by her panties.

"Oh, God, Graham. You're killing me." She squirmed against him, and a cold sweat broke out on his brow.

His body hummed with a need to make her his. He dropped her wrists and circled both arms around her waist, pressing her hard against him. Her arms wrapped around his neck and he took her mouth in his. His tongue invaded her mouth and she moaned as she greedily accepted him.

"Excuse me, is everything all right in there?" A deep, booming voice sounded over the intercom.

"Shit." His voice came out in ragged breaths. Mickey's chest expanded beneath him as she panted, her hot breath tickling his skin. He pulled himself away and she sank against the wall. He pressed the red button and spoke into the intercom. "Sorry, we're fine. We must have hit the stop button by accident."

"No, problem, sir. But if you could please pull the button back out, there are people waiting to use the elevator."

Mickey giggled as he released the button and the elevator churned to life. He stood beside her, his arm wrapped possessively around her, and held his breath until the elevator stopped on his floor. "Come on."

"What's your room number?" Her long legs matched his stride for stride as they hurried down the hallway.

He pulled his wallet from his back pocket and grabbed the hotel key inside. "Four twenty one."

They turned the wide corner and raced down the narrow hall until they reached the end of the hallway. His hand trembled as he slid the key in the bronze slot in the door. The green light flickered on, and he pushed down on the handle to open the door. He pulled her inside, slammed the door closed, and turned her to face him.

Damn, she was beautiful, and he'd wanted her for days. To hell with patience. They needed each other to ease the pain of the last few days. Ease it with the pleasure he'd been dying to heap onto her body. He scooped her in his arms and carried her to the king-size bed. He pressed his lips to hers and the mattress dipped low under their weight. Her hands slid under his T-shirt and her touch set his skin on fire. She grabbed the bottom of the shirt and pulled it up and over his head, tossing it to the floor.

Mickey crawled to her knees and sat on her heels. One strap of her dress fell off her shoulder and adrenaline spiked through his body like a stake in the ground.

"Wait." He reached his arm to the light on the nightstand and flicked it on. "I want to see every inch of you."

Focusing his attention back on Mickey, he slid the other strap from her shoulder, and then tugged the zipper that ran down her back. The soft material pooled around her waist, resting on the bed. He sucked in a sharp breath and his heart squeezed against his ribcage as the creamy flesh of her free breasts stole his attention.

"If you'd told me you weren't wearing anything under your dress, I'm afraid I might have embarrassed myself."

A wicked smile curved on her lips and she lifted herself high on her knees, letting the dress drop further down her lean body. Graham grabbed his chest and groaned. "Nothing sexier than lacy, black panties on a beautiful woman."

He tackled her to the bed. Her squeals of delight were music to his ears, and drove him even crazier with desire. He dipped his head low, taking one breast in his mouth. Mickey arched her back as his tongue circled her nipple, and then he lightly bit the tender flesh. His eyes locked on hers. "Payback for biting my thumb."

"Less talk, more action." She fisted his hair in her hands and urged him back to her breast. *My God, she's incredible.*

The phone started ringing.

Sonofabitch.

"Please tell me you're going to ignore that." Mickey's fingers played with the short strands of his hair, her voice husky with need.

"I'd like nothing better, but I can't." Her fingers slipped from his hair as he pulled away and reached into his back pocket. His palm closed around the hard plastic of his case and ripped it out.

"The ringing stopped. Put the phone down and get back here." Her words purred like velvet from her supple lips and every nerve ending in his body screamed at him to take her breast in his mouth again. But the only person he used that ringtone with was Eric. He couldn't ignore his partner.

"I'm sorry, babe, but it's Eric. I've got to call him back."

Mickey pulled back the white down comforter on the bed

and burrowed under it. He sighed as she covered her delicious breasts. He turned away. He couldn't concentrate on what Eric had to tell him if Mickey lay naked in front of him. He swung his feet over the end of the bed and called Eric.

"Hey, man, where are you?" Eric asked after picking up on the first ring.

"At my hotel in Playa Del Carmen. Just got in."

"Did you talk to Paula?"

Shit, he'd gotten so caught up in Mickey he hadn't gotten all of the details about her conversation with Paula. He'd need to find out what Paula had to say when he got off the phone. "I'm going to see her tomorrow."

"Good. Until then, you might want to meet me. I've gotten some leads on Pete, and we might be able to find the bastard tonight. Word is he likes to frequent Fifth Avenue and search for tourists to prey on. We might get lucky."

"Okay. Where should I meet you?" He leaned forward and grabbed his shirt off the floor.

"I'm at my hotel, right down the street from you. I'll meet you in the lobby in five."

Eric disconnected and Graham pulled his shirt over his head. He turned toward Mickey and his heart stopped beating for a split second. Her lips were swollen, her face flushed. He wanted nothing more than to crawl under the covers and finish what they'd started, but he had a job to do. If there was a chance they could find Pete, he had to take it.

"I'm sorry, but I've got to go. That was Eric, and he got some leads on Pete. We might be able to find him tonight."

Mickey sat up straight and clutched the blanket to her breasts. "Don't apologize. Go!"

"Do you want to wait for me? I don't know how long I'll be, but you'd be nice to come back to."

She beamed at him, but shook her head. "I'm having dinner with Vanessa and Allison. I need to go anyway." With one hand holding up the blanket, she leaned forward and picked her dress up off the floor.

He chuckled. "I've seen the goods. No need for modesty."

She laughed, dropped the blanket, and pulled the dress over her head. "Oh, I didn't tell you about Paula."

Graham stood and put his phone back in his pocket. Leaning forward, he pressed a kiss to her forehead. "Later. Right now, I need to focus on catching that bastard. I'll see you later, okay?"

"Okay. And, Graham, if you find Pete tonight, give him hell."

He nodded, gave a small wave, and walked out the door. He'd be giving Pete Bogart hell all right. For kidnapping three innocent girls, for using Mickey as a pawn in his sick game, and for giving him blue balls for the second night in a row.

Chapter Nineteen

"Have I ever told you two how much I love salsa?" Allison asked as she dipped a tortilla chip in the bowl of salsa sitting in the middle of the table.

Uneasiness pitched back and forth in Mickey's stomach like a sailboat in a storm. She glanced around her as her friends enjoyed their dinners. People of every age, color, and gender walked by their table. Mickey searched all of their faces, silently willing Pete to walk by. She hadn't heard anything from Graham since he'd left the hotel. She assumed Pete hadn't been found.

"Are you going to eat?" Vanessa asked. Her gentle tone matched a mother speaking to a child.

Mickey forced a smile and shrugged. "I'm not hungry."

"You've had a hell of a week, but you really should eat," Allison said.

Mickey picked up a taco, took one bite, and set it back down.

Allison chuckled and poured herself another margarita from the pitcher that sat on their table. She took a sip and set her glass down, her features turning serious. "Have you talked to Suzi?"

Mickey shook her head. She'd been too nervous to reach back out to her, fearing the rejection. Maybe she could have Graham call and tell Suzi he believed she wasn't involved. But would it even matter? She was still the one who had brought Pete into their lives. Tears sprang to her eyes and she dabbed them away with her cheap cloth napkin.

Vanessa reached out and grabbed her hand. "Are you okay?"

She drew in a shuddering breath and sniffed back a sob. Falling apart in the middle of Fifth Avenue wasn't an option. "I'm fine, just tired. I'm going to head back to the hotel."

Allison and Vanessa wore matching expressions of concern. Mouths drawn down at the corners, eyebrows dipped together in the center. "We'll go with you. Let me get the check," Allison said.

"No, don't do that. You two stay out and have fun. We're only here for two nights." Pushing her chair back from the table, she stood and put some money down. "I'll get a good night's sleep and be well rested in the morning."

"Are you sure? Do you want us to at least walk you back to the hotel?" Vanessa asked.

"I can see the top of our hotel from here. I think I'll be fine." Leaning down, she pressed a quick kiss to Allison's and then Vanessa's cheeks. "I'll see you both poolside in the morning."

Neither Allison nor Vanessa looked convinced, but she pushed their worried expressions from her mind as she walked toward the hotel. She hated to admit it, but she needed to get away from them. She hadn't told them the full story about Pete, or Suzi's reaction to her when she'd tried to explain. Hell, she hadn't even told them about Graham. Everything had happened so fast, and retelling the whole story to more people made her feel worse, not better.

But Lydia knew. She'd head back to the hotel, put on her pajamas, and call Lydia. She needed to fill her in on what had happened with Graham the last couple of nights anyway. At least she had one bright spot in her life right now.

Trumpets and guitars mixed together, blasting mariachi music from restaurants and bars as she walked past. Streams of people passed by, and Mickey caught herself staring into face after face, searching for the hazel eyes and light brown hair that had become so familiar to her over the past few months.

A flash of blue streaked by her peripheral vision at the same moment the scent of a familiar cologne and sweat seeped into her senses. She spun to the side, her eyes searching the blue hat that had caught her attention. Standing on her tiptoes, she craned her neck and peered over the crowd. A man with a Chicago Cubs baseball hat lurked down the alley veering away from the main street.

Pete!

Every instinct in her body screamed at her to run. To go back to the hotel, call Graham, and stay far away from whatever trouble Pete was looking for. But what if he'd lead her to Becca? She couldn't risk waiting for Graham and then losing him.

Turning in the direction Pete had gone, she grabbed her phone out of her purse and dialed Graham. She picked up her pace, struggling to weave through the throng of people.

"Hey, Mickey. What's up?" Graham asked when he answered the phone.

"I think I see Pete. I was heading back to the hotel when I noticed a man with his build wearing a Cubs hat. He's heading down a side street, traveling away from the ocean." Her breathing picked up the faster she moved and her heart pounded in her chest.

"Where are you?" Graham's voice was gruff, his words coming out fast.

She glanced around. The music and laughter of Fifth Avenue faded behind her, replaced by rapidly spoken Spanish inside tiny houses and crickets singing into the warm night air. "I don't know. I turned down some street a block or two away from my hotel. East of my hotel."

"Turn back around and get the hell out of there." His words were tight, as if he spoke with his teeth clenched.

"I can't. I already lost him. He'll get away if leave now. He can't be far." She spun in a small circle, cringing at the ramshackle houses and run-down businesses located so close to the glitz and excitement of the busy tourist attractions.

Moist, hot breath hit the back of her neck and a shiver ran down her spine. "Put the phone away, Mickey."

She lowered her phone to her side and slowly turned around. She swallowed hard and concentrated on keeping her breath even. Every muscle in her body tightened and she came face to face with Pete. She couldn't show fear. She glanced around and her stomach dropped. Not a single person loitered on the sidewalk around them.

Her gaze landed back on Pete. His hat was pulled low over his face, but even in the shadow his eyes were hard, his cheeks hollow. "Where is she? Where's Becca?" Her voice shook and she tightened her jaw to keep her chin from quivering.

A brittle laugh came out of his mouth and rage built inside of her. "Do you think I'd bring her here? No way. Becca's special."

Disgust turned to bile in her gut. Her fingers itched to smack his smug face, but she needed to keep him talking. Graham was still on the other line and she needed him to get to her fast. "If you don't have her with you, then why are you here? I know you're moving a human trafficking ring to Chicago. Why come back to Mexico if you already have things set up?"

His eyes widened for a brief second. No doubt he didn't expect her to know so much about his operation, but all traces of surprise left his face, and his features contorted into a nasty sneer. "I have some unfinished business to take care of before I leave Mexico for good. No reason to expose Becca to this world. She's safer in Chicago."

Alarm bells rang in her head. "Are you here for Paula?"

Pete took a step toward her. "What do you know about Paula?"

"I know she looks like Becca, and you've made her life a living hell since she was nine years old. Is that what you want to do to Becca, too? Take away everything she loves and ruin her life? She'll hate you. Just like Paula does."

Pete's hand drew back and slashed across her cheek so fast she didn't have time to react. Her head snapped back and pain sliced across her face. "You don't know a damn thing. Paula loves me. She always has, but everyone tried to keep us apart. But not anymore. We can be together, and we can keep Becca with us. It will be so much better than it ever was before."

Mickey rubbed the soreness from her face. The metallic taste of blood filled her mouth and she spit it at his feet. "You're a monster. I'll find Becca, and warn Paula, too. I've already talked to her. She wants nothing to do with you. She hates you just as much as I do."

Pete grabbed her phone from her hand and threw it on the ground.

Shit. She needed to have a way to reach Graham. Lurching forward, she reached for the phone, but Pete's foot swung forward and connected with the soft flesh of her stomach. Pain shot through her. She fell to the ground and curled onto her side. Pete grabbed a fistful of hair and pulled her to her feet. She yelped as her scalp screamed in agony. He pushed her backward and forced her into a deserted alley. Her legs backpedaled as quickly as they could, but her ankle twisted in her damn heels and she fell to the ground. Pete pulled her upright and then slammed her into the side of the building. The force of it stole her breath from her lungs. Her mind raced and her heart hammered so hard against her chest she was convinced it would break through the skin.

Keep him talking.

"You'll never get away with this. The FBI is searching for you right now. They'll be here any minute. You're wasting time on me, time where you could be getting away."

He pressed his face into her personal space. His sweat mixed with the stale smell of beer and she fought hard not to gag. "I've been getting away with it for years. No one's ever been able to stop me."

A slow smile curved on his lips. "I have missed you, Mickey. I didn't think I'd get anything out of the time we spent together, but you were so eager to please in the sack. Maybe one little taste of you before I kill you can hold me over before I get back to Becca."

His beady eyes traveled up and down her body like a dying man eyeing his last meal. Panic rang in her head and she fought to stay calm. His free hand grabbed her chin and lifted her face to the tiny sliver of light that poured out from an upstairs window. She wouldn't let this piece of shit touch her. She had to wait until the time was right to make her move.

He pressed his body against her and her back pressed against the hard brick of the building behind her. His mouth came down on hers and his tongue pierced through her closed lips. She bit down as hard as she could and her teeth sunk into his tongue. He pulled away, but she refused to let up. His closed fist came up and connected to her temple. Stars burst in her vision and she staggered to the side, releasing his tongue.

"What the fuck?" he screamed. Spit and blood flew from his mouth and splattered on her face. "I should kill you now."

Pressure built in her chest, making it hard to breathe. Fear heightened her senses and adrenaline coursed through her veins. Darkness misted her vision and she forced herself to focus on the fury etched on the planes of his face. Acting on instinct, her knee shot up and connected to his groin.

"Bitch!" he yelled and stumbled backward.

She swung her leg forward and connected the pointy toe of her shoe to his balls. His shrill scream bounced around the alley and he fell to the ground. His hands covered his injured area and he rolled to his side in front of her. Now was her chance, she had to get out of here. She jumped over him and ran toward the opening of the alley. Her lungs burned as she struggled to take in air, but she was almost there.

A tight grip circled around her ankle and she crashed to the ground. Her head smacked off the concrete and pain seared through every inch of her body. Her fingertips dug into stone and broken glass and she tried to crawl toward the light at the end of the alley. "Help me!" Her voice shook and her eyes searched the mouth of the alley for someone to help her, but no one passed by.

Strong hands pulled her backward, and concrete and God knew whatever else scraped against her body. Once he pulled her away from the opening, from freedom, he flipped her over on her back. He stood over her, one leg on either side of her stomach, and hurled a wad of spit on the side of her head. "You're going to pay for that."

He lowered himself to the ground, trapping her hands with his own. She thrashed around, kicking her legs and bucking her hips, but he only tightened his hold. "Get off me. Stop. Help! Somebody help me!"

"Nobody's coming, sweetheart. No one can save you now." He lowered his mouth so it was an inch above hers. "I want one little taste before I teach you not to fuck with me again."

Mickey lifted her mouth and bared her teeth. She bit into his bottom lip as hard as she could. He pulled away and grabbed his lip. "Sonofabitch." Blood coated his hand. He reared back and slapped her across the face. The sharp sting bit into her cheek and she clenched her jaw to keep from screaming. "Big mistake, bitch."

His hand dropped to his side and he pulled a small knife from his pocket. Her eyes widened in fear. He traced the side of the blade along her jawline and down her neck. "Keep your mouth shut and stay still and I might not use this. At least not yet."

Her body went lax. She wasn't strong enough to fight him, but she was smart enough. There had to be a way to get out of this. She laid her head back and stared numbly toward the opening of the alley as her mind raced.

A shadow appeared at the front of the alley. She blinked and focused on the upside-down outline of a man as it moved toward them. Her body went numb and her brain shut down. Now there were two of them. Luck obviously wasn't on her side. She closed her eyes and accepted her fate as the blade sliced through her tank top and the cold kiss of metal pressed against her skin.

Chapter Twenty

A dark figure huddled in the back of the alley. Graham peered into the darkness, but couldn't make out what the hell it was. Fear churned in his gut. He and Eric had split up, checking the streets on the north side of Fifth Avenue, away from the ocean. He'd heard part of Mickey and Pete's conversation, and panic had paralyzed him when the line had gone dead.

But something had caught his eye in the deserted alley. Drawing his gun, he inched farther into the alley. A soft whimper reached his ears and every muscle in his body tightened.

Mickey.

He inhaled a deep breath through his nose, and then blew it out slowly. He couldn't charge in and put her in danger, but he needed to move quickly. He walked on his tiptoes to minimize the sound of stones crunching under his feet. A large dumpster sat against the wall of the alley behind the kneeling figure. He crouched alongside it as he slithered behind Pete, who held Mickey to the ground. A flash of red hair sprawled against the brown dirt. The jagged edges of a knife pressed against her shoulder.

The metallic taste of fear filled his mouth and red invaded his vision. His hand trembled as he lifted his gun and stepped up behind the sonofabitch. He pressed the barrel of the gun to the back of his head. "FBI. Get the fuck off her."

Mickey's eyes flew open and his heart lurched. Tears streamed from the corners of her eyes. Blood trickled down her shoulder and dripped to the ground. Every fiber in his being yelled at him to scoop her into his arms and get her the hell out of here. But the asshole held the knife to her throat. If he shot him, he'd have no choice but to kill him and he needed Pete alive to find out where the missing girls were.

Pete stiffened, but didn't turn around. "I don't think you want me to hurt this lovely lady. Back up, put down the gun, and I'll let her up. Try anything stupid, and I'll jam this knife into her jugular."

He kept his eyes trained on Mickey, trying to convey a sense of calm for her. She lay as still as a statue on the filthy ground. Her cotton skirt hitched high on her thigh, revealing inches of pale, creamy skin. The tiny stream of light from an overhead window highlighted brown fingerprints that marred her thigh. Bile burned his stomach lining.

"There's no way out of this for you," he said. "Stand up slowly, and put your hands in the air."

"I have a better idea. I'll stand up with her, and we'll walk to the front of the alley. I'll give you Mickey, and you let me run. Or I cut her."

"You know that's not going to work, Pete. We've been looking for you for a while. I can't just let you go." Pete's shoulder blades bunched together and his body tensed as he said his name. "Where are the girls?"

Pete had to be weighing his options, which weren't good. He needed to get Mickey away from him. Mickey dipped her chin a fraction of an inch and stared into his eyes. His lip hitched up in amazement. She wasn't going down without a fight. He nodded, acknowledging her, before glancing around for something to use as a distraction. The alley was bare except for rocks and scattered trash. He bent down and picked up a large rock, making sure to keep the gun steady on the back of Pete's head. He jiggled it around in his hand as he stared up at the exterior walls enclosing him in.

A second-story window loomed on the wall opposite him. He tossed the rock up and down in his hand to test its weight. He glanced back down at Mickey and gave her one more nod. His pulse beat against his ears like a hammer. He had one shot; he couldn't miss. Keeping his gun trained on the back of the bastard's head, he cocked his other arm back and soundlessly hurled the rock toward the window. He held his breath.

Crash!

Pete lifted his head toward the window and Mickey brought her knee up hard. Graham lurched forward, grabbed Pete's skinny neck, and yanked him off Mickey. The knife slashed back, nearly nicking him in the side. He twisted away, spinning his captive to face him. He grabbed him by the neck of his shirt and trained his gun to his face. "I'll shoot you if you don't stop, you dumb fuck."

"I'm not going to jail." He waved the knife around and laughed like a lunatic.

A white spark of light flashed behind him and Pete's smile disappeared. Convulsions shook his body until he fell like a rock to the ground. Mickey stood behind the crumbled body, her eyes fixed on the motionless form. Her foot reared back and she kicked him in the stomach before looking up at Graham. "I had my taser in my purse, but I couldn't get to it before." Her voice shook as she locked eyes with him.

"Good job. Stand there for a second while I cuff him. We don't know how long he'll be out." He pulled out a pair of cuffs he had tucked in the back of his jeans. Once he slapped them on, he pulled Mickey into his arms and ran his hand over the back of her head.

Tremors shook her body and her tears gathered on his neck. "He said the girls were still in Chicago. He came here to get Paula."

"I heard your conversation with him. I about lost my mind when the call disconnected." He pulled away and grabbed his phone from his pocket. "Call one of your friends. I need to get Eric here and take this guy in. Do you need to be looked at? Did he hurt you?" His hands gently roamed over her, checking for hidden injuries. He ran the pad of his thumb over her split lip and she winced.

"I'm fine." Mickey smoothed down her skirt and lifted the torn strap of her tank top. Bloodstains marred the white material. "Just the cut by my shoulder. It's not deep."

"Take my shirt. Yours isn't going to stay up." He handed her his phone and then lifted the hem of his shirt over his head. The night air hit his bare skin and cooled the fire that had raged inside him.

"Thanks." She took the shirt, pulled it over her head, and winced.

"What is it? Are you okay?" Alarm sent his nerves on edge.

"I'm fine. The shirt hurt my shoulder a little is all."

A groan sounded at their feet. He glanced down and Pete's shut eyelids fluttered. He placed the heel of his shoe on his chest to keep him down. "Once I get Eric here and go over everything, I'll take you to get checked out."

"I don't want to go to a hospital. It just needs to be cleaned and covered." Even with clumps of dirt tangled in her hair and mascara streaking down her cheeks, she oozed a fiery confidence he didn't want to mess with right now.

"Fine. I'll look at it later. Call your friend."

Mickey lifted her finger to unlock his phone, and a glimmer of light from the screen shone down on her hand. She turned her hands toward her face and furrowed her brow.

"What is it?" He grabbed her wrist and lifted her palm to his line of vision. "Holy shit, what happened to your hands?"

She glanced down at her palms. "I got away and ran down the alley, but he tripped me. I fell and tried to crawl away. He dragged me to the back of the alley."

The heel of his shoe ground harder into Pete's chest. He coughed and squirmed under the pressure, but his eyes stayed closed. Graham took the phone back and wrapped an arm around her shoulders. He leaned in and kissed her temple, lingering a little to soak her in. His blood pumped furiously, and he calmed his quivering heart by breathing her scent. She was okay, but he needed to make sure she was taken care of. "I'm taking you in. You need those wounds cleaned."

He dialed Eric's number and pressed the phone to his ear.

"Did you find her?" Eric's words came out in a rush after the first ring.

"I did. And I have Pete. I need you to meet me and take this asshole down for questioning. We're down an alley just a block north of my hotel. Call it in on your way here."

He hoped like hell Pete would be extradited quickly. They might have caught the ringleader, but the girls were still missing and they wouldn't be safe until they were home. He needed Pete sweating in a cell in Chicago where he had all the time he needed to get the information of their whereabouts out of him.

Screw the cell. Let me put him in the back of a truck and I'll beat the information out of him.

"I'll be there in ten."

He ended the call and glanced at Mickey. "What's your friend's number?"

"I don't want to burden them with this. I can wait for you to finish."

"Okay. Let's walk to the front of the alley to wait for Eric and the police."

Mickey nodded and walked beside him. He needed both of his hands to maneuver Pete. He could place a little weight on his legs, but his feet dragged along the debris on the ground and his head rolled around his neck like a spinning top.

Light from the streetlamps poured down around them. He dropped Pete to the ground and used his toe to push him back against the wall of a building. Pete lifted his face and Graham grimaced. Dried blood coated his chin and swollen lips. His skin was ashen and his limbs twitched.

"What happened to his mouth?"

Mickey curled her lips and shuddered. "I bit him."

He chuckled and pulled her in close. "My little spitfire."

She placed her head on his shoulder as an ambulance pulled up beside them. Mickey pulled away and glanced up at him through narrowed eyes. "I told you no hospital."

"Eric must have called them. Speaking of which..." Graham nodded toward the end of the street. "There's Eric. Why don't you sit down and let them look at you while I talk to him? If they clear you to leave, I'll take you back to the hotel while Eric deals with this mess."

"What about Pete? Don't you need to question him?"

"He's not going to say much tonight. I'll get more out of him tomorrow after he spends a night in jail. Besides, Eric has more experience dealing with the Mexican authorities. It's better to let him handle it."

Mickey covered a yawn and eyed the paramedic who had stepped around to the back of the ambulance and opened the back door. "Fine. But I'm not going to the hospital. I'll sit here and wait for you."

He kissed her forehead and she scowled at him before

walking toward the ambulance.

Eric met him in the middle of the sidewalk, his eyes flicking toward Pete huddled on the ground. "What happened to him?" He kicked Pete in the foot and got a small grunt in response.

"Mickey tazed him."

"No shit." Eric smiled and shook his head before his features turned serious. He glanced over his shoulder, but Mickey's back was to them. "Is she okay?"

He blew out a shaky breath. The adrenaline from earlier trickled out, leaving him drained. Images of what could have happened ran through his mind. "She'll be fine, but thanks for getting the paramedics here. Did you call the local authorities?"

"Yeah. I'm surprised they're not here already." He tilted his head toward the ground. "If you want to look after Mickey, I can deal with him."

"Are you sure?" As much as he wanted to be with Mickey, leaving his partner to wade through the shit of an international arrest didn't sit right with him. Even if the last thing he wanted to do was shift through the bureaucratic bullshit.

Eric slapped a hand on his shoulder and squeezed. "Go. I'll send an officer to the hotel to talk to you and Mickey. She'll be more comfortable talking away from the scene. You can come in tomorrow to talk to this piece of garbage. From the looks of it, he won't be much use tonight anyway."

He hesitated, torn between taking care of Mickey and doing his job. He glanced down at Pete. Eric was right. This guy wasn't going to talk much tonight. "Thanks, man. I'll call Harper and fill him in."

He grabbed the keys to the handcuffs out of his front pocket and tossed them to Eric. He walked toward Mickey, stopping behind her and placing his hand on the small of her back. "How's she looking?" he asked the middle-aged woman who was checking Mickey's heart rate.

"I don't need to get checked out. I'm a little scraped up, that's it." She looked at him, her eyes rounded and lips pressed in a pout.

"*Si*, she just needs to be cleaned up. I can take care of it here if you'd like."

Mickey shook her head. "No thanks. I can do it at the hotel just as easily."

He glanced down at her and pushed a strand of hair off her face. "Are you sure?"

"I'm sure."

"Okay, let's head back. I need to make a quick call while we walk."

Mickey nodded and walked quietly beside him while he pulled up Harper's number and placed the phone to his ear. The shrill rings sounded in his ear, but no one answered. He didn't want to leave a voicemail, so he hung up and called the office instead. Two rings, followed by a sudden click vibrated through the phone.

"Hello, you've reached Lieutenant Harper's office."

"Mary?" Graham pulled his phone away from his ear and glanced at the screen to make sure he called the right number. Sure enough, Harper's office number, not his receptionist, was on the screen.

"Yes, this is Mary. Graham?"

"Yes. I'm looking for Harper. I have an update for him on the Bogart case."

"He's had all of his calls transferred to me for the next couple of days. He's asked all agents to write up any reports they have and send them to his email. He'll look at them when he gets a chance."

Graham's head spun. Harper never took time off. Hell, even if the guy was out of the office for the day he made sure all agents knew how to contact him. It didn't make sense Harper would just up and leave without letting everyone in on the details.

"Where is he?"

"I have no further information to pass along. Just send the lieutenant your report and I'm sure he'll be back in the office soon."

Graham hung up and put his phone in his pocket. His mind spun in so many different directions, he wasn't sure which way was up. In all of his years with the FBI, he'd never had his superior just disappear in the middle of a big case. Where the hell could he have gone?

They walked in silence toward the busy street full of life and laughter. Blue and red lights flashed by them on top of a squad car and a siren screamed into the night. The cops had finally showed up. He pushed Harper out of his mind. He needed to focus on Mickey right now, and making sure she was all right.

The sun had disappeared and the glow of the moon shone bright overhead. Music filled the air and people packed along the sidewalks to take in the sights. Funny how busy the street was mere blocks away from where Mickey had been attacked.

Graham swallowed past a lump in his throat. He could have lost Mickey tonight. Never in a million years would he have imagined she'd come to mean so much to him. He glanced over at her, and she looked up and her wide mouth curved into a smile. Even with her hair a mess and dried blood along the subtle bruises on her face, she was the most beautiful woman he'd ever seen.

She was a fighter, and now that'd he'd finally gotten Pete in cuffs, he'd do whatever it took to make her his.

Chapter Twenty-One

Searing pain scolded her shoulder.

Mickey pressed her teeth together, not wanting Graham to see how much she hurt as he inspected her. He gently pressed the peroxide-soaked cloth to the wound. Her toes curled into the plush carpet and tears burned her eyes. Rivulets of peroxide ran down her arm and dripped down on the wing-back chair, turning the cream color dark.

"I know it hurts," he said in a hushed tone. "We've got to make sure it's clean."

She nodded, looking away and squeezing her eyes shut. Her knees bounced up and down and she counted in her mind to focus on something besides the pain. The cloth lifted from her arm and a cold, wet one replaced it.

The coolness seeped through her skin and chased away the burning sensation from moments before. She turned to face him. "That feels good."

"Focus on that while I look at your hands and arms." He lifted her arms and placed them on his lap.

She leaned back against the chair and sucked in a sharp

breath when he picked up a pair of tweezers from the side table beside the bed. "What's that for?"

"You have some stones and debris in your cuts. I need to get it out." Her muscles stiffened and she tried to pull away, but he tightened his grip. "Trust me, okay?"

"Wait, do you have a mini bar in here?" She glanced around the room and searched for the tiny fridge that usually came in every hotel room. She needed a little liquid courage.

The lopsided grin that always made her weak in the knees hitched up on his face. "What's your poison?"

"I'd kill for another margarita, but I'll settle for tequila."

He stood from the bed and walked across the room to the fridge. She kept her eyes glued to him and focused on his high and tight ass as he leaned forward instead of the ominous tweezers lying beside her. Glass clattered together until he pulled out two small bottles and turned to her with a triumphant smile. "Tequila for both of us."

"I'm not sure I want you drunk while holding a deadly weapon to my damaged skin."

"If one shot of tequila gets me drunk, we've got bigger problems to deal with." He winked and she shook her head with a laugh. "Do you want a glass? Or are you going to take this like a champ?"

She lifted her hand in the air and grinned. "Like a champ."

He tossed the miniature bottle toward her and she snatched it out of the air. "That's my girl."

Warmth spread down to her toes, edging out the pain in her hand from catching the bottle. His girl? She'd only known him a short time, but the idea of being his made her stomach do cartwheels. Heat invaded her cheeks and she dropped her gaze to the floor.

Graham's feet padded toward her until they came into her line of vision. His fingers lifted her chin until her eyes locked on his. Concern etched fine lines in the corners of his eyes. "What's wrong?"

A small smile lifted her lips. "Nothing. Let's get this over with." She unscrewed the cap of her bottle and hoisted it in the air. "Cheers."

Clinking his bottle to hers, he smiled and then lifted the small bottle to his lips.

The tequila burned her esophagus as it trickled down her throat. The warm liquid pooled in the pit of her stomach and she took a deep breath. "I'm ready."

Graham nodded and sat down opposite her on the bed. He placed her arms on his lap and her muscles tightened. "I'll be as gentle as possible."

The cool metal pressed against her tender flesh and she jerked away. A strong hand clamped down on the crook of her elbow, pressing her arm back down. Tears filled her eyes and she bit into her bottom lip and looked away.

"What's your favorite song?" Graham asked.

Her head whipped around and she faced him again. "Excuse me?"

"What's your favorite song?"

"Why?"

A husky laugh rumbled from him and skimmed over her. "It's not like I asked about your stance on gun control. I want to know your favorite song."

A million songs popped into her head. Not one stood out as her absolute favorite. "I don't know. Anything by Journey I guess."

Graham focused on her arm, the tweezers poised above her skin, and hummed a few bars of a song. The metal pressed against her skin and she sucked in a sharp breath. His grip tightened and he croaked out the first verse of one of her favorite songs.

She smiled through her tears as his voice cracked to the

words of "Don't Stop Believing." "You're a terrible singer."

"Lucky for you I make a better medic."

She concentrated on the words and the horrible tone of the melody as he sang. Every time he pressed the tweezers to her palms and her muscles tightened, his voice cracked even more, making her laugh. By the time he'd finished butchering the song, all the dirt had been cleaned from her cuts.

"Thank God that's over." She slunk low in the chair while Graham wrapped her arm with a beige bandage.

"I hope I didn't hurt you too badly."

"The pain in my arms was nothing compared to my poor ears. If I hadn't known better, I'd have thought a cat was being murdered in here." Graham chuckled and released his grip. She studied his handiwork, turning her wrists to test her flexibility. "Not too shabby. I think I'll keep you around."

He cleared his throat, and she lifted her gaze to meet his. "I like the sound of that." Tears hovered above the rim of his lower lashes, and she reached out and cupped his cheek. His breath shook as he drew it in and out. "I was scared as hell when I saw you lying on the ground with that sonofabitch on top of you. I thought I'd messed things up again. That I'd lost you."

Moisture ran along the lines of her fingers, and she used the pad of her thumb to wipe his face clean. "Hey. I'm all right. And it was my own fault. I shouldn't have gone after Pete alone. You didn't do anything wrong. You saved me."

He squeezed his eyes shut and the lines of his face contorted. "I wouldn't have been able to live with myself if something happened to you. I couldn't carry any more guilt like that."

Pushing up from the chair, she shifted her weight and sat close to him on the bed. The mattress dipped low beneath their weight and his jean-clad thigh scraped against her smooth skin. "What do you mean by more guilt?" She kept her voice soft, urging him to confide in her.

"Something backfired on my last case." He shook his head back and forth. "I don't want to talk about it."

"Please open your eyes and look at me." He did as she asked, and the pain in his gray eyes deepened them to slate and split her heart in two. She linked her hand with his and squeezed, her gaze never wavering from his. "You can tell me. I'm here for you."

His gaze dropped to their joined hands and his shoulders slumped forward. "I've been with the FBI for the last eight years. I came in wanting to make a difference, and the human trafficking division seemed like an ideal fit. I've worked through the ranks and clawed my way to where I am today. Being a special agent, looking for the bad guys day after day, is exactly where I want to be. But it's not always easy."

Her heart hammered against her chest and anxiety zipped through her veins. She couldn't begin to imagine the things he'd seen. Hell, the nightmares hadn't left her since the night they'd found that damn house. "I'm sure it's never easy, but you're able to help so many innocent women and children. That has to feel good."

A half smile lifted his mouth. "It does. I've learned to cope with most of the bad I come across, but what happened in Austin has never left my mind. It was a couple of months ago, and my stupidity got an innocent man killed." His voice fell to a whisper and his hand hung limply in hers.

"I'm sure that's not true. You'd never be careless." She'd only known him a short time, but she was as sure of that as she was her own name. He was damn good at his job, and he would never compromise anyone's safety. He was too smart.

He pulled away and stood in front of her, tunneling his hands through his hair. "How would you know? You don't even know what happened."

"Then tell me." Her breath caught in her throat as she waited for him to say something. He stood, frozen in time, his gaze fixed to some unseen place.

"The case was similar to this one. Eric and I got a tip about a small but lucrative sex ring that planned on traveling to Chicago. We'd dealt with this type of thing before. A lot of traffickers bring girls up from Mexico. Eric and I started digging around, and I was convinced I'd found the right thread to pull to break open the case."

His voice broke off and she reached for him. He shook her off and paced back and forth, creating a well-worn path in front of the bed. Seconds ticked by before she asked, "What happened?"

"My sight was locked in so tight on one specific person that I missed the bigger picture. Eric had to practically do the job alone because I wouldn't listen to anyone or anything. By the time Eric opened my eyes to what was happening, we were forced to act quickly...too quickly." He stopped moving and the tips of his fingers dug into his eye sockets. "We pulled in the local police and raided the house. A good cop died, and I killed the only person who could have given us the answers we needed."

Her heart sank. "Was it the person you'd been investigating?"

"What does that matter? A good man is dead because I didn't open my damn eyes to what was going on."

She tucked her bottom lip into her teeth and weighed her words. What had happened was terrible, but he didn't need to put all the blame on his shoulders. She wanted to comfort him, not piss him off. "It sounds like your gut was spot on. The man you knew was responsible for being an ass hat was killed because you didn't take the time you needed to create a better plan of attack. That's not all on you."

"Eric found the house, he coordinated the raid, and he stopped them from moving those girls to Chicago."

"And you'd already found the ringleader and were forced to

abandon your plan to follow someone else's." Doubt darkened his irises, and she pushed on. "What happened was tragic and I'm sorry it happened, but you aren't wholly responsible. And it's not the same thing that's happening now."

"It feels the same. Even though we have Pete, we still don't know where the girls are. And you could have…" His voice trailed off and moisture filled his eyes.

Pushing herself up from her chair, she stood in front of him and framed his face with her hands. "Hey, look at me. I'm okay. Nothing's going to happen to me." She leaned forward and pressed her lips to his. His hand pressed against her neck, keeping her close. Her hand came down on his hard chest and she deepened the kiss. His tongue parted her mouth and she let him invade her warmth. A moan tore through her throat and a strong arm wrapped around her back.

They broke apart and he looked down at her with smiling eyes. Her heart leaped to her throat. She loved those eyes.

"Are you okay? Did I hurt you?"

Not yet, but he could. But did it matter? She was already a goner. "No, the tequila's wearing off and my shoulder's throbbing."

Leaning her backward, he laid her on the bed. The corners of his mouth tipped up in a delicious grin. "Maybe I can help take your mind away from the pain."

She swallowed hard. The pain he could inflict on her tender heart was much worse than the cuts and scrapes on her flesh. But as she stared deep into his kind eyes, the last strings of resistance fell away. Graham wanted to protect her, not hurt her. Raising her arms, she wrapped them around his neck. "Come on, tough guy, show me what you've got."

A low growl rumbled from his chest as he lowered on top of her. Her heart picked up its pace as he lifted himself up on his elbows and stared down at her. His T-shirt hung away from his stomach, and she let her hands roam over his hard muscles before peeling his shirt over his head. Shifting to her side, he grabbed her hand and laced their fingers together. He placed their joined hands on her breast and her skin tightened. The pad of his thumb brushed over her hard nipple and she sucked in her breath. Even over her shirt, she was sensitive to his touch.

He twisted their hands so his was no longer pressed against her nipple. Instead, her breast rested in her own palm. "We need to get rid of this." Releasing her hand, he tugged at the hem of the shirt and pulled it over her head.

His bare skin scorched her and he pulled her back down to him, resting her on her side. He tucked one arm under her while the other glided over the curve of her side. His hand slid over her knuckles, gently guiding it back to her breasts. "Do you like to be touched here?"

Her mouth became dry and she licked her cracked lips. His fingers manipulated hers as she rubbed and pinched the hard nub of her nipple. A moan hummed in her throat and she squirmed against the long length of his chiseled body. The hardness hidden beneath his rough jeans moved against her side and her mind raced with all the things she wanted to do to him.

Shifting her free hand behind her, she reached for him. A hiss sounded in her ear, and he grabbed her hand and brought it high above her head. "Not so fast. This is about distracting you. But if you're ready to speed things up a little…"

He lifted her fingers and moved them to her breastbone and then led her hand down her stomach. The center of her stomach dipped in as her fingers moved lower, leaving a trail of heat in their wake. Graham's hot breath caressed her neck, but not even his lips touched her body. "You might need to speed things up more than just a little."

Husky laughter tickled her ear and her breath came out in short gasps. He dipped her fingertips past her skirt and into the soft material of her panties, pressing lower until her fingers invaded her own warmth. All thoughts fled her mind and nature took over, pushing her to take what was hers.

His hand released hers and he stroked her skin. Up her back, down her arms, over her breasts...as if he couldn't figure out where he wanted to touch her. It only heightened the sensation building insider her. The arch of her back bowed and a firm reminder of Graham's increasing desire snuck into her empty mind. She turned toward him and took his mouth in hers. He met her hungry kisses head on, and his tongue pushed deep into her mouth.

She pulled the hand above her head free, wiggled out of her skirt and panties, and wasted no time in yanking his clothes off, springing him loose. She wrapped her hand around the base of his shaft, and his muscles tightened against her. He reached out and stopped her, gazing deep into her eyes.

Doubt nagged at her. "What's wrong?"

The light from above shone down, illuminating his face. Creases at the corner of his eyes showed his concern, and he reached out and cupped her chin, lifting it toward him. "I don't want to take this too far if you're not ready. I wanted to distract you, not trick you into sleeping with me."

Her heart swelled to the point of bursting as she stared back at him. He was a good man, a man who cared about her. A man she wanted more than anything right now, and dammit she would have him. She shifted onto all fours, her legs straddling him, her hands brushing against his elbows. Her eyes never wavered from his when she said, "Trust me, I'm more than ready for this. Now tell me where you keep your condoms."

Lust sparked in his eyes, darkening them to slate. He nodded toward his pants on the floor. "In my wallet in the back pocket of my jeans."

She stretched to the side and grabbed a condom. Sitting

back on her heels, she unwrapped the package and delicately slid it on. Graham groaned and his head dropped back on the bed. Mickey crawled back on all fours, leaned forward, and sucked his bottom lip. His mouth lurched up and he bit down with his top teeth.

Giggling, she pulled back. She traced her fingertips along his chest before she positioned herself above him, just to lower herself onto him. He filled her, stretching her until she'd taken in every inch. She rolled her hips and his fingers dug into the side of her thighs.

"My God, Mickey."

He closed his eyes as she rocked back and forth, up and down, riding the waves of pleasure whichever way they took her. Pressure built at her core and heat consumed her. She flipped back her head, letting her hair fall down her back. Graham's fingers dug deeper into her hips as she pushed him further and further until the heat caught on fire and she yelled his name during her release.

A primitive grunt roared from Graham and he pulled her mouth to his. Her hips rocked forward and his hands moved around to her ass. He ground her into him again and again until his body went lax from his own climax and he fought to catch his breath. She fell onto him, her chest raising and falling with each desperate attempt to take in air.

Graham's fingers snaked into her tangled tresses. She rolled to his side and propped her head on her fist. Her lips curved into a small smile. "Well, that was a hell of a distraction."

He kissed the top of her head. "Good. Did I hurt you?"

"Trust me, you did everything exactly right." Snuggling in closer, she closed her eyes. No nightmares invaded her thoughts as she drifted off to sleep. Instead, images of Graham and his smiling eyes stayed in her mind and in her heart.

Chapter Twenty-Two

Anxiety dipped low in his stomach like a sinking ship as he studied Mickey's face. Her freshly washed hair fell in soft waves around her shoulders, and the pale green tank top showed off her battle scars. He didn't want her to fly home by herself, but he didn't have much of a choice.

She'd been through hell last night, but she wasn't going to crumble to pieces and demand his protection. Instead, she insisted he give his full attention to talking to Pete and finding Becca.

His rental car idled on the curb near the arrivals at the Cancun International Airport. Cars crawled by his window, searching for their own spots to drop off friends and loved ones. The hard leather of the steering wheel bit into his hands. Every ounce of his being screamed at him to pull her close to him and refuse to let go until she agreed to stay. Instead, he kept his hands at ten and two and focused on the way the leather chafed against his skin.

"Any idea what time you'll take off?" A car honked behind him, and he peered out the window, waving the impatient bastard along.

"No. My boss understood why I needed to take a few days off, but she couldn't get me on a direct flight home. A few flights go to Chicago today, so hopefully I can weasel my way onto one of them."

"And if you can't?"

Mickey shrugged. "Then I'll be here waiting for you."

"You should be here with me anyway. Wait a little while and I'll book us a flight home together. You might not even be able to get home on standby."

"Don't be ridiculous. I'm sure I'll be on a flight in no time." She reached out and squeezed his forearm. Her touch warmed his skin despite the frigid air blasting from the vents and his muscles relaxed. "I'll be waiting for you when you get home."

The heat from her touch spread from his arm until it filled his whole body. The idea of her waiting for him was more appealing than he expected. "I like the sound of that."

Her full lips curved up and his heart constricted in his chest. "Me too."

His hands dropped from the steering wheel and reached out to frame her face. He rubbed the pad of his thumb over the mole above her lip and she grimaced. She was so damn cute. "I gotta go meet Eric. We need to talk about our next move. Did you program my number in the phone you picked up?"

"Yes. I'll text you when I know my flight time, and you keep me posted as well."

He pulled her to him and crushed his mouth on hers. He needed one more taste before he let her go, even though it would never be enough. A rush of emotion flooded his chest, warming him to his toes. He broke away, his forehead pressed to hers, and inhaled the smell of strawberries and citrus. "I'll let you know as soon I can."

Mickey sighed and her warm breath skimmed over his face. She pressed a quick kiss to his cheek and then turned to open the door. The hot morning air swept into the car and pushed back the cold air he preferred.

Leaving the car idling, he stepped outside. His dark aviator sunglasses blocked out the glare of the sun, but couldn't hide the brilliant blue of the sky. The salty ocean air swirled around the slight breeze, settling on his skin. Palm trees swayed along the wide sidewalk winding into the airport. He walked around to the back of the car, popped open the trunk, and grabbed Mickey's carry-on bag. The wheels squeaked over small pebbles as he rolled it to where she stood on the sidewalk.

"Thanks," she said and reached for the handle.

He pulled her close to him, wrapping his arms around her. "Have a nice flight," he said, his mouth pressed into a mass of hair above her ear.

"I will." She pulled away, offering him one last smile, before she turned and walked toward the entrance.

He stood watching after her like a puppy waiting for its master. When she stepped through the threshold and the doors shut behind her, all the air left his lungs. Damn, he had it bad. His phone vibrated against his thigh and he fished it from his pocket.

Dude, where are you? You were supposed to meet me ten minutes ago.

Shit. Between sex with Mickey this morning and getting her to the airport, he'd lost track of time. His thumbs moved over the keyboard with a reply.

Sorry. Leaving the airport now. Be there in five.

Somehow Eric had managed to have Pete sent to a prison in Cancun instead of Playa Del Carmen. Graham didn't ask questions, just took the small luxury of having a partner with connections inside Mexican jails.

He put his phone in his pocket, climbed back into the car, and took off for the coffee shop where he'd agreed to meet Eric. The small shop had parking in the back and he found a spot easily. Heat pounded down on him and sweat gathered at his temples as he stepped into the hole-in-the-wall coffee shop. The cool air was thick with the smell of freshly brewed coffee. Taking a deep breath, he let the coolness chase the god-awful heat from his skin. He glanced around the room and quickly spotted Eric at a table for two in the back corner. Caffeine called to him, but Eric's pinched face and rigid body had him walking straight to the table.

"Hey, man, what's going on?" he asked as he pulled out a chair and sat down. "Did you get Pete to talk last night? Any word on how long it will take to extradite him?"

Eric ran a hand over the day-old scuff on his chin and sighed. "He's closed up tight. He knows he's going to jail regardless of what he says. I couldn't crack him."

He hadn't expected anything different. He'd take a stab at him. No way he was leaving without sitting down with the bastard. Maybe he'd have better luck. Graham leaned back in his chair and rubbed the back of his neck. "I'll head straight there once we're done. Maybe I can pry some information out of him."

Eric set his coffee on the table, circling the cup with his hands. "Good luck. He knows he's screwed so there's no need to cooperate." Hesitation had him dropping his gaze and fidgeting with his cup. "I don't know if we'll find those girls if he doesn't talk. And you won't have much time to talk to him. I had to grease a few palms to get us access."

"Maybe I can slip the guards a little extra today to turn their heads. I'd love to get my hands on that piece of shit." An image of Mickey bruised and bloody popped in his mind and his blood thundered in his ears.

Eric snorted. "I wouldn't blame you for trying. Did you

get a hold of Harper last night?"

"No, I was connected to Mary when I tried to reach him. She said he'll be gone for a few days, but couldn't give me any details. Have you ever known Harper to disappear?"

All humor left Eric's face and his mouth dropped into a frown. "No, never. Where do you think he went? Vacation?"

Graham shook his head. "He would have given us a heads up. This is different. I can feel it in my gut. Harper's been weird about this case, and it's damn coincidental he drops off the map as soon as we catch a break. I don't buy it. He's hiding something."

Eric furrowed his brow and his eyes flitted around the room, as if searching for the answer. "I don't know, man. But I agree, it can't be a coincidence. I booked a flight home, so I'll do some digging once I get in. I'm going to head straight to the airport from here. All the paperwork to get Pete back to Chicago can be done at home."

"Let me know if you hear anything, but I shouldn't be far behind you. After I talk to Pete, I'll be able to jump on a plane home."

"You're not planning on talking to Paula?"

Graham shook his head. "Nah. There's no point anymore. We've found Pete." Not like he'd needed to anyway. Mickey had already told him everything Paula had said. But he didn't want Eric knowing about Mickey's involvement. She'd overstepped a few times, and leaving her name out of things was for the best.

"Makes sense." Eric grabbed his to-go cup of coffee and stood from the table, extending his hand. "Good luck. See you soon."

Graham stood and shook his hand. He hoped like hell his interview with Pete went fast, and he got the information he needed to find Becca and the other girls. Without Pete's cooperation, he'd be screwed.

• • •

Gravel crunched beneath his tires as he pulled into the parking lot outside of the jail Pete had been transferred to. Peering over his steering wheel, he gazed up at the large white walls jutting out in four different directions. A watchtower stood tall in the center. Two armed guards looked out the square windows, their assault rifles ready for action.

Graham stepped out of the car and checked to make sure his Glock was in the back of his waistband. Chances were the guards would make him take it off, but he'd at least try to get it inside. He'd only been inside a Mexican jail a handful of times, and it wasn't a place he wanted to be left unarmed. Shouts of undistinguishable Spanish penetrated the walls. He locked his jaw, kept his head high, and his mind alert as he walked into the jail.

The smell hit him first, and he struggled not to cover his nose with his hand. Sweat, urine, and feces mingled together in the stifling heat, making bile burn his stomach. He held his breath and walked up to the office Eric had told him to find. He knocked on the closed door, and was greeted by an overweight Mexican guard with an assault rifle dangling at his side.

"*Que deseas?*"

Graham searched his mind for the limited Spanish he knew, but came up blank. "*Hola, yo soy Graham Grassi. Yo necesito ver Pete Bogart.*"

A deep laugh rumbled up from the guard's belly and out of his mouth. He turned and sat down on his chair, leaning back and crossing his ankles on top of his desk. The chair squeaked under his weight, and Graham feared the chair would fall backward.

"I met your friend last night. He said you'd be around, and you'd have something for me." The guard's thick accent made the words come out slow and broken.

Graham nodded and pulled a wad of bills from his front pocket. "This should cover it." He extended his hand, the bills hidden in his palm.

The guard leaned forward and grabbed the money. Shifting through the bills, he nodded his head and a large, crooked grin showed off brown stained teeth. "This will do nicely. I will take you to a room where the prisoner will be brought in. You'll be alone, with one guard outside the door. You'll have twenty minutes."

"What if I need more time?"

"Too bad for you," the guard said with a laugh as he stood. "Follow me."

Graham followed the man out of the office and down a long corridor. Cells filled either side of the hall, and men shoved their hands through the bars and yelled as they walked by. Graham ignored them, his attention focused solely on Pete. Twenty minutes wasn't much time, but he'd have to make it work.

A young man with dark skin and dressed in military style fatigues stood outside of a white steel door. Dark stains... blood?... ran down the door and dents made it bow in several spots. One small window looked into the room. The man's lips were set in a grim line and he fixed his eyes straight ahead.

The head guard spoke to him in Spanish, and the young man gave one nod.

"Okay, he's already in there. If you need help, Hector will be right outside the door. Remember, *veinte minutos.*"

Graham reached out and opened the door. The room was small and the stifling air inside had to be close to a hundred degrees. Beads of sweat coursed down his face and gathered on his back. A rectangular table sat in the middle of the room and the only light hung down from the ceiling over the center. One empty chair sat pushed into one side of the table, and

Pete Bogart sat on the other side.

Graham's blood boiled hotter than the room.

Pete glanced up and met his eyes. Damn, he looked like shit. His ashen skin sunk into the hollows of his cheeks and dried blood lingered around his swollen lips. Clumps of dirt clung to his close-cropped brown hair and red veins ran like spokes in the whites of his eyes. His hands clasped together on the table. His gaze stayed fixed on Graham as he walked to the table, pulled out the chair, and sat down.

Graham sucked in a deep breath and the hot air burned his lungs. He crossed his arms over his chest and hardened his gaze. "Where are the girls?"

Pete never looked away, just shrugged his shoulders.

"Is this where you want to live out the rest of your days?" Graham asked and waved a hand in the air. "This is hell. Tell me where the girls are and we'll transfer you to the U.S. Better food, a clean bed, air conditioning. You can't be stupid enough to want to stay here."

"It doesn't matter where I am. Nothing matters anymore." Pete's voice held no inflection, no hint of emotion. His eyes stayed fixed on Graham, but they were looking through him.

"Why? Because you were caught? You can't honestly believe you'd have a better life here. Tell me where the girls are and I'll bring you home." Graham's mind raced. He needed an angle, a carrot to dangle in front of Pete's face to get him to give up the girls. If it wasn't being expedited back to a more comfortable cell, what was it?

"I have no life. Not anymore. Not when he has her now."

Graham's heart rate kicked up. "Becca? Who has Becca? Tell me where she is and I'll get her away from him."

"It's too late. I've lost her forever."

The words pierced Graham's heart like a dagger. "It can't be too late. I can find Becca, if you help me."

Pete's eyes cleared and pain contorted his face. "This has

nothing to do with Becca. Paula! He has Paula! I fucked up so he took the only thing that matters to me. I got too caught up finally having her. I used my real name, I let Mickey into my life. All so she would finally be mine. And now she's gone."

"Who has Paula?"

Pete tilted his head to the side and he sneered. "Did you think you'd finally caught the bad guy? That it was over now? You don't know shit."

Adrenaline kicked up his pulse. "What do you mean?"

"I'm not the man in charge. I don't have the answers you want."

Graham curled his hands into fists and pounded them on the table. "Then who's in charge?"

"Did you think it was dumb luck I found Mickey? You should know there are no such things as coincidences."

Realization hit him like a fist to the gut. Someone else was helping Pete, someone who knew how to find Mickey. Fear washed over him. Someone who was still out there.

Graham pushed up from the table, leaned forward, and grabbed the neck of Pete's shirt. He pressed his face into Pete's personal space. "Give me a name. Tell me who it is."

Pete hung limply in his hand, not giving him the satisfaction of a response. The blank look came back into his eyes, and Graham pushed him back in his seat. Panic clawed at him. He needed answers, and fast. He sat back in his chair and took a steadying breath.

"I already told you, it doesn't matter anymore. He has Paula and he'll never let her go. She's my everything."

As quick as lightning, Pete unclasped his hands and his palm curled around something, its sharp tip barely visible. He slashed it across first one wrist, and then changed hands and slashed the other. Blood oozed onto the table, and a razor blade fell from Pete's now open palms.

"No! Hector, get your ass in here, now." He shot to his

feet and his chair crashed backward to the floor. The door flew open and Graham yelled, "Get a medic in here. He slit his wrists!"

Pete's head lolled back, exposing his pale neck. Graham took off his shirt and used the razor blade to slice strips of material. He grabbed Pete's arm and wrapped one strip above Pete's wrist where the cut had been made. Grabbing his other hand, he did the same thing above the other cut. Thick, crimson blood continued to ooze from the wounds. Graham placed two fingers under Pete's neck to check his pulse. His pulse was so weak, Graham could barely find it.

He glanced up at Hector and he yanked his fingers off Pete's neck. "It's no use. He'll never make it out of here alive."

Wiping Pete's blood onto his ruined shirt, he grabbed his phone from his pocket. He needed to catch a flight back home as soon as possible. His main suspect was dead, he had no other leads, and someone on the inside was up to their neck in this shit. He had to figure out who, and fast. He ground his teeth together as he pulled up the flight schedule on his phone.

One thing Pete had said kept spinning around in his head. *You should know there are no such thing as coincidences.*

Chapter Twenty-Three

A dull ache thudded behind Mickey's right eye, matching the pounding in her shoulder.

She shifted in the small seat in the back of the plane, but she couldn't get comfortable. She hated the confinement of the chair. It wasn't natural to her. She wanted to stand in the front of the plane with the flight attendants working the flight, but she didn't know them very well. She usually worked with the same group of people, and had only met this crew a handful of times. They wouldn't appreciate her annoying them.

She inserted her earbuds and set her iTunes to shuffle. Exhaustion and pent-up emotion made her limbs heavy. Between almost being killed, Pete being behind bars, and her growing feelings for Graham...it was as if every emotion in her body screamed at her for attention. She'd kept her shit together when saying goodbye to Graham, and then waited hours for a flight. Now, all she wanted was to be home. Her eyelids grew heavy, and she leaned her head against the back of her seat to wait for takeoff.

A slight hesitation in the song made her eyes fly open and check her phone. A message from Graham hovered on her home screen. She must have forgotten to put her phone on airplane mode. Swiping open the message, she read the text.

Things didn't go as hoped today. I'll fill you in later. Catching a flight now. Should be back in Chicago shortly after you.

A sigh of relief eased some of the tension in her neck, but her stomach dropped. Had Pete not told him where Becca was? She quickly shot back a reply.

Sorry it didn't go well. My flight was delayed…again…so we'll probably land around the same time.

Three bubbles popped up below her message and she waited for his response.

Wait for me and I'll drive you home.

She sent back the thumbs up and kissy face emojis and then quickly set her phone to airplane mode before starting her music again. The plane jostled her sore body back and forth as it taxied toward the runway. She clenched her teeth and her fingers curled around the armrest. The engines roared to life and the plane sped down the runway until it lifted off the ground. Only a few more hours and she'd be home. Then she could find out what Graham had learned from Pete, and hopefully put this nightmare behind her.

The floor rumbled under her feet as the wheels tucked into the bottom of the plane. Her ears popped and the plane tilted as it turned toward its correct flight path to Chicago. The turquoise blue of the ocean and the tall buildings of Cancun came into view, and were quickly replaced by blue skies and white clouds as the plane straightened and climbed higher in the sky. She leaned her head against her seat, closed her eyes, and settled in for the flight.

The plane dropped down and Mickey's eyes flew open. Her heart lodged in her throat and her head swiveled around the cabin. Her breath hitched on a gasp, and a gentle hand covered hers. "It's just a little turbulence, dear. You can go back to sleep."

She smiled at the white-haired older lady next to her. "Thank you. It just startled me awake. I don't even know how long I've been asleep."

"We've been in the air about two hours. It won't be long now."

The woman lifted her book up and Mickey glanced around. No one else had been disturbed by the turbulence. Hell, she wouldn't have been either if she hadn't almost died in a plane crash a week ago. The plane dipped again and her nerves shook. She needed to get up and stretch her legs, do something to keep her mind busy.

Stepping into the small aisle, she smiled at the flight attendant at the back of the plane. Mindy? Mandy? She shook her head and walked toward the front cabin. It didn't matter what the woman's name was. She'd probably never see her again anyway. As she approached the middle of the plane, the door to the cockpit swung open and anxiety formed a tight knot in the pit of her stomach. The co-pilot stepped out and flashed a brilliant smile at her and she bit into her tongue to keep from screaming at him. He turned to walk into the bathroom, and her breath caught in her throat.

No, not again. Close the damn door.

As if he read her mind, he turned back toward the cockpit and closed the door before heading into the bathroom. Relief washed through her and her knees buckled. Her hand gripped the chair beside her and she swayed against the woman in the aisle seat. She glanced down to apologize, and shock rooted her to the spot.

"Paula? Is that you?"

The woman in the seat beside her glanced in her direction. Large, dark sunglasses covered her eyes and a wide-brim hat sat low on her head. Mickey had noticed how ridiculous the woman had looked when she'd boarded the plane, but hadn't given her much thought. But now, there was no doubt in her mind it was Paula sitting beside an older man who was definitely not Jose.

Her eyes were hidden behind the glasses, but if they were as blank as the rest of her face, Paula showed no signs of recognizing her. Mickey crouched down in the aisle so their faces were inches apart.

"Paula, why are you going to Chicago? Where's Jose?"

The older man beside her leaned over and held Mickey's gaze. "Excuse me, miss, but I think you're mistaken. This is my wife, Marcia."

Mickey straightened and looked down at the man with kind brown eyes and an easy smile. Something wasn't right. The woman by his side might be acting strange, and true she couldn't see her whole face, but it was Paula. She had the same bow-shaped mouth, the same small oval face. Her hair might be hidden by the hat, but wisps of blond showed at her neck, and her tan skin stood out in contrast to her white cotton dress.

The woman was relaxed and calm beside the older man, even if she wasn't answering any questions for herself. Nothing was adding up.

She forced a smile on her face and a bright note in her tone when she said, "I'm incredibly sorry for the confusion. Your wife looks so much like a friend of mine. I thought for sure it was her."

The man chuckled and waved away her apology. "No worries, my dear. She gets that a lot. Has one of those faces."

"I guess so. Excuse me." She gave him one more smile, her eyes landing briefly on the woman next to him, before turning back toward her seat.

She tried to put the weird encounter out of her mind

and relax for the rest of the flight, but the absurdity of it kept circling around. Not to mention the straw hat stayed in her line of vision every time she glanced toward the front of the plane. Something just wasn't sitting right. That woman was Paula Williams. So why was she pretending she wasn't? And who was the man pretending to be her husband? He had to be close to three times her age. Unless Paula had pulled one over on her yesterday, Paula was happily married to a very handsome man who hadn't been much older than her.

Mickey shook her head, instantly dismissing that train of thought. If Paula had lied to her about her marriage to Jose, she could have been lying about her relationship with Pete. That was a string she didn't want to pull.

Grabbing her phone from the pocket in the seat in front of her, she made sure it was connected to the in-flight wifi and opened her messenger app. Graham needed to know what had happened, and he needed to know as quickly as possible. He had said he'd be landing in Chicago close behind her, but if there was a chance he could reach out to Paula or Jose before she could, then she had to give him the information as soon as possible. She quickly sent him a message.

Paula is on my flight with a man I've never seen before. She wouldn't answer me when I asked her questions, and the man insisted I was mistaken and she was his wife. I know it's her. Something's not right.

She slid the phone back into the pocket in front of her and leaned against her seat. She would keep her eyes on Paula for the rest of the flight, just in case the woman tried to gain her attention. Graham had told her it was important for her to stay diligent, attuned to her gut telling her something was wrong. This was one of those times.

The rest of the flight dragged on, and Mickey's nerves crawled under her skin like annoying gnats by the time they finally touched down in Chicago. The sun dipped below the horizon and the pink and purple swirls of twilight danced across the sky. Pain pounded a steady rhythm through her wounds and her sore body yearned for a soft bed to lie on and Graham's firm arms wrapped around her.

Nodding a polite acknowledgment to the crew as she stepped off the plane, she kept her gaze locked on the straw hat that bobbed along in front of her. Crowds of people weaved between her and Paula once she stepped into the terminal. She quickened her pace and every muscle in her body screamed at her to slow down. Her carry-on bounced along behind her and she slipped in between harried travelers to keep the space between them close.

Her phone vibrated in her back pocket and she grabbed it, casting a quick glance at the screen to see who it was.

Graham.

She connected the call and pressed the phone to her ear while still keeping laser focus on the back of Paula's head.

"Hey. Did you land?" she asked, her words breathy as she tried to keep her lungs filled with air.

"Yeah. Where are you?" Voices clashed in the background. He must still be on the plane.

"I'm walking toward the exit. It looks like Paula and whoever the hell she's with didn't check any bags. What do you think's going on?"

"Nothing good. Pete slit his wrists when I was questioning him, after telling me someone has Paula. I don't think I'm going to like it when I find out who he's been working with."

Mickey's feet stopped working and she stood in the middle of the busy corridor, shock rooting her to the spot. Bile filled her stomach. People moved past her in a haze. "Oh my God. What happens now? How do we find Becca?" A weight sat on her chest, making it hard to breathe. She closed her eyes and pushed her teeth together to keep from crying. They'd been so damn close to finding Becca.

A whoosh of breath sounded through her speaker. "I don't know. Eric's meeting me later at the office. I want to take you back to my place, where it's safe, and then we'll come up with another plan."

Opening her eyes, she nodded her agreement. Not like he could see her. His apartment was a much better option than hers. Who the hell knew where Connie was? Disappointment crushed her, making her limbs heavy. With Pete in custody, the threat that had hung over her head the last few days had disappeared. But not anymore. "Okay. I'll meet you outside. I need some fresh air. I thought this was coming to an end."

"I did too. I'll see you in a few minutes."

Mickey disconnected the call and put her phone back in her pocket. As soon as she got to Graham's, she needed to call Suzi. She had a right to know what was going on. Graham might not like it, but she didn't care. Suzi was Becca's mother, and she had a right to know where things stood. And maybe… just maybe…it could help bridge the gap between them.

Glass doors whooshed open in front of her and she stepped into the warm night air. The warm temperature wasn't as bad without the life-sucking humidity that had been in Mexico.

Shit! Paula.

Her conversation with Graham had distracted her and she'd forgotten to keep her eyes on Paula. She walked over to the curb. Cars lined up, waiting to pick up passengers. Her pulse kicked into high gear and she turned in a circle, her bag tipping to the side beside her. She bent down to pick it up and the squealing of tires caught her attention. She turned toward the road, and her heart stopped. A black SUV screeched to a halt beside her just as the back door swung open. Her feet stood rooted to the spot, and fear turned her bones to cement. She opened her mouth to scream, but a large hand bit into her bicep, yanking her into the back of the SUV. The wind whooshed out of her lungs and pain shot through her chest.

The man from the plane pressed a rough hand holding a sweet-smelling rag down on her mouth before she could make a sound. The door slammed shut behind her. She flailed her arms and legs, trying to connect with the man who'd grabbed her. Her head thrashed from side to side until she faced the wide blue eyes of Paula. She lifted her hand and reached toward Paula, but her arm fell to her side. Lead weighed down her limbs and her eyelids fluttered closed.

In the darkness, the cackle of a woman rang in her ears. "It's about time someone took this bitch down."

Chapter Twenty-Four

Hysteric voices and crowds of people clumped in small groups greeted Graham when he stepped out of the airport. Phones were pressed to ears and mothers clutched their children to their side, their eyes wide with fear.

Great. What now? I don't have time for this.

Biting back a sigh, Graham walked over to the chaos. A black carry-on bag lay on the sidewalk in the middle of the mess. "Is everything okay?"

A brown-haired woman with a small child on her hip turned to him. "No. A car just pulled up, grabbed a woman, and took off. It happened so fast. No one had time to help her."

The hairs on his arms stood on ends. "What kind of car?"

The woman shook her head. "I don't know the specific make. But it was one of those big SUVs. Black."

Graham muscled his way to the middle of the group and crouched to the ground beside the abandoned bag. He held his breath and turned over the luggage tag tied on the handle. Mickey's name and address stared up at him. His stomach dropped.

Panic squeezed the air from his lungs and he stood, turning to stare at the busy lanes of traffic leading out of the airport. "How long ago? Did she have red hair?" He turned back around to face the woman who had spoken to him.

The woman hesitated and took a step back. "It happened less than five minutes ago. And I didn't get a good look at her hair."

"I saw her," a man next to him said. "She had long red hair, very pretty. I called the police, but it looks like airport security is coming now." He nodded past Graham's shoulder.

Airport security? Graham snorted. What the hell could they do? And he didn't have time to wait for the police to show up and go after them. He had to act now. "I'm Agent Graham Grassi with the FBI. The woman who was taken is in grave danger and I need to go after her now. Does anyone have a car I can take?"

The crowd stared at him with concern etched on their faces…and their mouths closed. Fear clouded his mind and his blood thundered through him. "Please," his voice cracked. "I have to find her. I can't lose her."

Screw it. He pushed past the crowd and ran toward the taxi line. Cutting to the front, he rounded the corner of the cab, grabbed the startled driver from his seat, and tossed him to the ground.

"Hey! What the hell, dude?" The man yelled as he stood and brushed dirt from his jeans.

Graham held up his badge. "FBI. I need your car. Now get the hell out of my way."

He jumped into the idling car, slammed the door shut, and peeled away from the curb. He glanced in the rearview mirror and the cabbie stood on the sidewalk, his fist hoisted in the air. He refocused on the road in front of him. Worrying about the cabbie was pretty low on his list of priorities right now. Scanning the cars in front of him, he blasted on the horn to get the slow-moving traffic out of his way.

It didn't help.

Brake lights flashed in front of him and angry drivers blocked his path as he tried to snake between them to get out of the congested traffic. His eyes darted in every direction, willing the black SUV to come into view.

Come on, dammit. Where are you?

He slammed the heel of his hand against the steering wheel and hopelessness oozed into him. He'd never find the car, not like this. He needed to figure out where the car had taken Mickey, but how the hell could he do that? He didn't even know who he was looking for anymore.

Yanking his phone from his pocket, he dialed Eric. Maybe he'd have an idea.

"Hey, man. Did you land?" Eric asked, his voice heavy with fatigue.

"Someone took Mickey from the airport." He jerked the wheel to the left and came around a slow-moving van. He had nowhere to go, but for the life of him, he couldn't stand still. He had to keep moving or his heart would explode from his chest.

"What? When? Where are you?" Confusion laced through Eric's words.

"I don't know. Pete told me he was working for someone else, but he wouldn't give up a name."

Eric whistled through the phone. "Sonofabitch. Did he give you any clues? Do you want me to talk to him, or have the guard rough him up a little bit?"

"He's dead. And the only clue he gave was the person he worked for had a lot of knowledge about what's going on with the investigation. He told Pete where to find Mickey last night."

"Holy shit, dude. This isn't good. Do you have any idea

who it could be?"

His stomach dipped and his mind worked. The entire flight home he'd gone over every piece of information they'd uncovered. His gut had told him something was off, and he needed to follow his instincts. "Did you find out where Harper is?"

Silence filled the phone and he blasted his horn to make the bastard in front of him get out of the way. "You don't think he has anything to do with this, do you?" Eric asked.

"I don't know what to think. All I know is I need to find Mickey and I have no clue where to look."

"I'm on my way to the office now. Let me do some digging. We'll find her, Graham. I promise."

Eric's oath rang hollow in his ears the farther away from the airport he drove. His eyes never stopped scanning the busy streets, but nothing caught his attention. The hard leather bit into his calloused hands and he fought to keep panic from controlling his thoughts.

His gaze landed on a green traffic sign overhead. The exit for Old Town loomed on his right. The house he and Mickey had found flashed in his mind. It might be a long shot, but it was the only one he had. Cranking the wheel hard, he cut off two lanes of traffic to get to the exit. Gritting his teeth, he held his breath as horns blared all around him and a car spun out, barely missing being hit by his back bumper. His tires skid and a pile of trash in the musty cab slid across the floor.

Graham glanced behind him at the havoc he'd left behind and winced. Thank God no one had been hurt, but he couldn't dwell on it. He had to get to Cleveland Avenue. He had to get to Mickey. Traffic died down once he got off the highway, and the lights of the city whirled by in a haze. All the scenarios of what could happen to Mickey pushed to the back of his mind, and he called up all the training he had to keep his breath even and his nerves steady.

Streetlights cast shadows down on the empty streets of the neighborhoods around Old Town. His knuckles turned white as he pulled onto Cleveland Avenue and slid beside the curb of the old Victorian house with the dark gray porch and green raining down the sides. A shiver ran down his spine. He'd never understand how Mickey thought this place was beautiful. Even the paint cried for the sins that happened inside.

Putting the car in park, he cut the engine, stepped into the night, and ran toward the house. Glancing around, he checked to make sure no neighbors loitered on the porches or watched him from down the street. The last thing he needed was some nosy pedestrian questioning his motives. He crouched down low and slithered alongside the overgrown shrubs. No cars sat in the driveway and no lights beat back the darkness inside the house. But that didn't mean no one was there. Staying low to the ground, he climbed the creaking porch steps and walked up to the door. He ran a hand around the edge of the doorframe and relief washed over him. Still broken.

With one more look over his shoulder, he opened the door and stepped inside. Stale air mixed with the smell of rotted food assaulted him. Nothing had changed since the night he'd been there with Mickey. His gut told him Mickey wasn't here, but he had to check. Pulling the gun from the waistband of his jeans, he crept up to the second floor and checked every room. Cobwebs and dust bunnies greeted him everywhere he looked, and he cleared every room in the house in ten minutes.

Except the basement. The one place he'd never wanted to set foot in again, but the only place that held the secrets he needed. With his gun positioned in his hands, he stepped down the old stairs and onto the dirt floor. He ducked his head low and walked straight toward the opening in the wall. The bookcase stood away from the opening, just where he'd left it. But something was different. He shifted his gun to his right hand and turned the flashlight on his phone on. Boot marks imprinted the tightly packed dirt. He moved the light across the floor toward the stairs and sucked in a breath. Someone had been down here.

Adrenaline spiked in his veins. This was it, the way to the girls...and hopefully Mickey. With the light from his phone shining in front of him, and his free hand gripped around his gun, he made his way down the narrow tunnel Mickey believed was used as part of the Underground Railroad. A tunnel he was convinced led straight to hell. Dust lifted from the ground with every frantic step, coating his skin and seeping into his mouth. His lungs burned and sweat poured down his back.

Just a little bit further. Keep going.

The low ceiling grazed the top of his head and something fell into the front of his shirt. Without breaking his stride, he pulled his shirt from his chest and shook whatever the hell was in there out. He didn't have time to stop. The blast of cool air rushed at him, cooling his skin and lifting his spirits. The opening was near. He prayed it'd be clear what set of tracks to take once he reached the open cavern. Whispers of bats echoed around him, and he hurried toward them. The corridor opened wider, little by little, until he finally stepped into the wide cavern with three sets of tracks.

He walked to the closest tracks and crouched down to study them. The light from his phone tried to battle against the dark, but it hardly made a dent. His face was inches from the ground, his knees pressed against the hard steel of the tracks, but nothing appeared out of place.

He hurried to the middle tracks, keeping the light trained on the ground. A scattering of loose pebbles caught against his foot and flew into the dark pit of the track. He glanced down, noticing the small stones for the first time. They littered the floor in small clumps, except when broken up and randomly cast around the ground as if carelessly kicked about.

That's it! The stones.

Graham ran back to the opening of the first tunnel and crouched down to study the stones. Nothing but small groups with only a couple of loose pebbles thrown here and there. He stood and ran past the middle tunnel to the last set of tracks. Leaning down, he lifted the light and his heart pumped wildly against his chest. Stones scattered all around the ground, no groups or small clumps of pebbles lingered undisturbed over the dirt floor. This was it.

Keeping himself in the center of the tracks, he ducked his head and ran in at full speed. The light bounced around the stone walls, lighting the way down the mouth of the tunnel. He took it all in. His eyes searched every crevice they landed on, every inch bathed in the soft light of his phone for a sign of where this path would lead him. He slowed his pace, taking in air to fill his lungs. His hands fell to his knees and he doubled over, gasping for breath. A sharp pain jabbed into his side and he straightened to pinch the pain away. His head fell back and his hands dropped to his sides, the light shooting upward and settling on a vent on the ceiling, an old piece of plywood pushed to its side.

What the hell?

He stretched his hands over his head and ran them along the rusted grates of the vent. His fingers brushed against the plywood, and it fell to the ground at his feet. Using the palms of his hands, he pushed up against the vent and it popped out of place. Standing on his tip toes, he squeezed his arms through the vent and pulled himself up through the tight space. The sharp edges scraped against his sides and the muscles in his arms screamed as he burrowed through and brought himself through the floor and into an old, deserted room.

Dirt and dust clung to his face and stained his clothes. The cold air blasted up from the hole he'd just come through, giving a chill to the eerie room. Gooseflesh danced on his skin and he stepped farther inside. A large hole took up the far end of the room, but a wooden stage sat proudly in front of it. Rows of red velvet chairs faced the gaping hole, with aisles leading through the chairs. An old movie theater.

Something shifted on top of the stage, and he ducked down behind the last row of chairs. His breath caught and his blood pounded so loudly in his ears he was surprised it didn't bounce around the high ceiling above him. A beat passed and he lifted his eyes over the seat. The stage was too far; he couldn't see what was on it. Staying low to the ground, he walked on the balls of his feet and moved as quietly as possible toward where the screen must have hung years ago. The dirty carpet on the aisle muffled his footsteps and he squinted his eyes to see clearer. A tiny light illuminated the first few rows, along with the stage, but he was still too far away to make out what was up there.

Row by row, inch by inch, he moved closer. He held his breath, afraid even the whisper of air from his lungs would be heard in the large space. As he approached the third row, the silhouette on the stage took shape. His cheeks puffed out as he held his scream trapped inside. On the stage, huddled together on a blanket, were the three missing girls. Becca sat in the middle, her arms wrapped around a girl on either side of her. She held her chin high, and when she caught sight of him, her eyes widened.

He lifted his finger to his lips, but it was too late. A beast of a man sitting in the front row stood and turned toward him.

"Run! He has a gun!" Becca shouted.

Graham stood tall, pointed his gun at the man, and pulled the trigger. The shot rang loud in the stillness of the room. The girls shrieked and the man dropped to the ground. Graham ran up the aisle and paused long enough to make sure the man was dead before leaping onto the stage. The two girls shrank away from him, and his heart broke, but Becca met his eyes with a defiant sneer. Pride blossomed in his chest.

"I'm with the FBI. I've been looking for you three. Is there anyone else here with you?"

Her face softened and tears hovered in her blue eyes. Dirt caked her round cheeks and her blond hair fell limply past her shoulders. She shook her head. "He's been the only one here for a while. There's a woman that's usually here, but she left a while ago. She said she'd be back soon to take us to a new house. He was supposed to make sure we didn't run. And Pete." Becca's face crumbled as she mentioned his name and Graham fought the urge to pull her into his arms. That might scare her right now.

"I already found Pete. He won't hurt you anymore. Was there ever anyone else? Any other name mentioned in front of you?"

Becca sniffed back a sob and shook her head. The other girls buried their heads in Becca's side and their little bodies shook from the force of their tears. Even though all the girls were close to the same age, Becca had obviously become their safe place to hide in the last few days.

Dammit. Where the hell is Mickey?

"Okay," he said and glanced at his phone. No service. "I need to call the police and they will be here soon to help. The man down there is dead, so don't look at him, okay?"

Becca's gaze flickered to the floor and then back up to Graham. Her pupils dilated with fear. "Aren't you staying with us until the police come? What if someone comes back?"

"No one's coming back. I promise. But, Becca, the woman who was here, she has Mickey. I have to find them."

"Mickey?" Becca's voice broke and fat tears slid down her dirty cheeks.

Graham blew out a breath. He couldn't leave them here. "I want you three to come with me. We'll walk outside and I'll call for help. I'll wait with you until they get here, okay?"

Becca nodded and whispered into the other girls' ears. All three stood and slowly walked toward him. His blood pumped furiously as they walked down the stairs and he ground the heel of his foot in the ground to keep from kicking the sonofabitch on the floor. "Follow me."

Turning around, he walked back up the aisle and into what used to be the lobby. Broken glass littered the floor and beams of moonlight shone in through cracked windows. He led the way to the front door and kicked it open with his foot. Fresh air welcomed him outside, and he held the door open for the girls to walk through. Once the door was closed, he unlocked his phone and called the police.

"911, what's your emergency?" The dispatcher's no-nonsense tone spoke through the phone.

"This is Agent Graham Grassi with the FBI. I've found three missing girls who were all taken by Pete Bogart within the last three weeks. The latest being Becca Stanley taken on Sunday morning. I need backup ASAP, as well as their families notified."

"Okay, Agent Grassi. What is your location?"

That's a good question.

He turned in a circle and tried to find a street sign or landmark, something to tell him where in the city they were. The tree-lined streets were quiet, not a pedestrian in sight. Brick townhouses and mom and pop restaurants came into view and the world shifted under his feet. Fury tunneled his vision until only one thing stood out in his mind.

Lieutenant Harper's townhouse.

Chapter Twenty-Five

A door banged shut and Mickey flinched as the sound penetrated through the darkness of her mind and assaulted her pounding head.

A groan rumbled deep in her throat but stopped before she could let it escape her cracked lips. Her tongue moved against the dryness of her mouth and nausea rolled around in her stomach. Her eyelids fluttered and her stiff muscles ached for relief. Shifting to the side, she rolled her shoulders and arched her back. Joints cracked with the movement, and she stretched her arms high above her head.

Her shoulder screamed in protest and her wrists refused to come apart. Reality crashed down on her and her eyes flew open. Fear bit into her with the strength of a pit bull, quickly turning her nausea to bile. Her head spun and dizziness blurred her vision. She blinked, trying to adjust her eyes to the darkened room, and her gaze fell on a woman curled into a ball in the corner.

Paula!

Pushing away the blinding pain piercing through her, she

shifted her body weight from side to side and anchored her joined hands on the ground to push herself up on her knees. She inched her way over, swaying as she tried to regain her equilibrium. Was the room spinning, or was that her head? Saliva pooled in her mouth and she pushed it back down her esophagus. She couldn't lose it, she had to push on and figure out where the hell she was. The carpet rubbed against her bare knees as she made her way across the room to Paula.

Leaning down to whisper in her ear, Mickey said, "Paula, are you okay?"

No response.

She leaned closer and Paula's breath caressed her cheek. Mickey sank down so her bottom rested on her heels. At least Paula was alive, but how could she get them both out of here?

"Don't worry about her. She'll be fine," a hard voice said from behind her.

Mickey craned her neck around, taking in the bare room. Gauzy curtains on the lone window let the moonlight shine through its thin material. At the open doorway stood Connie. Her thin lips pressed into a tight line and a nasty purple bruise circled around her eye.

"What happened to you?" Mickey asked. Connie's battered appearance made her less threatening somehow.

Connie snorted and cocked her head to the side. Her arms crossed tightly across her chest. "A little punishment for not killing you when I was supposed to."

The coldness of her words caused a chill to settle over Mickey's skin. "Who hit you? Pete?"

"Come on. I thought you were smarter than that." A brittle laugh pushed past Connie's lips and she stepped into the room. Mickey didn't move a muscle. She refused to show her fear. "Pete was just another pawn who outlived his usefulness."

"Then who?"

"Why do you think I'd tell you?"

Mickey shrugged and her shoulder screamed. "Why not? I'm going to be dead soon anyway." Connie didn't answer, just continued to stare at her through narrowed eyes. Mickey needed a different approach to get her to talk. "Where are we? Are the girls here?"

Amusement widened Connie's eyes and her lips curved into a small smile. "You really are stupid. Do you think we'd take you to them? No, they're tucked away safe and sound right where I left them."

Mickey's blood burned hot. "You're a monster. How do you justify hurting innocent little girls?" Her voice shook as she spoke.

"You don't know me and what I've been through."

"Then tell me. Help me understand why you'd do this." Mickey softened her voice and rested her hands on her knees. The zip tie cut into her tender flesh, but she slowly twisted her wrists to try to loosen the restraint. It didn't budge.

"I don't need your understanding." Connie's words held less fire than before, and Mickey pressed on.

"You're right. You don't. But I'm going to die no matter what you tell me. It'd be nice if I had just a shred of clarity before that happens."

Connie sighed, walked to the windowsill, and leaned the small of her back against the wooden ledge. "I'm a survivor. I do what I have to do to keep living. Plain and simple. I had to learn that lesson at a young age, figure out how to give myself at least a small choice of what to do with my life. I could either let men touch me, hurt me for their sick pleasure...or I could use what I had to get what I want. I could choose who touched me. I didn't have to be a victim stuck in some god-awful trailer with my mother and her bastard of a boyfriend. I could just walk away. Live my life the way I wanted to."

The ice around Mickey's heart melted just a fraction for

the broken woman in front of her. Connie was wrong. She was a victim. A victim who was so heartless and so damn brainwashed she chose to inflict pain on others in order to lessen the pain inflicted on herself. Connie was right, Mickey had no idea what her life had been like, but she wasn't a survivor. She was another lost soul.

"Can't you see how you've used the horrible things that happened to you as an excuse to do horrible things to others? Let me help you. Let me get you out of this life and into a better place."

"I don't need help, especially yours," Connie said.

"So this is your big choice, the life you're so happy to live? You help kidnap little girls and just stand back while they're abused? That's not a life, it's a nightmare." Mickey's heart raced and her skin burned as she continued working at the ties on her wrists. They weren't loosening at all, just digging deeper and deeper into her flesh.

"What the hell's going on in here?" A dark shadow loomed in the doorway, his deep voice booming with disapproval. Mickey stopped moving.

Connie straightened and turned toward the door. "Nothing. I just came in to see if either of them had woken up."

"Is that why I heard you bitching about your sad little life? Don't talk to them, Connie. No one wants to hear your shit."

"I…I'm sorry." Connie dropped her chin to her chest. "I wanted to explain to her."

"Explain what? That you've always been a whore and you like getting roughed up?" The man strode toward Connie, and Mickey recoiled at his words.

"No. She wanted to help me, but I don't need help. I've got you." A wide smile splashed across her face.

The man's long legs closed the distance between them

and he pressed his face into Connie's, his silhouette blocking the light from the window. "You have me?" he growled. "That's what you think this is? Some fucked up little fairytale where you get your man? You're just a dumb bitch who I have to keep putting in her place."

His hand reared back and slammed against Connie's face. Her head whipped around and she fell to the floor. Mickey's breath caught in her throat and she fixed her gaze on Connie's unmoving form, willing her to get up. But nothing happened. Horror grabbed her by the throat when the man turned to face her, his lip hitched up in a sneer.

"Hello, Mickey. I've been looking forward to meeting you."

He walked toward her and she fell to her butt, her legs stretched in front of her. She tried to use her heels to push herself backward, but the awkward movement caused her to tip to the side. The man chuckled and crouched down in front of her.

"I've heard an awful lot about you. First from Pete, and then from Graham. Stupid Graham, running around trying to catch the bad guy. Not knowing I've been under his nose this whole time."

Terror rippled over her, but she refused to let it take hold of her. "He'll figure it out. He's already putting pieces together. He won't stop until he finds me."

The man tilted his head to the side, an amused smirk played on his face. "Do you know who I am? I don't think you do, or you'd know I've already gotten away with everything. It wasn't until you showed up that things started going wrong. But you'll pay. I'll make sure of it."

Floorboards creaked from outside the room and the man stood straight, his ears tuned toward the door. The groans of the house grew louder, and her pulse quickened. Someone else was here.

As fast as lightning, the man dropped his hand to her head and grabbed a fistful of hair. Her hands shot up to stop him, but she couldn't fight him as he yanked her to her feet. The roots of her hair all but pulled from her scalp and she bit back a shriek of pain. Something hard pressed into her back and her stomach sank. He had a gun. "You're coming with me. Can't be too careful now, can we?"

Pushing her in front of him, his grip tightened on her hair as they walked out of the room and stepped into a dining room. Wooden floors squeaked beneath her flip flops and a rectangular table dominated the room. A crystal chandelier hung from the middle of the ceiling and a man sat tied up at the head of the table.

She craned her neck forward and squinted into the darkness. With no windows, it was hard for her eyes to adjust. She closed them for a few seconds, praying Graham wasn't the man at the table, and opened them again. Her vision sharpened, the picture in front of her becoming clearer. The man at the table seemed older than Graham, his posture drooped and his hairline receding. "Who is that?"

Her captor turned them toward the table. "A friend of mine. He's going to play a key piece in my escape. Because of you, things got a little messy this time around. I won't be able to pick up the pieces and move onto the next thing. I need to make a big bust to clear any lingering suspicion of my department."

The truth of who held her life in his hands slammed into her like a punch to the gut. "You're with the FBI?"

He let go of her hair and clapped slowly into the quiet room. "Very good, Mickey. But, I mean, it shouldn't have been too hard to figure out. How do you think Pete knew you were in Mexico? Or how I got Paula to let me into her home when she was alone before I could drug her and get her on a plane? When you have as many years as I do in the FBI, it's easy to slip through the cracks to get what you need."

The light flicked on and Mickey squinted to protect her eyes from the sudden brightness. "Don't you mean slither?" Graham's gruff voice sounded behind them and the man's body stiffened against her back.

"I wasn't expecting you here so quickly. I didn't even get a chance to call and tell you what I had found." The man turned her so they faced Graham, who stood in the arched doorway, a gun pointed toward them. "But this will make things much easier."

Graham nodded past them at the man hunched over at the table. "Is Harper alive? Or did you kill him too, Eric?"

"I didn't kill anyone. Just because Pete was smart enough to use the razor blade I gave him, doesn't mean his blood is on my hands."

Mickey's eyes devoured Graham. Her heart slammed into her ribcage and every muscle in her body yearned to fly into his arms. But she couldn't. Her hands were still bound together and Eric stood at her back. He'd let go of her hair, but there was no telling what he'd do if she tried to move.

Her mind snapped to attention and focused on what Graham had said. "Eric? As in your partner?"

A dark scowl covered Graham's face and anger flared in his eyes. "One and the same. How did I not see it sooner?"

Eric's hot breath skimmed over the back of her neck and she shuddered. "I made sure you always looked somewhere else. Who do you think's been pulling the strings all these years? Why do you think Harper was so pissed at you? I was feeding into his misgivings about your ability to run the case. 'Graham's head just isn't in it, sir. He's too caught up with this girl, Mickey. Wants to follow his gut again and not use his head.' It was too easy. But Harper started to question my word and poke around. I needed someone to place the blame on, and you were already looking in that direction. It would have been a nice, easy way to clean up the mess Pete left me."

Mickey ground her teeth together and asked, "What about what happened in Austin?"

"You told her, huh?" Eric chuckled. "Man, watching it eat you up inside the past month has been the funniest shit I've ever seen. And knowing I was the one who put the whole thing in motion. It killed me keeping it to myself. But then Harper started asking questions and Pete had to fuck everything up. I couldn't keep it hidden much longer, so I figured why not let Harper take the blame? You've been bitching about how unfair he is like a whiney girl. Thought you might find some poetic justice in it."

The lines in Graham's face deepened and he clenched his jaw. "Why? Why would you do any of this?"

A moment of tense silence passed before he said, "It started for the money. I made dick with the FBI, and day after day I chased after drug dealers rolling in dough while I pinched pennies to make ends meet. It didn't make sense. When I switched over to the human trafficking division and I saw a chance to break into the market, I jumped in."

"You jumped into the market?" she asked through clenched teeth. Her stomach rolled. "You steal children from their mothers and sell them for sex. You are the lowest form of filth on this planet."

Eric's large hand shoved hard between her shoulder blades and she fell head first onto the floor. Her conjoined wrists shot out in front of her to break the fall, but they pushed into her stomach and stole her breath as she landed on the floor. Feet scurried behind her, and ragged breaths filled the air.

Bang!

"Motherfucker," Eric yelled.

Bang!

Another shot rang out and Graham dove to the floor.

Eric's words barely broke through the ringing in her ears, and she glanced up to see blood pouring down one arm, a gun poised in his hand. Turning onto her back, she shifted her gaze to Graham. Anger, hot and red, colored his face and his chest expanded with every breath he took. His long body spread out on his side, and his gun trained on Eric's head.

Eric fell toward the table and rested his heavy frame on the back of a chair. His gun never faltered as it stayed aimed at Graham. "You're going to pay for that, you dumb shit. I planned on killing you quickly, but not anymore. Now I'll make you watch while your little whore girlfriend begs for her life."

Mickey squeezed her eyes shut and tried to erase his words from her mind. She opened them again and glanced at Eric. All of his anger, all of his attention, was focused on Graham. She couldn't get caught up in the fear that threatened to paralyze her, she had to do something. Using her core, she pulled herself into a sitting position, her legs still stretched out in front of her and her hands on her lap. She slowly inched her feet toward her until her legs were crossed beneath her.

"But first," Eric said. "I need to make sure you won't get in the way." He shifted the barrel of the gun and aimed it at Graham's kneecap.

"What makes you think I'm going to let you shoot me?" Graham asked, as he got to his feet. "My gun is pointed right at you."

"Because you're an idiot in love."

Mickey jumped up on the balls of her feet, lowered her head, and rushed head first toward Eric's soft middle. Her aching shoulder connected with the spongy tissue and rammed him hard against the dining room table.

Bang!

A bullet pierced her flesh and pain burned into her chest,

spreading like wildfire through her body. She hit the ground hard, but she was so numb she didn't register the impact. Her eyes blinked and she tried to keep them open. All the air left her lungs, but she didn't have the energy to fill them back up. She stared up from the floor and darkness misted around her vision.

Bang!

A man's face hovered over hers and she willed her muscles to move…but it was no use. Her eyes drifted closed and before she gave into the comfort of escape, one thought fluttered through her mind.

She was the idiot in love, and now Graham would never know.

Chapter Twenty-Six

Mickey's body lay limply on the ground, her head turned away from him. Blood oozed on the floor from her wound and his entire world stopped spinning. His heart shattered and the broken pieces ricocheted around his body.

She was gone.

Mickey had grown to become a huge part of his life, and now she was gone before they'd even gotten a chance to have a life together. Before he could tell her he'd fallen in love with her.

Rage battled against the anguish inside him and demanded him to focus. A loud groan caught his attention, and he rushed to the floor and dropped to his knees. Eric withered beside Mickey's still form, his bad arm reaching for the gun she had knocked from his hand. Eric might have been able to move out of the first shot he'd taken, managing to only get an injured shoulder from the bullet, but he hadn't been so lucky with Graham's second shot. Eric wouldn't be a threat to anyone anymore.

Eric's bloodshot eyes gazed up at him and he grimaced.

"Just kill me already."

Ignoring his partner's plea for mercy, he cradled Mickey's head in his hands, his gun dangled loosely from his fingers. Her limp body melted into his arms and blood coated his skin. No breath fell from her lips, no movement lifted her chest. Eric had done this to her, he'd taken her away.

Graham's sweat-slicked hands gripped his gun and aimed it at the center of Eric's forehead. His finger trembled as it grazed the trigger. He squeezed his eyes shut and a scream tore through him. He wanted Eric dead, needed revenge on the lives he'd destroyed...on the ones he'd taken.

"Graham?" A small voice croaked out his name and his eyes flew open.

He glanced up, his eyes searching for the voice speaking his name. Harper lifted his head. Dried blood caked the corner of his lip and ran down the side of his face. He dipped his chin toward the fallen bodies of Mickey and Eric, his eyes intense and focused.

He sighed. Harper was right. Killing Eric wouldn't solve anything. His body ached to gather Mickey into his arms, but he should make sure his boss was all right before he fell apart. He gently placed Mickey's head back on the ground and heaved himself to his feet. His eyes bore into her, willing her to move...but it was no use.

His chest tightened and guilt swam in his veins. He should have been here sooner, shouldn't have missed Eric when he had the chance to take him down. Turning toward Eric, he shot his foot forward and smashed it into his face once, twice, three times. Blood spurted from his nose and his head went lax. Graham lowered his gun and walked around to Harper. He grabbed a switchblade from his pocket and cut the bindings at his wrists and ankles. "Are you okay?"

Harper cleared his throat and opened his mouth to speak. A cough rattled through him and he doubled over, gasping for air. Graham pounded on his back, but Harper shook his head, reached around, and pulled at his hand. He lifted a shaking finger, pointed toward Mickey, and Graham's heart lodged in his throat. Her long eyelashes fluttered and her finger tapped slowly against her palm.

She's alive.

Hope soared in his chest as he dropped to his knees and pressed his fingers against the delicate skin under her jaw. A weak pulse thudded against his fingers. He whipped his head around the room and his mind raced. He pulled his phone from his pocket and pressed redial.

"911. What's your emergency?"

"This is Agent Graham Grassi. I need an ambulance and a squad car on Orchard Street. Now."

"What's the address, sir?"

"What's the house number, Harper?" he asked without turning away from Mickey.

"Five seventy-two."

Graham repeated the number to the operator and disconnected the call. The pool of blood grew under Mickey, soaking through her clothes. He had to find the bullet wound. She'd bleed out if he waited for the paramedics to get here. He needed to put pressure on it to make the bleeding stop.

"Graham," Harper said, but he ignored him as he glanced around to find something to help him take care of Mickey. "Graham!"

"What do you want?" Tears streamed down his face and hopelessness weighed down his mind. Mickey might still be breathing, but she wouldn't be for long. He had to figure something out, and fast.

A hard hand landed on his shoulder, and he glanced up at Harper's warm eyes. "Take a breath, son. You can't help her if you're a mess. You've been trained for this. Stop, look around, and form a plan. But first, we need to get that bastard in handcuffs. We can't risk him waking up, even if you did beat the shit out of him."

Harper was right. Graham blew a large breath in through his nose and pulled handcuffs from his back pocket. He brought Eric's wrists together and snapped the cuffs in place. Harper yanked on the cuffs and dragged him away from Mickey. Using the switchblade, Graham cut the zip tie that bound her hands. Deep gashes marred her smooth skin around her wrists. A new wave of anger washed over him, and he ground his teeth together until it passed. He couldn't focus on Eric...or what he wanted to do to his sorry ass...he needed to help Mickey.

Crimson stains made her tank top appear more red than green. His hands grazed over the thin material, searching for the source of the blood. The shirt had to come off. He lifted the hem of her shirt over her pale skin and sucked in a sharp breath as the material peeled away from her stomach. A hole pierced her skin on her right side. His fingers gently skimmed the backside of the wound...no hole.

"Shit. The bullet's still in there. We need to get it out." Sweat broke out on his brow and his hands shook.

Harper crouched down beside him with white gauze in his hands. "Don't be an idiot. You're not a doctor, and moving the bullet around might cause more damage. We pack the wound with sterile gauze and try to stop the bleeding as best we can."

He used the back of his hand to wipe the moisture from his face and reached for the gauze. Harper shook his head and pushed him aside. "Let me do this. You talk to her until the paramedics get here. You never know what she can hear."

Graham nodded, sank to the floor beside her head, and folded Mickey's hand in between his own. His teeth bit into the inside of his mouth to stop more tears from coming. He had to keep his composure, had to be strong for her. "Help's on the way, baby. You're going to be fine." He held his breath and waited for a response...but nothing. Her arm came off the ground as he lifted their hands to his forehead and closed his eyes against the soul-crushing pain.

A knock sounded at the door, followed by hurried footsteps. "Police and EMS in response to a gunshot wound," a loud voice called out.

He opened his mouth, but emotion lodged in his throat and no sound came out.

"In the dining room," Harper called. "We have one suspect cuffed and unconscious with us, two women in the back bedroom who'll need medical assistance, and one critical civilian shot in the side who needs immediate medical help."

Two police officers ran into the room with a medic on their heels. One of the officers whistled and asked, "What the hell happened here?"

Harper stood and authority vibrated from him. He took charge of the scene while Graham sat paralyzed with fear beside Mickey. Another medic rushed in with a gurney and stopped beside them. He glanced at Graham and said, "We've got her now. Please step back."

"No," he whispered. He couldn't bear to let her hand go, to sever the connection. The two men in their white uniform tops and blue pants carefully shifted her onto the gurney, raised it, and started for the door. Graham kept pace beside them, his grip never wavering from Mickey's cold hand. He helped them load her into the back of the ambulance and he sat beside her.

Please God, don't let her die.

The sirens blared and they sped through the city. The ambulance screeched to a halt and the back door banged open. "You have to let her go now, sir."

They pulled the gurney out of the ambulance and his grip

slipped from her fingers as they took her away and rushed her into the emergency room. Graham's mouth dropped open and he stared into the dark city outside the open door. He couldn't move, couldn't think.

Dropping his head in his hands, he let the dam break. His shoulders shook and his lungs burned as sobs racked through him. He might have just lost the love of his life and he'd never gotten a chance to tell her.

. . .

The hard cushions of the chair in the waiting room shifted under his weight. Time had stood still as he waited to hear from Mickey's surgeon. The staff at the hospital had made a fuss about only letting family know about her condition, but Harper had shown up and smoothed the way for him to get whatever information they had.

And then he'd stayed. He still couldn't believe it. The man who'd made his life a living hell the past month, the man who he had thought capable of horrible things, had come through for him in more ways than one tonight.

Graham leaned back in his chair and folded his hands behind his head. He stared at the clock. Two hours had passed since Mickey had been taken into surgery. His toe tapped against the cheap carpet under his shoe.

Harper walked in with two cups of coffee in his hands. He offered one to Graham. Heat penetrated the white Styrofoam and Graham set the cup on the floor. Anxiety bounced around in his stomach. No way could he drink caffeine right now.

A surgeon with green scrubs walked into the waiting room and glanced around. His tired eyes landed on Graham and he shot to his feet. Harper stood next to him and rested a hand on his shoulder as the surgeon walked toward them.

"How is she? Can I see her?" Graham's voice shook as he spoke and his eyes searched the man's face for answers.

The doctor sighed and rubbed a hand over his face. "She made it out of surgery and is in the ICU. She's not awake, but you can go in and sit with her for a few minutes."

Graham nodded and followed the doctor out of the room. He stopped at the doorway and glanced back at Harper. Harper waved his hands as if shooing a fly. "Go on. I'll be here when you're done."

He drew in a large breath of sterile air into his lungs and tried to steady his nerves. He braced himself as he rounded the corner and passed the flurry of activity in the ICU. Nurses rushed in and out of rooms, doctors checked charts, and the steady beeps of life rang out from the rooms.

The doctor led him to the second room from the nurses' station. Graham took a step inside and his knees buckled. Mickey lay in a large hospital bed with an IV attached to her arm. A machine beside her bed showed her vital signs, and beeped along with the rest of the activity outside. A blanket had been pulled under her armpits and her long, red hair fanned out on her pillow. The bruising on her cheek from where Pete had hit her had deepened and bandages covered her hands.

"The bullet missed any internal organs and I was able to get it out. She lost a lot of blood, but we gave her a transfusion. We've done all we can for her. The rest is up to her. Does she have more family coming to see her?"

Graham's head spun and he tried to focus on the doctor's words, but all he wanted was to see Mickey. "I called her parents when she went in for surgery, but they were out of town. They're on their way, but it'll be a few hours before they get here."

The doctor gave one stiff nod and then left him alone with Mickey.

His feet moved toward her as if a magnet drew him to her side. Her pale skin was ashen under the florescent lights and he reached out and brushed a strand of hair from her forehead. A chair sat beside the bed, and he all but fell back into it. He propped his elbows on his knees and leaned toward her. He laid his hand over hers, warming it with his touch.

"Mickey? Can you hear me? I found Becca." Moisture filled the corners of his eyes. "The girls are safe and back with their families. We did it, Red. We got them home."

Beep...beep...beep.

Disappointment smothered him. What did he expect? It would take time for her to wake up. He couldn't really think she'd open her eyes the moment she heard his voice.

"Are you still calling me Red?" Her voice was small, her words rough as if spoken through quicksand.

He straightened and his pulse quickened. "Mickey?"

She opened her eyes and then grimaced, shrinking away from the light. She turned her neck to look at him. "Did you really find Becca?"

He nodded and joy burst inside him. "I did."

Her lips curved into a small smile and she closed her eyes again. "Good job, G.I. Joe."

"How do you feel?" He had so many things he wanted to say to her.

"Like I was shot."

He chuckled and then turned serious. "You could have gotten yourself killed. You shouldn't have done that."

Her eyes fluttered open and her amber irises bore into him. "I had to do something."

"You should have let me handle it."

Her eyebrows arched high on her face. "And why's that? Because you're a man and I'm a woman?"

"No," he said, gathering his courage. "Because a man should always rescue the woman he loves."

Mickey's mouth dropped open and her eyes searched his. "You love me?"

"More than I realized. When I saw you lying on the floor and I thought I'd lost you…" His throat closed up and words failed him. The moisture lingering in his eyes coursed down his face. He stood, leaned over the bed, and framed her round face with his hands. "I love you, Mickey. I don't want to ever lose you."

"I love you too, Graham. Who would have ever thought something so good could have come out of all of this."

"Lord knows I didn't," Graham said with a laugh.

"Can you promise something?"

"Anything," he said, as his thumb caressed her cheek.

"When I get out of the hospital, can we leave the excitement behind us? I don't think I can handle any more drama."

"You got it. I'll do my best to make sure your life is as dull as possible." He laughed and then pressed his lips to hers. His heart soared and he pulled away and stared down into the most beautiful face he'd ever seen. A face he planned to see every day for the rest of his life.

Mickey's husky laugh skimmed over him and set his blood on fire. "I'm going to hold you to that, G.I. Joe."

He grinned and took her mouth in his. No matter what the future held for them, life with Mickey would never be boring.

Epilogue

Mickey's eyes fluttered open and she blinked to adjust to the morning sun streaming in through the window. They'd forgotten to close the curtains last night. She stretched her arms high above her head, and only a dull ache lingered in her body.

Between physical therapy and a little TLC from Graham, her body had healed nicely from the trauma from a few months ago. Thank God for that. Being stuck in a bed, hopped up on pain medicine, hadn't been for her. Now that Becca was home, Paula was safe, and Eric was locked behind bars for the rest of his life, things could get back to normal.

A strong arm wrapped around her waist and pulled her against a hard wall of muscle. Her toes curled and she leaned into him. Graham kept his eyes closed, and she reached up to run the pad of her finger along the whiskers on his jaw.

"Why are you awake?" he asked and she snuggled closer to his side.

"I need to go home and change. I came straight from work, and I'm meeting Becca and Suzi at the zoo in a couple of hours. I don't have any more clothes here."

His hand gripped her hipbone and his fingers inched their way inside her shirt. "Just wear your uniform. Becca likes it when you look professional."

"Really? She's never mentioned that before." Mickey laughed and she sucked in her stomach as his fingers brushed against the bottom of her breast. "Besides, even the uniforms I have here are dirty. Do you mind if I pack a bag and leave more stuff here? I'm staying with you most nights, so it'd be nice to have more of my things around."

Graham rolled on top of her and captured her mouth in his. Her heart rate picked up and she wrapped her arms around him. At this rate, she'd never get out of here. But that was okay. In her wildest dreams, she never imagined she could be this happy.

He pulled away and stared down at her, his lip hitched up in his cocky half-ass smile. "I was thinking you should bring it all over here. It's hard to be married when you're living in different apartments."

She gasped and Graham slid off of the bed and down onto one knee. The hard muscles on his bare chest bunched as he turned toward his nightstand and pulled open the drawer. A small velvet box sat in his hands when he faced her. Mickey covered her hands with her mouth and sat up on the edge of the bed. Her eyes looked from Graham to the box and back up to Graham. This couldn't be happening.

"Mickey, I knew I loved you a week after meeting you. It didn't take much longer for me to realize I don't want you to just be a part of my life when we find the time. I want you in my life all day, every day, until the day I die. I want you to be my wife."

Her heart leaped in her chest and she threw herself into his arms. "Yes. Absolutely yes!"

He leaned back and pulled the diamond ring from the

comfort of its box. Her hand trembled as he slid it onto her finger. Her heart swelled with joy and tears misted her eyes. How could the man who had dragged her into a nightmare be the one to make all her dreams come true? "It's a perfect fit," she said.

"You bet it is. And, Mickey, you might want to call Suzi."

She glanced up from the ring sparkling on her finger and raised her brows. "Why?"

"Because you're going to be late."

He sprang to his feet, picked her up, and threw her on the bed. Laughter erupted from her mouth and he trapped her beneath him. He smiled down at her, his gray eyes alight with love. His wide smile transformed into a wicked grin. He lowered his mouth to hers and began to show her just how much he loved her.

Oh, she'd be late all right. And it would well be worth it.

Acknowledgments

First and foremost, I'd love to thank my amazing family. I wouldn't have the courage to sit at my computer if it wasn't for your constant support and encouragement. To my husband, Scott, thank you for being my biggest cheerleader and giving *Bound by Danger* your official stamp of approval. I can't begin to tell you how it feels to hear you hype up my work to anyone and everyone who will listen. To my children, Abigail and Vaughn, thank you for your patience and understanding. I know it's hard to share me with the characters I make up in my head, and the guilt I have for not giving 100% of my time to you will never go away. But seeing the beautiful books you create, Abigail, and hearing the amazing stories you tell, Vaughn, shows me I'm doing something right by teaching you both to always follow your dreams and pursue your passions.

To my mom, thank you for being my most avid listener as I read chapter after chapter to you. I know it can't be easy to listen to me stumble through my words, making corrections and talking to my children as I go. And to Celeste for being by my side through this crazy journey! Even if that means an across the state road trip to be a part of my first author event. Without you in my life, I'd have crumbled into a million pieces by now. To my awe-inspiring critique partner, Samantha, thank you for pushing me into Romantic Suspense. This book started outside of my comfort zone, and you helped me realize my passion for writing fast-paced romantic suspense books. You also helped me wade through the hurdles and road blocks along the way to getting this book published. I also want to thank my cousin, Jessica, for her inside knowledge of Chicago and my beta reader, Angela, who pointed out the crucial errors that needed fixing. Without both of you, *Bound by Danger* wouldn't be half the book it is today.

A huge thank you to my amazing editor, Alethea. You breathed life into this book, and to me, when you pulled it from the slush pile and took a chance on it. I will forever be grateful to you. Also, to Jessie, my agent, thank you for holding my hand through this daunting process of publishing my first book! Your support and knowledge have kept me as calm as I could possibly be.

And finally, to my readers! Publishing this novel was something I doubted many times would actually happen. Even as I sit here writing out my gratitude, I still can't believe this dream is coming true. There are so many amazing and wonderful stories out there to be read, and the fact that you picked my book is mind boggling! I hope you fall in love with these characters and this story as much as I did. From the bottom of my heart, thank you for reading *Bound by Danger*. I hope you enjoy it!

About the Author

Danielle Haas resides in Ohio with her husband and two children. She earned a BA in Political Science many moons ago from Bowling Green State University, but thought staying home with her two children and writing romance novels would be more fun than pursuing a career in politics. She is a member of Romance Writers of America, as well as her local North East Ohio chapter. She spends her days chasing her kids around, loving up her dog, and trying to find a spare minute to write about her favorite thing: love.

Discover more Amara titles...

SLEIGHT OF HAND
an *Outbreak Task Force* novel by Julie Rowe

College students are dying and no one knows why. The CDC's former army nurse, pragmatic Joy Oshiro, and her combustible, but sexy, partner Dr. Gunner Anderson will need to learn to trust each other to figure out the terrorists behind the deaths. But each new clue keeps them one step behind the killers, with buildings and evidence destroyed just as they near. They're in a race against time to not only find a cure but also avoid becoming the next targets.

LOCK 'N' LOAD
a Federal K-9 novel by Tee O'Fallon

During a routine assignment, CIA analyst Trista Gold stumbles across a cryptic exchange. She doesn't think much of it...until someone tries to murder her—twice. But now she has to hide. And her new bodyguard, Matt, and his K-9 are the only hope she has against the powerful forces that want her dead.

WARRIOR NIGHTS
an *Odin's Bastards* novel by Sheryl Nantus

Liam Wolfson has worked hard to hide all traces of his old life, but Kara rips old wounds open as their old feelings for each other come rushing back. But it's not just Kara who's come to town looking for answers. When mercenaries arrive looking for Liam, he'll need Kara to remember what she's capable of if either of them is going to survive...

DARK WATER
a novel by Tricia Tyler

Nick Garrison's opinion of so-called psychics is carved in stone, as well as on his heart, which puts his best friend's little cousin squarely off limits, regardless of how much the sassy, Cajun, spitfire turns him on. But when Evangeline Broussard supposed sixth sense, and a leak in the local police department, put her in the crosshairs of the killer, she's the only one who can save them all.

Made in the USA
Lexington, KY
06 February 2019